Advance]

Atacama is historical fiction ... ...
and minds of those seeking change in tumultuous times. Carmen
Rodríguez's new novel is a deep dive into the life of revolutionary
activists, journalists and artists in Chile and Spain during the first
half of the twentieth century. From the fight against fascism in Chile
to the Spanish Civil War, we experience these historical battles
through the intimate lives of Lucía González and Manuel Garay,
the novel's two main characters. Set a century ago, the resonance for
today's changing times is stunning. A great read.

— Judy Rebick, journalist, activist
and author of *Ten Thousand Roses* and *Heroes in My Head*

In *Atacama*, Carmen Rodríguez opens a view that will be unfamiliar
to most Canadians — that of Chile in the first half of the twentieth century, which makes her book as much a history primer as a
novel. *Atacama*, however, is firmly of this century, as Rodríguez
paints a sprawling scene whose twists and turns span decades and,
through the Chilean diaspora, find echoes in contemporary Canada.
An astute reader might discern the influence of Eduardo Galleano
— using story as a tool for intellectual discourse. But *Atacama's*
greatest strength is in scope and cinematic feel — reading it makes
me crave a screen adaptation.

— Anna Marie Sewell, Edmonton Poet Laureate 2011-13
and author of *Humane*

Carmen Rodríguez's illuminating historical novel is an homage to
human resilience and to everyday people's ability to stand up to terror
and oppression. Poignant, layered, and absorbing, *Atacama* demon-
strates that biology doesn't have to shape destiny and that it is possible
to choose individual values over the complex bonds of family.

— Ava Homa, author of *Echoes from the Other Land*
and *Daughters of Smoke and Fire*

Atacama brings to life a variety of intensely moving, creative, dedicated characters whose lives intersect and fulfill one another in surprising ways, even under the shadow of unrelenting threat. It takes place over the span of a century, beginning during the mining strikes in the northern Chilean desert in the 1920s and moving through the artistic world of Valparaíso and Santiago and on to events of the Spanish Civil War. It reaches deep into Chilean history to reveal the courage and endurance of its people, whose rights have been repeatedly crushed by the military and the oligarchs that control it, but whose voices have never been silenced and that speak to us here.

— Hugh Hazelton, writer and translator, author of *Antimatter* and winner of the Governor General's Award for Translation

Atacama may be a novel, but it's written with the authority of memoir, the directness of history, and the magic of poetry. A story of heroism and depravity in politics, and the struggle of two young people caught between the two.

— Susan Crean, cultural critic and author of *The Laughing One* and *Finding Mr. Wong*

Atacama presents two of the twentieth century's great struggles for democratic freedom, in Chile and in Spain. From childhood on, Lucía and Manuel embody human efforts everywhere to make the world better and to make art. In telling their life-stories, Carmen Rodríguez has written a real page-turner — complete with an unexpected ending.

— Cynthia Flood, fiction writer and award-winning author of *My Father Took a Cake to France* and *Red Girl Rat Boy*, among others

From the mining camps of northern Chile to a dance studio in Valparaíso, and on to Barcelona during the Spanish Civil War and Pablo Neruda's office in a Parisian consulate... Carmen Rodríguez's new novel, *Atacama*, is wide-ranging and ambitious. At its centre are the inter-twined stories of an unlikely pairing: Manuel Garay, son of a poor family of activists and union organizers; and Lucía Céspedes, daughter of the military officer responsible for Manuel's father's death (and many others). The novel's narrative switches deftly between these two characters' stories, as it takes us from the 1920s to the 1940s, a period of heroic struggle but also brutal repression in Latin America and around the world. Just when all seems lost, a glimmer of hope takes us to a surprising twist set in the present day. Rodríguez's narrative is ultimately a story about the power of writing, the power of art, both to dramatize grief and to encourage remembrance. As drama and as remembrance, this novel succeeds admirably.

— Jon Beasley-Murray, professor of Latin American Studies
and author of *Posthegemony*

This is an extraordinary book. While it spans over seventy years of a personal drama, it also portrays—both accurately and poignantly — Chile's reality in the first half of the twentieth century, as well as that of the Spanish Civil War. But *Atacama* is much more than a sweeping historical novel, as it also delves deep into the psyche of its protagonists — Lucía and Manuel; who, as children, face up to horrendous personal tragedies and yet overcome them through their love of art and the written word, and their commitment to social justice. The crackling dramatic tension, the twists and turns in Lucía's and Manuel's lives, all the way to the conclusion of the story in present time Vancouver, Canada, are masterfully crafted. I cannot speak too highly of this work.

— John M. Kirk, professor of Latin American Studies and author
of eighteen books, including *Cuba at the Crossroads*
and *José Martí, Mentor of the Cuban Revolution*

ATACAMA

San Francisco, July 7,
2022

ATACAMA

a novel

CARMEN RODRÍGUEZ

For Nicole,

with love,

Carmen

ROSEWAY PUBLISHING
an imprint of Fernwood Publishing
Halifax & Winnipeg

This is a work of fiction.
Any resemblance to actual persons or events is coincidental.

Copy editing: Brenda Conroy
Design: Tania Craan
Printed and bound in Canada

Published by Roseway Publishing
an imprint of Fernwood Publishing
32 Oceanvista Lane, Black Point, Nova Scotia, B0J 1B0
and 748 Broadway Avenue, Winnipeg, Manitoba, R3G 0x3
www.fernwoodpublishing.ca/roseway

Fernwood Publishing Company Limited gratefully acknowledges the
financial support of the Government of Canada through the Canada Book Fund,
the Canada Council for the Arts, the Province of Nova Scotia
and the Province of Manitoba for our publishing program.

Library and Archives Canada Cataloguing in Publication

Title: Atacama : a novel / Carmen Rodríguez.
Names: Rodríguez, Carmen, 1948- author.
Identifiers: Canadiana (print) 2021025601X | Canadiana (ebook) 20210256281 | ISBN
9781773634777
(softcover) | ISBN 9781773634920 (EPUB)
Classification: LCC PS8585.O373 A83 2021 | DDC C813/.54—dc23

The history of all existing societies
is the history of class struggle.
— *Karl Marx*

They haven't died! They're in the heart of the battle,
standing, like burning torches.
Their shadows have come together
on the copper coloured plain
like a shield made of ironclad wind,
like a barrier the colour of fury,
like the invisible chest of the sky itself.
— *Pablo Neruda*

Another world is not only possible, she is on her way.
On a quiet day, I can hear her breathing.
— *Arundhati Roy*

For Carmen Cortés, my mother,
and Armando Rodríguez, my father

Y también para la Primera línea

PART I

1925

MANUEL

· · · · · · · · · · · · · ·

March – July 1925

La Coruña

THE *PAMPA* WAS STILL. The acrid smell of the saltpetre fields filled my lungs while my eyes feasted on the outline of the Andes against the pearly sky. Soon they would be trimmed with sunlight.

I heard its hissing before I saw it — the buzzard chick I had been eyeing for days had finally decided to take a look at the world. It was standing on the jagged edge of the rock that hid its nest, flapping its wings and cranking its neck. My sling was stretched and loaded; all I had to do was aim and shoot. The bird shuddered and dropped. I picked it up and ran. This was my first day of work and I couldn't be late.

The chick was still warm when I got home. Without a word, my mama snatched it from my hands, dumped it in a pot and poured a kettle of boiling water over it. When the water started to cool down, she would take the bird out, pluck it and gut it. My mouth watered at the thought of the stew we'd eat later that day.

The sun was up now, and the chill of the desert night was starting to give way to the heat that would set everything on fire by the time the afternoon came around. My papa walked in the door, a pail of water in each hand. His hair was slicked back.

"Time to go," he said to me, putting down the pails.

He walked up to my mama wanting to kiss her on the cheek, but she turned her head and pushed him away.

I grabbed a piece of bread off the table and followed him.

"I bet you'll be smiling and asking for kisses when the boy brings home his first pouch of tokens," my papa said as he walked out the door.

"No, I won't. I'll be smiling and asking for kisses when he's back in the classroom, where he belongs," she yelled back.

Halfway down the lane I could still hear her banging pots and pans.

My mama had high hopes for me. She had taught me how to read and write way before I started school and wanted me to go to high school in Iquique.

"You can stay with Aunt Asunta," she'd say, her hands busy at the stove, a smile on her face and her eyes dreamingly contemplating her younger days, which seemed to reside on the other side of the window.

Aunt Asunta was my mama's best friend, who she called an "organizer and agitator." Because of her, my mama had got involved in politics and had turned into an organizer and agitator herself.

"Asunta showed me how to use my noodle," my mama would say, pointing to her head. "First as my teacher at school and then as a comrade; she made me see that the Catholic Church is in cahoots with the capitalists — the priests and the nuns are in charge of doing the brainwashing, of making sure that people stay ignorant and dumb, especially the women. 'It's God's will,' they'll tell you, a fake smile on their face. God's will, my ass! It's *their* will to keep us all praying and hoping to go to heaven instead of fighting for a decent life right here on earth," she'd add, raising her voice and punctuating every word with a knock on the table.

That's how in 1912 she had set foot in La Coruña — to organize the women and form a new chapter of the National Women's Council. My papa, three years her junior and a good four inches shorter than her, was smitten by her smarts, haughtiness and boisterous laughter. In that order. It took him five days to muster the courage to ask her to marry him.

By the age of six I knew the story by heart, but once in a while felt the urge to hear it again and my mama was quick to comply; the ending was always the same.

"What about you, Mama? Did you fall in love with Papa too?" I'd ask.

"At the beginning I wasn't sure," she'd respond. "I loved my freedom and to tell you the truth, I didn't like men."

"What do you mean you didn't like men!" I'd shoot back.

"Well, most of the men I knew in Iquique were either sleazy or violent, and often both, like my dad. He'd stay out till the wee hours, come home drunk and proceed to yank us all out of bed and beat us up. That is until I grew to be stronger than him and sent him flying across the room one night. That was the end of his shenanigans. And in the street? Men would say gross things to us girls and even grope us. But as much as they tried, they couldn't get *me* — I would punch them and kick them until I ran out of steam. It helped that I was taller and stronger than most of them," she'd chuckle.

"But what about Papa? He isn't sleazy or violent!" I'd counter.

"No, you're right. He's not. That's why as much as I tried not to, I did fall in love with him. Because he's gentle and strong at the same time, like you," she'd answer, ruffling my hair. "Besides, he didn't mind that I was tall and plump and that I looked like a skunk," she'd chuckle again, referring to the naturally white tuft that split her black mane in two, right at the centre of her head.

My papa *was* gentle and strong. He was also smart. While I liked the idea of going to high school in Iquique, what I really wanted was to follow in his footsteps. He had worked in the saltpetre mines since he was a kid and had climbed the ladder to the best job of all: blaster. Blasters concocted the formulas for the explosives, assembled their own fuses and knew how to set everything up so that they could blast the exact patch of *pampa* they had picked out, no more, no less. They *had* to be smart. Also, they had to know how to handle their power.

At twelve years old, when I finished primary school, my papa gave me a choice: go to high school in Iquique or stay in La Coruña and start working at the mine. To my mama's dismay, I chose to stay.

But that first day of work, I wasn't so sure about my decision anymore. The clashing and pounding of the machinery were deafening and the fresh, salty air I had breathed earlier that morning had been replaced by thick clouds of crushed rock and black smoke.

I had been to the mine a few times before and had felt exhilarated by the engrossing din and bustle of the place. Now that same din and that same bustle were getting on my nerves. Mama's descriptions of Iquique went through my mind — sandy beaches under a clear sky and a beautiful, quiet square with large, leafy trees like the ones in my geography books. The pictures in my mind certainly looked a lot prettier than the one I had in front of me. But it was too late for a change of heart. I'd rather die than disappoint my papa.

When he clapped me on the back by way of saying goodbye and pointed the way to the crushers yard, I lingered and watched him join the small group of blasters standing on the field. They all had a ball of juicy coca leaves inside their cheeks and a smoke dangling out of their mouths. Smiling with glee I reminded myself that now that I was a worker, soon enough I would be allowed to have a ball of coca leaves inside my own cheeks and a smoke dangling out of my own mouth. As for joining the blasters, I would have to wait another few years.

Like all kids, I had been hired as a crusher cleaner. When I got to the crushers yard, there was a large group of boys messing around while they waited for the boss. A handful of them were my friends; quite a few, my enemies — there were only so many buzzard chicks, vizcachas and iguanas up the *pampa* to hunt and trap but a lot of families to feed. So, territorial lines had to be drawn and defended. Fighting was not my strength — I was small and skinny — but I could outsmart the bullies. I had won over the younger kids by sharing some of my tactics with them, and now, whenever I was attacked, they didn't hesitate to come to my rescue.

My friends and the boss gave me pointers on how to do the job, but the first few times I dove into the crusher all I did was scream and kick around. I couldn't breathe and felt trapped inside the ugly beast — a clunky creature made of steel with the jaws of a crocodile and the tail of a rat, never mind its black and stuffy insides. When the boss finally pulled me out, I was gasping for air and falling over. He set me down on my feet, held me upright with one hand and slapped me on the face with the other until I started breathing again.

I was the laughingstock of my enemies, but not for long. By the second day, I could follow the steps to a T: fill your lungs with air before going in, hold your breath, keep your eyes peeled, use your poker and brush to get rid of the rocks and dust stuck inside the machine, and finally, when you feel yourself going woozy, use an economical one-two scissor-kick to let the boss know that you want out. At the beginning I wasn't able to stay in for long, but by the end of the first week I could hold my breath and keep my eyes open long enough to actually clean the beast's insides.

At the end of my first workday my papa took me to a workers' assembly. He was one of the union leaders and La Coruña's rep at FOCH, the Workers' Federation of Chile.

That evening we walked up the *pampa* and into the sand dunes, where we wouldn't be seen from town. I could hardly contain my excitement. I had been to political gatherings before — my mama had taken us kids to her meetings at the Women's Centre many times — but this was different. Now I was a worker myself and was joining the miners to discuss strike action.

Hundreds of men and boys were already there when we got to the dunes. I caught sight of a couple of my friends and a few of my enemies in the crowd. I couldn't help but see them as such, even though on our way my papa had explained that in the union there weren't any friends or enemies — just fellow workers striving for a single goal: justice.

By the time my papa made his way up a hillock and began to

address the crowd, the sun was nothing but an orange smudge on the horizon. A quarter moon had just started to rise from behind the mountains and dozens of torches pierced the growing darkness. My papa's outline against the twilight sky was barely visible, but his voice boomed with fortitude and truth.

"Comrades! Fellow workers have been walking out of the job all over the *pampa* to protest our living and working conditions. They have said 'Enough' and *we* say 'Enough.' Enough is enough! We can't go on living in shacks that turn into ovens by day and iceboxes by night, working twelve to fourteen hours a day, getting ill and dying from all the dust and smoke we breathe in and watching comrades suffer horrible deaths by falling into uncovered smelters! And to top it all off, our meagre wages are paid in tokens that can be used only at the company store!

"The time is ripe for a general strike, comrades!

"When we all join the strike, when we bring the Atacama region to its knees, they'll have to listen to us, comrades! Without us, they're nothing. Nothing! We make their profits, we pay for their luxuries, and we are the wheels that make their capitalist world turn.

"They exploit us, they abuse us, and they kill us. They treat us and our families like beasts. But we're not beasts, comrades. We are human beings. We are workers. We are smart workers. We know better. We are the pro-le-tar-iat. We know that life doesn't have to be like this. Let's not forget the Russian Revolution and the Soviet Union, where the state is in the hands of the proletariat and their allies. Let's also remember the Winnipeg General Strike, the Battle of Blair Mountain, the Guayaquil General Strike and all those *organized* workers who stood up to the bosses before us and are still struggling for justice all around the world. Let's follow in their footsteps.

"Today, we're asking for better working and living conditions *and* for the Chilean state to nationalize the mines. We don't want any more Norths, Gildemeisters, Nietos and Graces owning our places of work. They don't give a damn about us, comrades! All they care about is their profits — profits that we Chileans make for them and that they're quick to take back to their countries — to England, to Germany, to Spain. And what about the Chilean state? Instead of making sure that these foreigners treat us like human beings, the state condones and supports their actions! This must stop. Saltpetre is Chilean and it must benefit Chileans, not foreigners!

"Comrades, we have to prepare for the long haul. This is only the beginning of our struggle because once we fulfill these demands, we must go on; we cannot rest; we will not rest; we will join forces with workers from the north, from the centre and from the south, and will keep on struggling until we realize our most cherished dream: to crush capitalism and establish a workers' socialist state. The future belongs to the working class, comrades!!"

The crowd was on fire and I was on fire. There and then I stopped having second thoughts about staying in La Coruña instead of going to school in Iquique. I was in the right place and had become the person I had always wanted to be — a proud miner and a member of the proletariat. Not only that, now I was also my father's comrade in arms. Under the Atacama night sky, my heart pounding, I joined my fellow workers in an impassioned rendition of the "Internationale," an anthem my mama had taught me as soon as I could string two words together. I looked at my papa, standing on his rock, his left fist up in the air, and promised myself that I would fight under his leadership and alongside my comrades until final victory.

FOLLOWING A FEW WEEKS of negotiations, unions representing an array of trades reached an agreement and the whole region went on strike. Miners, railroad workers, cart operators and the longshoremen in the port of Iquique joined in. Everything came to a halt.

It didn't take long for the government to side with the companies. The army was deployed to key points all across the land, and the minister of defence declared a state of siege and sent five warships with reinforcements to Iquique.

On June 3, our whole camp walked up the *pampa* to Alto San Antonio to attend a meeting called by FOCH. As we were stepping out the door, my mama handed me a black-and-red *chuspa* filled with coca leaves.

"You're a man and a miner now," she said. "Use just a few leaves. It'll be enough to keep you going," she advised.

Since starting work, I had been expecting to get a *chuspa* woven by my mama especially for me, but still I was taken by surprise. I admired the rows of tiny llamas and the playful tassels hanging from the corners before pulling the little bag's shoulder strap over my head.

"It's beautiful! Thank you, mama!" I said, planting a kiss on her cheek.

The walk up the *pampa* under the scorching sun took us more than three hours, but the bitter coca leaves worked their magic and I didn't feel thirsty, hungry or tired at all. My mama carried baby Rufina on her back, bundled up in her *aguayo*, and papa and I took turns giving my brother Moncho and sister Eva piggyback rides whenever they got tired. We also had to help some of the other families and their kids, but in the end we all made it to Alto San Antonio in one piece.

Thousands of people from other camps were already there, waiting to listen to our leaders' reports. There was optimism in the air, but it didn't take long for it to fade away. A delegation had travelled to Santiago and presented our demands to the president himself. The president had listened attentively and made promises. But nearly a month later, nothing had changed.

The crowd became restless. Some wanted to put an end to the strike, but most of us called for more serious actions. "Let's march to Iquique! Let's take our demands to the governor himself!" many of us shouted. "Let's blow the bastards up, set their houses on fire, kill their women and their kids," a few men yelled. My papa and mama had warned us that there would be company-paid agitators inciting violence and causing disturbances. Sure enough, next thing we knew, there was pushing and shoving, shouting and swearing, and in the blink of an eye skirmishes had erupted everywhere.

The mounted police, which until then had remained cool and composed, charged into the crowd. People started to run, tripping over each other, shrieking and crying. My papa and mama were up front, on the speakers' scaffold, and I was down below in charge of my brother and sisters. I held on tight to little Rufina and ordered Eva and Moncho to hang on to my pants. We managed to get away from the chaos and meet up with our mama, who had jumped off the platform, while my papa yelled "Stay calm, comrades, stay calm..." from up top.

It turned out that as he yelled into the megaphone, the police were being attacked by a mob. By the time the crowd dispersed, two policemen lay dead on the ground.

That afternoon, we walked back to La Coruña in bitter silence. There was no question about what would happen now: the government would revenge the policemen's deaths by sending in the troops.

We worked that whole night and the next day and night. By the early morning of June 5, everything that could be done had been done: we had occupied the mine; taken over the company store and parceled out provisions to every household; set up explosives in key spots; and dealt out borers, picks, shovels, pitchforks and hand bombs. Everything was in place and everybody knew what to do.

My parents were at the helm of the operations — my papa, as union leader and FOCH's representative at La Coruña; my mama, as president of the Women's Centre and member of the executive committee of the National Women's Council. I was there too, at union headquarters, listening to the urgent discussions on strategies and tactics, and running errands all over town.

One of those discussions had to do with the children. What to do with the children. My papa, supported by most, proposed that a few women take all the children up to the dunes, well out of the reach of the army. My mama countered that the children must remain in town and act as a shield. After all, the soldiers were working class boys, just like the young men employed at the mine. They would not fire against their own, and particularly not against children, she argued.

"What about the Santa María School massacre??!! They didn't care then; why should they care now??!!" some called out.

But my mama argued that the Santa María slaughter had happened eighteen years earlier and since then, the troops had become much more aware of their own exploitation as working-class boys and of the oppression they were subjected to by the officers.

In the end, it was agreed that it would be up to the parents to determine whether their children remained in town or went to hide in the dunes. My parents decided that Moncho and Eva would stay, but Rufina, the baby, would go up to the dunes with a neighbour.

Then my papa charged me with a very important task: to go out on the open *pampa*, watch the horizon and report back if I saw any signs of the troops coming. As I was walking out of the building, I saw my mama plant a peck on my papa's cheek, which he reciprocated by taking her face in his hands and kissing her on the lips. This was their first display of affection since the morning I'd started working. I ran back in and gave them both a hug.

I hurried to the *tamarugo* forest at the edge of the camp. As far as I could remember I had been coming to this place whenever I wanted to be on my own. It had taken me a while to learn to navigate the thorny branches without ripping my pants or tearing my skin, but now I could climb my favourite tree — a particularly tall *tamarugo* with thick limbs shooting high up into the sky — in the wink of an eye. Sitting on its highest branch I pondered life and surveyed La Coruña and the landscape beyond.

Our collection of shacks on one side of the square was a sorry sight compared to the tidy blocks of cement row houses where the white-collar employees lived. But nothing paralleled the sprawling grounds of the bosses' residences on the other side, not to mention their fancy theatre, social club, tennis courts and a riveted-steel swimming pool filled with clear water, which sat further back.

The soccer field, the train station and the mine were behind our camp, and beyond all that, the *caliche* fields covered the *pampa* with an uneven, motley crust. Past the dunes, the Atacama Desert spread out like the rugged skin of an old man's face, all the way up to the foothills of the Andes, where it gave way to the shimmering lagoons that nourished flamingoes, llamas and vicuñas. Finally, my eyes came to rest on the pointy snow-capped volcanoes and jagged peaks of the *cordillera*.

I had never walked that far, but one day I would — maybe after we won the revolution, and the mine, the swimming pool, the big houses and the theatre belonged to all of us miners and our families. Before then, there was no time to spare — we had to keep up the struggle.

As I pondered all of this, I scanned the *pampa* for anything unusual — vizcachas hopping out of their burrows, iguanas and lizards abandoning their sunny posts and scrambling under a rock, birds becoming restless... Those were signs that would signal the approach of the troops.

Soon enough a black-head lizard dashed off a rock and disappeared, while a family of finches began to trill and flew out of another *tamarugo* tree. I trained my eyes on the horizon, and sure enough, a barely discernible cloud of dust traversed the *pampa*. I didn't hesitate. I climbed down the tree and ran.

When I got to the union office I was so out of breath that I could hardly speak, but I did manage to shout "The troops are coming" as I burst through the door.

My papa handed me a burlap sling bag filled with hand bombs and sent me off to the soccer field to join my mama, the rest of the women and the kids. "If they start shooting, hurl the bombs right at them," he said.

The soccer field was crammed. The women had gathered in small groups and the kids were running around laughing and screeching as if this was just another normal day. The crusher cleaners were there too — standing in clusters, kicking the dirt and talking among themselves. I felt the weight of the hand bombs in my bag, pondered the power and responsibility that came with them and approached one of my enemies' groups. They made no attempt at tongue-lashing, just looked at me with slanted eyes.

"We're in this together," I said. "We're fellow workers now, comrades in arms."

I dipped into my bag and handed each one a few hand bombs. Then I repeated my papa's words: "If the troops start shooting, throw the bombs at them with all your strength."

It took me a while to find my mama, but as soon as she saw me she knew that I'd come to tell her that the troops were on their way. She cut through the crowd, grabbed her horn, stood on a soap box and began to shout: "Women, women! Women and children! The troops are on their way. The troops are on their way! We have to get ready. Remember: they have the weapons, but we have the truth! We all know that we cannot keep on living like this. Our men and our boys cannot keep on working like this. Our demands are just. So, be ready to face the soldiers with dignity. We will stand together. We will hold hands. We will hoist our banners and flags up high. We will chant our slogans loudly and with conviction. When the troops see and hear us, they'll understand that what we're asking for is nothing more than a decent life for our families. The same kind of life they want for *their* families. When they realize that we are as human as they are, they will not shoot! But if they do, you know what to do: those of us who chose to use hand bombs will throw them at the troops and the rest will retreat up the *pampa* and into the dunes. Are we ready??!!"

A resounding "Yes!!" erupted from the soccer field.

Soon after, we heard the first claps of the horses' hooves on the saltpetre fields. The banners and the flags went up and we all reached for our neighbours' hands. My mama began to chant: "We want justice, we want justice."

It didn't take long for everybody to join in.

That first slogan was followed by many others: "No more tokens." "Decent housing for all." "Workers to power." "No more oppression." "Saltpetre is Chilean."

The tapping of the horses became louder and louder, and now we could also hear the wheels of the military carts crunching the *caliche* as they got closer to the mine and the camp. Then we saw them: hundreds of them coming towards us, on horseback and on foot.

"We are your mothers." "We are your children." "You are workers, we are workers." "We are your brothers, we are your sisters," we shouted.

I hardly had any voice left when the explosions began at the mine site, and as if on cue, the soldiers started shooting.

"Don't shoot! We're your mothers, we're your sisters, we're your children," I heard my mama and other women shout. But by then, I had already reached into my bag and begun hurling the hand bombs until there weren't any left.

They kept on shooting.

Bodies were falling all around me. I was petrified. In the midst of the inferno I heard Eva gasp. I reached out for her hand, but she wasn't there. She was on the ground, flat on her back, her eyes wide open and blood spurting out of a hole in her chest. I covered the hole with my hands, sat on it, got up, tore off a piece of my shirt, pressed the cloth against the wound. But the blood kept gushing out.

Then I heard my mama shout: "Manuel! Eva! Moncho! Run! Let's run!"

"Eva," I muttered, pointing at my sister.

My mom stopped in her tracks and fell on her knees. She looked at Eva, looked at me and then began to scream and shake Eva with both her hands.

"Mama, she's dead! Let's run!!" I shouted.

She picked Eva up, I grabbed Moncho's hand, and we ran. Ran like crazy, urging the other women and kids to run too, while the bullets kept whistling past our ears.

After what felt like an eternity, we made it to a rock ridge that sat at the back of the soccer field. We scrambled up to the top and over to the other side, tripping, falling, crawling on our hands and knees, any which way we could. Then, right in front of us something fell out of the sky and exploded. I felt myself go up in the air and hit the rocks with a thump. I don't know how long I was lying there, but when I opened my eyes, it was already dusk and everything was quiet.

I sat up. There were bodies everywhere. Some were squirming, others weren't moving at all. A few women were walking around, calling their children's names. Kids were crying. I got up. My whole body hurt, but I wasn't bleeding anywhere. I called Moncho's name. A little voice came back from between the rocks. I found him in a ball, all shaken up, but unhurt. I picked him up and carried him around as I looked for my mama.

When we found her, the first stars were starting to twinkle in the sky. She was sitting on a rock, her legs splayed out. She was holding Eva in her arms, against her chest, as if she were a baby.

I sat beside her, put Moncho on my lap, and we stayed there, in a daze, listening to the kids and women cry and call out. When the full moon — plump and shiny, as if nothing had ever happened — came up from behind the mountains, my mom laid Eva down on the ground, got up and began to speak.

"What did I do? What did I do? I sent my own child to her death. I sent all these children and all these women to their deaths. What led me to believe they wouldn't shoot? What? How could they, the bastards! And to make sure that they'd finish us off, they sent the artillery in. The cannons. The deadly cannons!"

A few women started to yell at my mama, blaming her for the

massacre. A couple of them even tried to punch her and kick her. But I punched and kicked back with all my might, and a few other women also came to her defence.

"Flora didn't kill your children. The army did!" Señora Carmela, one of my mom's friends from the Women's Centre shouted. "Don't blame her! Blame the capitalist state!"

My mama dropped to the ground. Her teeth were chattering.

Señora Carmela took over then and ordered me to run to the mine site and come back with a report on the situation there.

Half the camp was flattened. The union office was in ruins. My papa should've been there because this was the centre of operations, but now there was no office. Had he been killed? Was his body trapped underneath the rubble? I turned a few pieces of debris over and looked underneath but found nothing.

Then I saw a few people heading towards the soccer field. They looked like phantoms in the silvery moonlight.

"Papa!" I called. "Papa, is that you?"

The phantoms stopped and turned, but only one opened his arms. I ran like crazy, tripping and jumping over the rubble.

"You're alive, you're alive!" I shouted when I finally felt his arms close around me.

"And you're alive too!" he responded, squeezing me tight.

Then he asked: "Your mama, Eva, Moncho?"

I told him that the bastards had killed Eva.

He didn't react. He just stood there. Then he asked: "Are they still on the soccer field?"

"No. We found cover behind the rock ridge at the back of the field," I responded.

"Go tell your mama that I'll be there soon. In the meantime, she has to round everybody up. We'll take care of the wounded, bury our dead and then we'll leave for the mountains. Well, *we* won't leave. You guys will leave," he said, starting to walk again. Then I noticed he had a limp.

"What about you, Papa? Aren't you coming with us?" I asked. He didn't respond.

"Is it because of your foot? What happened to your foot, Papa?" I pressed on.

He cleared his throat: "No, well, yeah... my foot hurts. I twisted my ankle... that's all."

Then he pointed to the dark void down the *pampa*: "The troops set up camp over there, on the other side of the tracks. They'll come back tomorrow at dawn, but by then everybody will be gone. Now, run!"

When my papa arrived, he stood on a rock and told the women what he had told me. He said that the wounded would be carried to town and taken care of as best we could; the dead would be buried in the soccer field, and then everybody would collect food and water and leave for the mountains.

Then he said that as soon as everybody was on their way, he would cross the tracks and turn himself in on condition that the troops not attack our people again and that the wounded be taken to the clinic in Alto San Antonio.

Before taking off, he knelt down and kissed Eva on the forehead.

By then, the women and the kids who had been hiding in the dunes were starting to come back. When we finally saw our neighbour walking towards us with Rufina in her arms, my mama and I ran to meet her, Moncho in tow. I had never loved my baby sister as much as I did that night.

The school was still standing, so we took the wounded there. In the meantime, the men dug graves for the dead in the soccer field. Many women went crazy when it was time to bury their kids, including my mama. She didn't want to let go of Eva. Finally, I took my sister out of her arms and placed her gently in her grave. Oddly enough, the soap box my mama had stood on earlier was intact and in the same place. I pulled a plank off it and wrote with a pointy rock: Eva Gregoria Garay Zelaya, 1915–1925.

By the time the mass burial was over, the soccer field was covered with crosses. Eva's grave was one of the few without a cross because we didn't believe in god or in crosses.

People started to leave for the mountains, but my mama, papa, Moncho, baby Rufina and I went home instead. We sat quietly around the table, a candle flickering at its centre and an empty chair next to Moncho's. My mama broke the silence: "We're not leaving, José. We'll stay here with whoever else wants to stay. Carmela and other women have already said they won't leave either. Those who haven't found their dead and who have to take care of their wounded are also staying."

My papa tried to talk her into leaving, but she didn't budge. "You're a leader and I'm a leader. You're not leaving and I'm not leaving either. I can't just abandon the wounded, the women who haven't found their husbands and their children. I can't leave."

As soon as the first rays of sun made their way through the slats on the window, my papa kissed us all and left the house. By then, Rufina and Moncho had fallen asleep, so my mama bundled the baby up in her *aguayo* and tied her to my back, hoisted my little brother onto her shoulder, and we left for the school.

"We'll help out with the wounded and wait for news of your papa," she said, closing the door behind her.

News came about an hour later, when hundreds of soldiers took over the camp, rounded us up, made us walk, wounded and all, to the slaughterhouse and locked us up in the stockyards.

They left us there for a whole day and night. The soldiers had also gone after the people who were leaving for the mountains, so they rammed them into the stockyards with the rest of us. A lot of them were wounded, and we heard that many had been killed.

The next morning at dawn they brought my papa out from the tripe room. He was limping so badly he could hardly walk. His clothes were torn and his face black and blue. They blindfolded him and made him stand against the tripe room's brick wall. Several soldiers were already standing on the other side of the yard, right across from him. Then a tall, square-shouldered military officer came out and strutted towards my father. He stood beside him, looked in our direction and grinned. His nostrils were flaring, one of his thick eyebrows was arched, and his eyes glowering with hatred. He took a piece of paper out of his coat pocket and began to read: "Yesterday, a war tribunal was convened and prosecuted José Cunac Garay Quispe on charges of crimes against the state and treason to the fatherland. The tribunal was unanimous in its verdict and sentence: José Garay was found guilty of all charges and condemned to death by firing squad."

The women began to wail and the men to roar. As the military man raised his arm, my papa shouted *"Viva el proletariado!"* — "Long Live the Proletariat!" An indignant *"Viva!"* exploded from the crowd. For an instant, the army officer seemed to hesitate, but then he hollered "Fire!" at the top of his lungs.

The barrage of gunfire sent me up into the expanse of the bluest sky. Down below, in the desolate vastness and beauty of the *pampa*, our ruined camp and the mangled mine looked like nothing other than mistakes of nature. But they weren't. My papa had explained it to me many times: La Coruña had been created by human greed and was just a sorry excuse for "progress" and "civilization."

As I hovered over the *pampa* and watched the camp's and the mine's remains, I realized that they had always lived inside me as much as I had lived in them. But not anymore. No matter what, even if we were allowed to go back, I would take my family elsewhere and start a new life. What I didn't realize then was that the space that La Coruña had occupied within me would become an everlasting black hole in my chest.

My mother's wailing brought me back to the slaughterhouse. The stockyard gates burst open, and we were ordered to walk out. I put my arm around my mama's waist, sat Rufina on my hip and urged Moncho to hold on to my pants. Tripping and stumbling, prodded by the soldiers, we were carried to the train station by a sea of wobbly bodies.

A cargo train was waiting, wrapped in clouds of steam, its engines revved up. The cars were meant for carrying saltpetre, so they looked like big, open cages. By the time everybody got on, we were squeezed so tight together, we could hardly breathe. Then we heard the howl of the whistle, and the train began to move. Rumour had it they were taking us to Iquique.

Iquique

THE FIRST TIME I saw the ocean, I didn't have enough eyes to take it in. We had been on the train for hours, breathing in dust and getting our heads baked by the sun, when Moncho started pulling at my pants: "What's that, what's that?" he kept asking.

I looked through the mesh. Down below and far away I saw a huge mass of blue shimmering in the sun. "Moncho, that's the Pacific Ocean," I responded in my most solemn of voices.

I knew because my mama had described it to me many times.

"How big is it?" I would ask her.

"Very big," she'd reply.

"Can you see where it ends?" I'd press on.

"No," she'd answer.

Now I understood. It was so big that it didn't fit inside my eyes.

"What's the Peciffy Oshan?" Moncho was asking now.

"It's that," I replied, pointing at it. "It's water. Tons of water. All that blue water is the Pacific Ocean. It's so big that we can't see where it ends," I explained.

"Oh!" Moncho commented, opening his eyes and his mouth as if that would help him see better.

"That's where we're going, Moncho, to all those houses down there, by the water," I went on. "That town is called Iquique and that's where our mama grew up," I added.

"Oh!" Moncho commented again, his eyes and mouth still wide open.

As the train switched back and forth, making its way down the steep mountain, I offered my face to the breeze. It felt moist and fresh.

From the train station we were made to walk to the barracks. Even though it was the middle of the afternoon, there wasn't a soul in the streets because the word was that the government had imposed a day-long curfew so the city workers couldn't go to the station to greet us. When we got to the barracks, the wounded were taken to the infirmary and the rest of us herded into the training grounds.

For the first time in days we ate: we were given a bowl of beans, bread and water and told to wait. So, we waited. After two days, the same military man who had commanded my father's execution came out and stood on a platform in his fancy uniform, his boots as shiny as mirrors. He surveyed the scene from up there, the same contemptuous look in his eyes, an arched eyebrow, nostrils flaring and a derisive smile across his face. He sniffed the air and continued to stand ramrod straight while the soldiers prodded us with their rifles and made us get on our feet.

As I looked at the clean, well-fed, arrogant man on the platform, I saw the crowd through his eyes: our filthy bodies, our clothes in rags, our hungry eyes. Only then did I realize that after so many days of misery we didn't only look like paupers but also smelled like pigs. I don't know what came over me, but the next thing I knew I was yelling: "Murderer, dirty bastard! *You* are the pig! You! Not us!"

He turned his head in my direction, but my mama had been quick to pull me down, and now I was sitting on the ground, her hand weighing heavily on my head.

The crowd stirred. The soldiers ordered people to stop shuffling and shut up. My mama made sure I stayed put, so from down there, surrounded by smelly feet and grungy pants and skirts, I listened to the pig speak to us as if we were the criminals and the murderers and not him and his troops. I can't remember exactly what he said — I was too busy feeling a kind of fury I had never felt before, but I did hear him say that we would not be released until our leaders signed a piece of paper agreeing to accept the government's orders.

There was one sentence that stuck with me: "We will not tire until every Bolshevik agitator in Chile is neutralized." I had never heard the term "neutralized" before, but I understood right away what it meant: "killed."

We were kept at the barracks for several more days — long enough for everybody to get sick and for a few more people to die. Fortunately, even though we were all burning with fever and coughing our lungs out, we didn't give the pig the satisfaction of being "neutralized" by the grippe.

When I asked my mama where we'd go when we got out, she didn't think twice about it: "Asunta's, of course! She'll know to come and get us."

Sure enough, the day we were released, there she was, all four-foot-eleven of her, a silver bun on top of her head, and her bright, blue eyes looking big and round behind a pair of glasses that could've been made with the bottoms of beer bottles.

She gave us all a hug and then examined us as if she were a doctor. She inspected our eyes, ears and mouths, even asked us to stick our tongues out, her glasses now balanced on the tip of her nose. Then she concluded that the repressive, capitalist state had not only treated us like shit, but also that we had high fevers and most likely, tonsilitis.

"Those bastards," she repeated in her weird way of speaking, as if her tongue kept getting caught in between her teeth. My mama had explained that Aunt Asunta had come to Chile from Barcelona and spoke like a Spaniard.

"No!" she replied, raising her hand when my mama suggested that we walk to her house. "You're all too ill. You can't walk."

Then she put her right thumb and index finger in her mouth and let out a whistle so loud that even the La Coruña foremen would've been impressed. In no time a horse-drawn cart was picking us up. A huge sense of relief washed over me. Aunt Asunta would take care of us.

Iquique looked like a metropolis compared to La Coruña: cobblestoned streets as opposed to dirt roads, street cars, a central square with palm trees and flowers, grandiose buildings all around it, all kinds of stores where Aunt Asunta said that you could buy whatever you wanted with *real* money instead of tokens (that is, if you *had* any money, which we didn't) and of course, my very favourite: the Pacific Ocean right around the corner from Aunt Asunta's place.

I don't think I had the concept of "ugly" and "pretty" until I got to Iquique. For me, La Coruña was the place where I had grown up and I had never stopped to think whether it was big, small, pretty or ugly. It was what it was. But now, after seeing the big city, I had no choice but to conclude that my hometown was ugly. Very, very ugly — a cluster of run-down shacks criss-crossed by narrow, dirt roads. I guess you could say that the bosses' part of town was pretty, but that was a different world, completely separate from ours. La Coruña was our camp and the mine.

As soon as we got to her house, Aunt Asunta ordered us to bathe. Moncho and I were already out the front door, looking for the public bathrooms at the end of the block when she ordered us to get back in the house and directed us to a tiny box of a building in the back yard: the bathroom. We had our own bathroom! Right in the middle, there was a cement tub with a brass gadget attached to the edge, which let water out of a spout when you turned the handle! And in the corner, a contraption in the form of a huge cup with a wooden lid where you went number one and number two! Not only that; right above it, there was a water tank connected to the cup by a pipe and when you pulled on a chain, all the water came rushing down and took the waste away! No wonder the bathroom smelled fresh and clean! I had read about drinking water and sewage systems in my schoolbooks, but seeing them at work with my own two eyes was something else altogether. Moncho and I might have been feverish and achy, but still we managed to have fun opening and closing the tap and pulling on the chain over and over again until Aunt Asunta showed up and ordered us to stop.

The private bathroom was not the only luxury in the house. There were many others: instead of dirt floors, there were wooden ones, where you could skid and slide to your heart's content; a large room with a dining table, a kitchen cupboard, a sink and a kerosene stove, instead of a coal-burning one; uninterrupted electricity (in La Coruña the power was turned off between nine at night and five in the morning) and a bedroom separated from the main room by an actual door (not a curtain, like in our La Coruña house). Also, there were large windows with glass panes that let the light in.

Aunt Asunta gave her bed to my mom and Rufina, put down a mattress on the bedroom floor for herself and set one on the front room floor for Moncho and me. As soon as we were all clean and shiny, she fed us *cazuela* and then sent us to bed.

"Don't worry about anything. Rest and get better," she ordered. She also commanded us to drink a horrible concoction called Bulgarian herb tea, and sure enough, after a week or so we were all back to normal.

Then, she began to enforce the second phase of her campaign: fattening us up. Moncho, baby Rufina and I responded to the new game plan with enthusiasm; we became bottomless bags — we could keep on eating forever. My mama was a different story. She hardly touched her food, and slowly, her portly self was replaced by a thin, older woman with salt and pepper hair and narrow eyes. It was as if she was afraid of what she might see if she opened them wide. She moved slowly, spoke little and could sit for hours looking at the wall. Perhaps that's where her past life resided now — La Coruña and everything that had happened there.

So, Aunt Asunta put phase three of her campaign in motion and focused on bringing my mama back to at least a semblance of her old, strong self. My aunt owned an ancient Underwood Number 5, on which she turned out the leaflets and newsletters she used in her political work. She started to leave my mama stacks of papers, which she *had* to finish typing by the end of the day. She also assigned her a few house chores, and when Aunt Asunta came home from work, made sure that they cooked together.

By then my mama's dream had come true: I had started attending high school, so I left the house early in the morning and didn't come back till early afternoon, when we ate our main meal together. Then, I left for the beach to forage for food, Aunt Asunta took Moncho along as she attended to her different projects, and my mama and Rufina stayed home with strict orders of taking a good, long nap.

Little by little my mama got her physical strength back, but not her combative spirit and hearty laugh. A few things put a smile on her face — helping me with my homework, teaching Moncho to read, listening to Rufina's nonsensical chatter. Most of the time though, she was quiet and withdrawn.

I liked my new life — how predictable it was and how safe it felt. At Aunt Asunta's house I seldom felt hungry, I was never too hot or too cold and I thoroughly enjoyed taking a daily bath in the privacy of our own bathroom. Mornings at school were full of surprises — like learning that turtles can live up to a hundred and fifty years or that in Egypt there are mummies just like the ones buried in the Atacama Desert.

But nothing topped my afternoons by the ocean. I could spend hours watching the waves come and go, the water rise and ebb, the foamy surf creep over and steal seashells from their sandy bed. It took me a while to learn how to read the ocean's hidden moods — coy, honest or deceitful, stingy or generous — all lying in wait under a sheet of glass suddenly shattered by a gust of wind, a gentle pulse turned thunderous without warning. I had to resist the temptation of outsmarting the ocean and learn to wait and take what it offered me.

The beach was a busy place: fishermen worked on their nets, kids hopped and shrieked in the waves, grownups combed the beach for unexpected treasures, and bums slept their drunkenness away splayed on the sand. Also, there were plenty of boys my age foraging for food. At first, I walked around and studied their ways out of the corner of my eye. They dug for clams, searched the rocks for mussels and sea urchins, set up fishing lines by sticking the poles in the sand and combed the surf for kelp and seaweed. Before coming to Iquique I had never eaten seafood, but Aunt Asunta's chowders and casseroles got me hooked. Besides, why pay for food when you can get it for free? As soon as possible then, I would join the other scavengers. But first, I would have to figure out how to win them over. They had come close a few times, stared at me shamelessly, and one of them, a blondish, ruddy-faced jackass twice my size had talked loudly to the other ones, making sure I heard him: "Have you ever come across such an ugly tadpole? If he thinks he can come to our beach and do whatever he wants, he'd better think twice. Well, I guess we'll just have to show him whose beach this is."

A couple of days later I decided to try my luck and started digging for clams. Next thing I knew, the tongue-lashing, brawny jackass had given me a mighty shove and I was in the water, battling the waves. Finally, I managed to get to my feet, gasping for air and coughing up the water I hadn't already swallowed. The bully and his buddies were laughing their heads off.

A few hours later I had a plan. Up in the *pampa*, I had enlisted the desert animals themselves to protect my territory. Whenever my enemies crossed the line, I shot a small rock at a flying buzzard, which reacted to the attack by regurgitating a thick shower of food. The stink was so revolting it sent the trespassers packing. There were no buzzards by the ocean, but I was sure another animal would help me stake out a place for myself as a forager on Bellavista Beach.

Earlier that day I had overheard a fisherman say that at night, the beach swarmed with crabs. "I got more than a dozen last night, enough for my mom to make a delicious *chupe*! But one of the damn beasts got hold of my toe and wouldn't let go! Look! It even broke the skin and my toe still hurts from the bite!" he said, lifting his foot for his friends to see.

That afternoon, I came home early. A while back Aunt Asunta had shown me a gadget she was particularly taken by — a modern, battery-operated flashlight. I had never seen anything like it before and asked if I could take it apart to figure out how it worked.

"Over my dead body!" she'd said, snatching it from my hands, walking into her bedroom and putting it away in one of her dresser drawers. "That's a valuable revolutionary tool, Manuel. It's a life saver when I go to the shanty towns at night to do my political work. Don't forget, those poor people don't have electricity."

That evening, I found the revolutionary tool, slipped it into my pocket and, after everyone had gone to bed, headed to the beach, a bucket in hand.

The tide was low and every receding wave revealed dozens of scampering crabs . I scooped water into my bucket, got on my knees, combed the wet sand with my hands and in no time at all I had three big crabs in the bucket. It could've been four, but the last one pinched my pinky and wouldn't let go. I tried pulling it off, hitting it, turning it over, shaking my hand, but with every new attempt to get rid of it, the crab tightened its grip even more. The fisherman was right; the beasts stabbed you with their pincers as if they were knives and then latched on for dear life. I dipped my hand in the ocean looking for relief from the pain, and within a few moments, the crab let go of me.

The next day I got to the beach early. I sat up high on a rock with my bucket of crabs and watched the regulars trickle in. The bully was one of the last ones to come. As usual, he was loud and obnoxious, making sure everyone knew that the king of the foragers had arrived. While he was busy bossing his minions around, I made my way off the rocks and onto the beach. Bucket in hand, I started digging for clams.

When he saw me, he marched in my direction. "Hey, tadpole! Do you want to drown for sure this time?" he yelled.

I ignored him.

He started running.

I got ready. I watched him with the corner of my eye, and when I figured he was a few seconds from me, I jumped to the side. He fell flat on his face, his arms and legs splayed out. I dropped a crab on each of his hands and one foot. For a moment I wished I'd had a fourth crab to make things symmetrical, but then decided it didn't really matter. Three crabs were already doing the trick.

The bully was now lying face down on the beach, squirming and writhing like a worm, his muted shrieks accomplishing nothing other than filling his mouth with sand. His minions came to his rescue and pulled him up. His face and the front of his body were plastered with wet sand and his eyes looked like bloodshot platters. While he jumped around and shook his hands and foot, the three crabs fastened on tight, he tried to yell something, but what came out was gibberish.

I felt the urge to laugh. I had to laugh. I couldn't help it. So, I laughed. I laughed loudly and I laughed with gusto. The scavengers, the fishermen, the little kids and whoever else was on the beach that day were all staring at the bully now, and when they heard me laugh, little by little they joined in until everybody was laughing.

I had expected his minions to help him, but they were too busy laughing. So, I decided to put the bully out of his misery. I grabbed him by the arms and pulled him into the ocean. He didn't resist. A good-sized wave dragged us into deep water. While I had taught myself how to stay afloat, I hadn't really learned how to swim yet and for a moment, I panicked. But soon enough another wave returned us to shore. The bully's face and clothes were clean now and the crabs had let go of him. We stood side by side in the surf.

"My name is Manuel Garay," I said. "I'm the only man in my family and I have to take food home. I won't take more than I need."

He looked at me sideways while he shuffled his feet. Then he turned to face me and extended his hand. "I'm El Rucio. Welcome to Bellavista Beach."

AS I WENT THROUGH my days, memories of my former life would cross my mind — the immutable, ochre expanse of the *pampa*, so different from the capricious, blue ocean; the sight of a fat iguana caught in my trap; the howl of the wind rushing through the saltpetre fields; Eva skipping rope with her friends, the warmth of her hand in mine, her hair parted on one side and held down with a barrette; the light in my papa's eyes, his calm demeanour, his speech at my first and only union meeting, his broken body when they took him out of the tripe room and the sound of the barrage of gunfire that killed him... Sometimes these memories cropped up as flashes or a series of pictures; at other times, they were a simple thought or a mumble-jumble of feelings. But no matter how they came to me, they always found their way into the hole in my chest. At night, in the amber light of a candle, I would turn them into words and spill them onto a blank page until the hole was empty and the page, full. By the time I blew the candle out, I was awash with a sense of serenity. Writing had become my new *tamarugo* tree.

LUCÍA

. . . .

March – July 1925

TACNA

. . . .

MY MOTHER WAS LIKE a hummingbird, always in motion, bustling about, organizing banquets and fashion shows at the Officers' Wives Club, going to cocktail and tea parties, shopping for this, that and the other. I longed to be like her, envied her bubbly personality, admired her fashionable clothes and stylish collection of shoes, and was enthralled with her jewellery and the heavenly fragrance she wore like a vaporous halo. I don't know if that could be called love. Perhaps, but I really don't know.

What I do know is that I adored my father and he adored me. He was handsome and dignified, and his self-confident poise made me feel safe and protected. He could also be very funny but most important of all, he called me "my princess" and he treated me like one. Not a day went by that he wouldn't compliment me on something — my hairdo, a new blouse, my rendition of Couperin's "The Little Trifle" on the piano...

Quite often my mother and I would go shopping for the latest fashions, so my wardrobe was always well supplied. But if something caught my fancy in between outings, she would insist that I wait until our next shopping date, claiming that she was too busy. Then, I knew exactly what to do.

"Mariana was wearing a pair of beautiful satin pointe shoes at ballet class yesterday," I would say in my most innocent of voices at the dinner table.

"Antonia, take Lucía to that place where she gets her dance costumes and shoes," my dad would instruct my mom.

"Pavlova's," I'd clarify.

"Yes, Pavlova's. You do want a pair of those shoes for yourself, don't you, my princess?" he'd ask me.

"Yes, Daddy, I do!" I'd respond.

Sure enough, the following day my mom would take me to Pavlova's, and I would be showing off my new pink satin pointe shoes at my next ballet class.

My father also used to give me exquisite presents for no reason whatsoever: a silver and ivory locket, mother-of-pearl barrettes, a pair of gold studs, a lace handkerchief, a music box that played Tchaikovsky's "Dance of the Sugar Plum Fairy."

"Why are you giving me such a beautiful present, Daddy?" I would ask. "It's not my birthday, it's not my saint's day, and it's not Christmas!"

"Because I love you, my princess," he'd say.

I cherished hearing those words, so every time he showed up with a new gift, I would ask him the same question and he would give me the same answer. Undoubtedly, he did love me.

I looked forward to late afternoons, when my mother was at one of her tea parties and my father picked me up to take me to Copihue Cultural Centre for my piano and ballet lessons. On the way there he would entertain me with funny stories and riddles.

"Miss Orange was crossing the street, but all of a sudden she stopped in her tracks. Why???... Because she ran out of juice!

"What do you call a cow that argues with her husband???... A bull fighter."

I would laugh with glee and ask for more.

The Centre was always bustling with children and mothers, so he'd use the opportunity to strut around.

"What a wonderful father you are, Major Céspedes! I wish my husband took such an interest in our children's education!

"You have a beautiful daughter, Major!"

"Lovely girl!"

"Pretty as a picture," the mothers would call out.

"Thank you! Fortunately, she takes after her mother," my father would respond, a hint of modesty in his voice.

"Oh, no! Look at that Grecian nose, Major! Identical to yours," the women would lie, smiling and flirtatious. He'd swagger about and I'd swagger about because I wanted to believe them, even though I knew that I didn't look like him at all. I wanted to believe those women because I could see how handsome he was and thought that if we looked alike, of course I had to be beautiful.

On Sunday mornings the three of us would go to eleven o'clock mass at Catedral de Nuestra Señora del Rosario, Tacna's cathedral, and then for a stroll at the Paseo Cívico. My mother would dress to the hilt, I'd dress to the hilt, and my dad would wear his formal military uniform, with all his medals pinned to his breast.

I treasured those mornings because not only did I get to wear a stylish outfit, but I also played fashion advisor to my mother. Over the years, she had coached me on how to opt for the styles best suited to my body type, combine colours and textures, and pick the most appropriate accessories for my outfit. Not only that, she had also taught me to be aware of the occasion I was dressing for.

"You can't show up at a charity event in a sequined dress, my darling! For those kinds of occasions, you have to dress modestly — a low-key shirtwaist dress in a solid colour, for example. But if you're going to a New Year's ball, bring on the sequins and accessorize generously!" she would advise, as we leafed through fashion magazines or pored over outfits during our shopping sprees. Before long she had come to trust my judgment enough to ask *me* for advice.

"What do you think, darling? Is this trimmed flapper too bold for church?" she'd ask, turning this way and that in front of the mirror.

"Well, if you wear your royal blue and aquamarine fringe shawl, it'll be perfect because it'll cover your shoulders and brighten your beige dress," I'd respond, taking the shawl out of the wardrobe and displaying it on my own shoulders for her to see.

"You're absolutely right, my darling," she'd say.

Then we'd move on to choose a complementary pair of T-strap shoes from her collection and a hand purse to go with them, decide between a cloche and a bucket hat, and select appropriate stockings and gloves. At last we would get to my favourite part: picking the perfect jewellery for my mom's outfit.

"What you have to do is choose jewellery that will *complete* your outfit by adding the right dose of colour and sparkle; no more, no less. No matter how expensive or beautiful a piece of jewellery is, if it doesn't go with your outfit, it'll wreck it," she'd explain. "Same thing with the size and amount of jewellery you put on. Too little will suggest that you're a penny pincher, too much will make you look like a Christmas tree," she'd add matter-of-factly.

Her jewellery box was the material of a girl's dreams: a miniature rosewood wardrobe with tiny drawers at the bottom and double-leaf doors at the top, carved jade inserts and brass hinges and handles. Her dad, a merchant marine, had brought it home from one of his trips to Japan, and my mom had inherited it from her mother. Sunday after Sunday, the ritual of choosing the right jewellery was repeated.

"Can I open it, Mommy?" I would ask, as I put my fingers on the wardrobe's door handles.

"Of course, my darling!" she'd respond absentmindedly, sitting in front of the vanity, her face close to the mirror as she fussed over her makeup.

The doors would whine as if saddened by the prospect of revealing the treasures they concealed. But all *I* could do was smile at the sight of my mom's strings of pearls, chains and gems, while I searched for the perfect colour and size to complete her outfit.

"What about your sapphire pendant with this delicate silver cable chain, Mommy? It's perfect for church because it's not glitzy, and it picks up on the blue threads in your shawl."

"You're right, my darling. Perfect. Now find the earrings that match the pendant. The last time I saw them they were in the bottom drawer," she'd respond, as she slipped her shoes on.

The pendant had a tear-shaped stone framed by a silver filigree trim, and I knew exactly what the earrings looked like: miniature versions of the trim.

The last step before meeting my dad at the front door was to spray ourselves with a touch of Shalimar.

"A lady never wears too much perfume, my darling. A scent must be an insinuation, not an intrusion," my mom would say as she squeezed the atomizer twice for me — front and back, twice for her — chest and neck, and then asked me to give her a third spray on her back.

The Paseo Cívico was the place where Tacna's Chilean and Peruvian crème de la crème met every Sunday at noon to exhibit their riches and exchange smiles and small talk. Only, Peruvians did it with their fellow Peruvians, and Chileans with their fellow Chileans. In fact, the two groups walked up and down on opposite sides of the boulevard so as not to bump into each other.

According to my dad, my teachers and the history books, during the War of the Pacific, the Chilean Armed Forces had "liberated Tacna from the clutches of backward Peru and endowed it with our country's superior customs and values." Both my great-grandfather and grandfather had been high-ranking officers in the Chilean Army, so my father had grown up surrounded by uniforms, flags and marches. He never tired of praising our fatherland and speaking ill of Peru and Bolivia. It seemed like all his stories and childhood memories had to do with military-related issues. For instance, he would boast that before turning two years old, he had memorized the last words pronounced by Navy Captain Arturo Prat aboard the *Esmeralda* during the War of the Pacific and that by age four he could recite by heart Major Rafael Segundo Torreblanca Dolarea's lengthy poem "My Heroic Regiment!" — something he still did with gusto at social gatherings.

When we had visitors for dinner, I would eat with Mercedes in the kitchen and listen to him brag about how he had trained as a military officer since he was a teenager and, after graduating from the National Military School, had had a "meteoric" career.

"You are so young to be a major!" one of our guests would say.

"And to be in charge of all military operations in Tacna is just extraordinary!" someone else would add.

"Thank you. Just serving the fatherland the best I can," my father would reply.

But now, his post was in jeopardy.

"My friends, as you well know, the Chilean government has yielded to Peruvian and international pressure and has called a plebiscite: the citizens themselves will decide whether they want Tacna to stay within Chilean territory or be returned to Peru. This is most certainly a sign of weakness on the part of our leaders, but I am sure our Chilean superiority will prevail, and Tacna will remain ours," he added, offering a toast to the fatherland.

I didn't really care whether Tacna was Chilean or Peruvian. All I wanted was to live in my town forever. I loved its clear, blue sky; its ample boulevards lined with tall, proud palm trees; the clusters of jasmine and honeysuckle that perfumed the air in springtime; the clear waters of the Caplina River; and the colourful bougainvillea that crept up fences and framed front doors, including our own.

Most of all though, I loved Tacna because of Mercedes. Mercedes had brought me up. Since I was born, she had taken care of me. I was her "Lovely" and she was my "Loly." She never called me Lucía, but "Lovely" instead. Then, when I started to talk, I wanted to reciprocate, but what came out of my mouth was "Loly." So, for the rest of our lives together, Mercedes was my "Loly" and I, her "Lovely."

In the morning, she would help me bathe and dress, feed me

breakfast, braid my hair and send me off to school with a big hug and a kiss. At bedtime, she would tuck me in, but not before telling me a story.

"*Los antiguos* — the old ones — relate that many, many years ago, a terrible drought punished the land. Not a cloud could be seen in the sky, not a shadow on the earth. The ground was parched and the air was hot. All plants and animals started to die. The *qantu* had only one bud left, hanging from a dry stem. Realizing that soon her last baby would also die, the *qantu* set it loose, but instead of falling on the ground, the small, red bud went up in the air and became a hummingbird.

"The hummingbird flew all the way to the top of the highest peak of the highest mountain, Waitapallana. Waitapallana was watching the sun come up when he smelled the sweet perfume of his favourite flower, the *qantu*. He looked around, but all he saw was a very tired, tiny hummingbird. The hummingbird came to rest in his hands and whispered, 'Mighty Waitapallana, have pity on the land of the Quechua.' Then she folded her wings, closed her eyes and died. Waitapallana looked down to the land below and saw how dry and desolate it had become. He felt so sad that without even realizing it, he shed two tears, which rolled down his cheeks and rushed down his body like gigantic waterfalls. Waitapallana's tears plunged thunderously into Wacracocha Lake and woke Amarú up.

"Many centuries before, Amarú had submersed her head and wings in the water and gone to sleep but had left her body and tail on the land, wound around the Andes mountains.

"Amarú had the head of a llama with a red snout and crystal eyes.

"Amarú had the body of a serpent and the tail of a fish.

"Amarú's body was covered with scales of all colours.

"Amarú had powerful wings.

"Amarú unwound her body and her tail and rose over the land. She opened her wings and blocked the sun. She breathed in all the hot, dry air and when she let it out, a cool, misty blanket covered the earth. Then she started to fly. As she flapped her wings, all the water they had soaked up while Amarú was asleep in the lake, rained over the land.

"When Amarú saw that the people, the animals and the plants had come back to life, she folded her wings and rested. The colourful scales on her body were lit by the sunlight and a beautiful rainbow appeared in the sky. The drought was over.

"Then Amarú wound her body and her tail around the mountains, plunged her head and her wings in the lake and went back to sleep."

The problem with Mercedes' stories was that instead of putting me to sleep, they'd perk me up and get my imagination going. In no time at all the hummingbird would turn into a ballerina in a scarlet tutu and matching pointe shoes, flapping a pair of shimmering wings as she glissaded and pirouetted her way across a stage. Amarú's llama head — a huge and elaborate headpiece held up by four dancers — would emerge from a flood of blue light. Mmmm... what about Amarús body? It was gigantic, so four dancers wouldn't do. Okay. The four dancers holding the magnificent llama head with the flaming snout and crystal eyes would be inside the head, so they wouldn't be seen. Amarú's body then would be made up of dozens of dancers in iridescent costumes. Every dancer would represent one scale on Amarús skin. All the scale-dancers would stick together and move as if they were one body slithering across the stage, as they followed Amarú's head. What about the wings? I imagined them as huge ovals covered with silver feathers, but how would they appear on stage? I would have to think about that. I would also have to figure out how Amarú would take flight and flap her wings. What I wouldn't have to think about was the music because I knew exactly what it would be: Rachmaninoff's Piano Concerto Number 2. A few weeks before my piano teacher had taken a few of us students to the Municipal Theatre to listen to it performed by Claudio Arrau and the Chilean Symphony Orchestra. Since then I hadn't been able to get it out of my head, and now I could see the little hummingbird rising from the parched land to the opening chords and flapping her wings desperately to the piano's cascading waterfall runs as she flew up to the top of Waitapallana. Long after Mercedes had kissed me goodnight, I would still be humming and seeing the dancers in my head.

As much as I cherished Mercedes' stories, nothing gave me more joy than our early evenings together. When I came home from Copihue Cultural Centre, we'd sit at the kitchen table over a cup of tea and homemade *buñuelos*, talk about anything and everything and then move to the living room and dance.

When I was in my mother's and father's presence, I enjoyed my "darling" and "princess" personas, but when I was with Mercedes, I felt free to be just myself. I didn't have to think about who I was or how to behave. I was just her "Lovely." It also made me happy that for that couple of hours, she didn't have to act like my parents' subservient maid but simply be Mercedes, my "Loly."

One of the last conversations we had was about the upcoming plebiscite that would decide Tacna's future as a Chilean or Peruvian city.

"Loly, are you Peruvian?" I asked.

"Yes and no, my Lovely. I'm Quechua because my *antiguos* and my family are Quechua, but I'm Peruvian too because I was born and live in Peru," she responded.

"But you don't live in Peru, Loly. You live in Tacna and Tacna is Chilean," I countered.

She took a bite of her *buñuelo* and sipped on her tea before answering. "Yes and no, my Lovely. I was born in my *pueblo* up the valley and that's in Peru. But you're right, I live in Tacna, which now is Chilean because Chile took it from Peru after the war. But Peruvians say that it still belongs to Peru."

"What do you think, Loly?" I interjected.

"I don't know. *Los antiguos* say that way back, before Peru and Chile even existed, all this was Quechua land. But not anymore. I don't think it matters much whether Tacna is part of Chile or Peru. I just wish that everybody would get along, live together in peace, and that Chileans weren't so mean to Peruvians."

"What do you mean, Loly?! We're not mean to Peruvians! You know that I love my Peruvian friends, the ones I play with at the river..."

"I didn't mean you, my Lovely, of course I didn't mean you. I meant other Chileans. Some terrible things are happening, my Lovely. There are lots of rumours going around, " she said.

"What terrible things?! What rumours?!" I asked, puzzled.

Mercedes took my face in her hands, smiled and looked me in the eye. "Nothing that my Lovely needs to worry about. Now, let's dance!"

We finished our tea, went to the living room and turned the radio on. As usual, we tuned it to Haykuykuy, Mercedes' favourite radio station, which broadcast in Quechua and played cheerful *huayños*, *supaypas* and *tarkadas*. I loved the beat of the *bombo*, the haunting sound of the *sikus* and *kenas*, and the nimble strumming of the *charango*.

As expected, Mercedes took my hand, spun me around, caught me by the waist with her other hand and led me forward, our feet flying and our bodies swaying to the pulse of the music.

"I want to go to your *pueblo* and dance in the *plaza* with you and your friends," I said as we swirled our skirts and stomped our feet. "When will you take me, Loly?" I asked, hoping that one day she would say "Next week" or "Next month."

All she did though was repeat what she always said: "Someday, my Lovely," which obviously meant "Never." While this made me sad, I knew, and I knew that Mercedes knew, that our world did not and could not extend beyond the house's walls and the few hours we spent together every day. She was the maid and I was the daughter of her well-to-do bosses; I was a fair-skinned Chilean and she was a dark-skinned Quechua; I wore the latest European fashions and she wore multilayered skirts and sombreros. We belonged to different worlds that were not supposed to come together. Somehow though, Mercedes and I had managed to create our own world, which, in spite of being small and limited, occupied the largest space of all in my heart.

But at age twelve, Mercedes' and my precious world was pulled from under our feet.

EVERY DAY AT TWO o'clock, my father took a nap and my mom glued her ear to a new episode of her favourite radio soap, *The Right to Live*. I would spend that time in my room, playing with my dolls, practising my dance routines and colouring. But a few months before turning twelve, I started to feel the urge to break free and get out of the house on my own. I talked to Mercedes about it.

"You're getting older and it's only natural to want to do your own thing once in a while, Lovely. Why don't you take a walk to the river? Just be careful and make sure to come back before three o'clock," she said.

When I was younger Mercedes and I would go down to the river together. I had loved those outings, but in the last few years, life had become so busy with school and my music and dance lessons that I couldn't even remember the last time we'd done that.

I hadn't expected to come across anybody at the river, so I was taken aback when I saw three girls playing with a red ball. I stopped in my tracks and was about to turn around when I heard one of them say: "Do you want to play with us?"

"Yes, join us!" another one said.

"We need a fourth player for Piggy in the Middle," the last one added, a big smile on her face.

By their accent, I knew right away they were Peruvian. I hesitated, but they seemed so friendly and welcoming that I walked towards them.

"I'm Chilean," I said.

They shrugged their shoulders. "Who cares!" they sang in unison and next thing I knew the ball had landed in my hands. We all laughed and kept on playing until finally, out of breath, we sat on a log and made our acquaintances.

Fresia, Susana and Laura lived not far from my house, but no matter how close to each other our houses were, we all knew that my world was completely separate from theirs; if we hadn't met at the river, our paths would never have crossed. Undoubtedly, our parents wouldn't have approved of our playing together either. But that afternoon we didn't mention any of that; they welcomed me into their circle, and I was happy to join them. That's how my outings to the river became a daily occurrence.

On a beautiful afternoon in April 1925, I winked at Mercedes, slipped out the kitchen door and dashed to the river. The day before my dad had given me a beautiful porcelain doll — silky blonde hair, rosy cheeks, a red button mouth and huge green eyes. She was dressed in an emerald green outfit that matched her eyes, and best of all, she said "Mama" when you sat her up. I couldn't wait to show it to my friends!

Fresia and Susana were waiting for me under our jacaranda tree. If I'd had to pick my favourite place in all of Tacna, this would've been it. The space was shaded by a canopy of trees and overlooked the crystalline river, with meadows, vineyards and cornfields stretching out forever on the other side. To the east, past the foothills of the Andes and the steep ravine that channelled the mountain waters into our valley, lay the Atacama Desert, and beyond it all, the snow-capped peaks of the Andes themselves reached up to the sky.

I took the doll from under my arm and offered it to my friends. Fresia studied it and then commented that it looked like Laura's. Susana sat her in her lap — "Mama" went the doll — and declared that she was exactly the same.

My enthusiasm fizzled, not only because my new doll hadn't

impressed my friends but also because I was reminded that Laura had abandoned us; for four days now, she hadn't come out to play. I sat on a rock and rested the doll on my lap. Fresia and Susana sat down on either side of me and for a few moments we listened to the sparrows trilling and fluttering in and about the trees and watched the river skipping the rocks. Finally, I broke the silence.

"She left without even saying goodbye..."

"Maybe she didn't have a chance. My dad says that a lot of Peruvian families are leaving town in a hurry because of the plebiscite and that we may have to leave too," Susana said, lifting a twig off the ground and doodling with it in the dirt.

"She may come back when the plebiscite is over," Fresia said, taking the doll off my lap and inspecting her glass eyes.

Two days before, the three of us had walked over to our friend's house. There were no signs of life; all the windows were shut and the blinds down. But the strangest thing of all was that a black cross had been painted on the front door. We'd knocked and knocked but to no avail. We'd called Laura's name. No response. Rested our ears on the door. Nothing. No voices, no noises.

There we were, pondering all these things when we realized that the trilling and fluttering of the birds had turned into a hellish racket. And, as if that weren't enough, it seemed like all the dogs in the city had decided to howl in unison, while all the cows in the countryside had started a chorus of moos.

What was going on? We exchanged puzzled glances and attempted to ask "What's that... why..." but now, over and above the birds, dogs and cows, we could hear rolls of thunder erupting from the earth itself. For sure it was a train on the other side of the river. The biggest train to have ever come to Tacna.

We skipped from rock to rock wanting to reach the other bank but were stopped in our tracks by what we saw upriver; an enormous swirl of something dark and sinister was bouncing and tumbling down the ravine, rushing towards us.

We ran as fast as we could and without thinking twice about it, clambered up to the highest branches of the great jacaranda. Down below, in a pool encircled by a few rocks, we could see the porcelain doll, floating on her back nonchalantly, her vacant, green eyes staring at the empty space.

Every hundred years or so, the mountain rains extend towards the west and also fall on the Atacama Desert. Then, the rivers swell, overflow their beds and run madly towards the ocean. It turned out that 1925 was one of those years and our Caplina, one of those rivers. It carried with it everything it met along the way and finally arrived in Tacna like a ball of thunder, a gigantic swirl of water, mud, rocks and sand, crops and trees, llamas and vicuñas. But not only that. Also, human corpses.

From the top of the jacaranda, we watched them go by. We saw heads, torsos, legs, hands sticking out of the jumble. One of those hands tapped the porcelain doll and for a short while continued to push it along before the vortex sucked it up. Once in a while, complete bodies emerged from the slush — bruised, swollen, mutilated, in rags, covered in mud.

When we heard our own cries, we realized that everything else was calm. No more roaring, no more howling, no more birds trilling and fluttering about, no more mooing cows. We climbed down the tree. The only sound in the midst of the eerie silence came from our teeth, chattering like castanets.

Holding hands, we began to walk away from the river. The mud came up to our knees and we could hardly breathe — the air was fetid. The street was not far from the riverbank, but our struggle to get up there took forever.

When we finally made it, we realized that we were barefoot. Our shoes had been sucked up by the mud. There wasn't a soul to be seen, but we could hear people calling, crying out. Still holding hands and shivering we started to walk. We were half a block from my street, when we saw Mercedes turn the corner. She called out my name and ran towards us. She urged Susana and Fresia to keep on walking gingerly towards their homes and took my hand in hers.

"Heaps and heaps of dead people came down the river, Loly," I told her. "We saw them... heads, hands... and they smelled... and I lost my new doll... and my shoes..."

"My poor Lovely," Mercedes said, picking me up and hugging me tight. "Your father is very angry. But don't worry because I told him it was all my fault." Then she whispered in my ear: "Amarú woke up, Lovely. Amarú woke up."

My mom and dad were standing at the front door. We had hardly got there when my father began to yell. My mom was snivelling. She hugged me and kissed me, but my dad just stood there, yelling. Then, all of a sudden, I felt a horrendous pain on my calves, thighs and buttocks, as if somebody was slashing me with a knife. It was my father. He was giving me a thrashing with his leather belt while he continued to holler at the top of his lungs.

"This is what you get for leaving the house without my permission, you disobedient little girl! You almost gave us a heart attack, do you understand? Do you? Eh? Until you learn how to behave yourself, no more outings, no more presents for you!"

Then he started thrashing Mercedes and yelling at her: "And you, stupid woman, ignorant Indian, where the hell did you get the idea that you, *you* could give permission to the girl to go to the river? In this house I'm in charge. You're just the maid. Do you hear me? I'm the boss, not you!" The last thing I remember is Mercedes' piercing screams.

When I woke up, I was in my room and the sun had already gone down. Mercedes and my mom were sitting at the edge of the bed, holding my hands. "What happened?" I asked.

"The river, you went to the river, Lovely, and you saw all those..." Mercedes responded.

"What did she see?!" my mother demanded, looking at Mercedes.

"Lovely will tell you..."

But I couldn't talk. I felt an explosion inside my head and began to hear the roar again and to see the jumble of dead people. I closed my eyes and covered my ears wanting to put a halt to the nightmare, but it didn't work. On top of everything else, I started to feel the brush of the dead against my legs and to breathe in the putrid smell of the river. Then, everything went black, until the next day.

The sun was already high in the sky when I came to. Mercedes was lying beside me, snoring away. I was very thirsty and needed to pee, so I crawled out of bed and went to the bathroom. My legs were stiff and pulsated all over with a stinging pain. I looked behind me and saw that they were covered in huge, red welts. Then I remembered my father's beating. Yes, I had disobeyed him, I had misbehaved, but I never imagined that he would punish me like that. What had happened to the immense love he claimed to feel for me?

I was on the toilet when I heard Mercedes calling my name. Soon after, my mom was calling out too. They both showed up at the bathroom door at the same time.

My mom approached me first. "Darling, tell me what you saw at the river," she said softly.

In between sobs, I told her about the roaring swirl of slush bouncing down the ravine, the corpses and the stench that I couldn't stop smelling. My mom hugged me, patted my head and left to turn the radio on in search of news.

Mercedes held me for a long time. "Amarú woke up and as horrible as it was, you were meant to see what you saw at the river, my Lovely," she said. "Don't forget what you saw. Don't forget."

I was soaking in the bathtub when my father arrived, giving orders at the top of his lungs: "Mercedes, get the suitcases out of the wardrobe and start packing our clothes. As soon as you finish, go make lunch because we'll be eating early today."

Then he turned to my mother: "Antonia, we have to move fast. Get all our valuables. Your jewellery, the girl's jewellery, the silverware, my medals, everything. And the photo albums. We're leaving.

We're being picked up at two o'clock.

"And Lucía? Where is Lucía? Lucía, put a few toys in a bag. We're leaving, my princess. Hurry up!

"Mercedes, pack your things too. You're going back to your village."

Mercedes came into the bathroom, helped me out of the tub, patted me dry and dabbed my legs with arnica water. We hugged and sobbed in each other's arms. She kissed my wet cheeks and I kissed her wet cheeks. We held hands and looked at each other in the eye. I don't know what she saw in mine, but hers were filled with fear and sorrow.

"We'll be back soon, Loly, you'll see," I managed to say. What I really wanted to say was "I don't want to leave. I want to stay with you." But I didn't say it.

She shook her head and repeated: "My Lovely, my Lovely..."

At two o'clock a military jeep arrived and off we went. Mercedes stayed behind, standing at the door, her arms wrapped around her little wicker suitcase as if it were a child, a bundle tied to her back and a few bills in her pocket.

The jeep took us to the train station. My mom and I were ushered into a small room and told to wait. It was dark outside when my father came to get us. We travelled through the night. There were three other families in the same sleeping car as ours, but we didn't mingle with them during the trip. My mom and I just sat inside our own compartment, holding hands and staring out into the night. Once in a while my dad would open the door and stick his head in.

"Everything is okay, my darlings. Don't worry because everything will be just fine," he'd say, looking in our general direction and blowing us kisses before closing the door again.

At ten o'clock an attendant came in, changed the seats into a bed and pulled down a wooden box from up above, which turned out to be a bunk bed. My mom took the lower berth; I climbed up onto the bunk and tried to go to sleep. My legs still hurt from my dad's beating.

I felt terrible about not having said goodbye to Susana and Fresia and even worse about leaving without knowing anything about Laura's whereabouts. I didn't know how I would survive without Mercedes, and to top it all off, I couldn't stop thinking about the dead people in the river.

"Amarú woke up. You were meant to see what you saw," Mercedes had said. "Don't forget." I promised myself that I wouldn't.

My mom's steady breathing told me she was asleep. I climbed down from the bunk and went to the bathroom.

At this late hour I didn't expect to see anybody, but my dad and a few other men were sitting in a lounging area at the end of the car, smoking, drinking *pisco* straight from the bottle and talking in hushed voices. They didn't even notice me going in and coming out of the bathroom. I sat on the floor, my back against the bathroom door.

They seemed angry — they were cursing the Caplina River and the desert rains, exchanging information about the flood, wondering if their work had been in vain and if the plebiscite would ever take place now that the cat was out of the bag. Once in a while they'd also swear their allegiance to each other and promise to stick together no matter what. I heard phrases like "Long live the Chilean Armed Forces," "Mazorqueros Patriotic League forever," "Filthy *cholos*," the pejorative word that Chileans used for Peruvians, "*Viva Chile, mierda!*" — "Long live Chile, damn it!" Their voices would go up then, but right away they'd start shushing each other and go back to whispering.

Then my father began to speak in a loud, clear voice and nobody made any attempts to hush him. I understood then that he was these men's boss. "We're heroes, comrades! We responded to the fatherland's call for action, worked hard, and because of it, Tacna is now more Chilean than ever before!"

I heard him gulp a swig of *pisco* and take a drag on his cigarette. "Our contribution will not only be recognized but also praised and honoured! Mark my words!" my father continued.

I could picture him in my mind — standing, his back straight, his chin up, his brow curled, intimating that he was deep in thought, and his gaze directed straight into the eyes of his audience. I had always loved this self-assured stance of his; it filled me with pride and admiration, but that night, listening to his words, I didn't know what to think. What was he saying? Was he truly my dad?

"How many *cholos* did we eliminate? A thousand? More than a thousand? Plebiscite or not, Tacna is now a cleaner place, a more civilized place. We swore to rid it of as much Peruvian scum as we could, and we did!"

My stomach heaved as I thought of the bodies in the river and understood right there and then that they belonged to Peruvian families, and that my father and his cohorts had killed them. They had buried the corpses up the valley, believing they would never be found, but the flood had unearthed them and dragged them down all the way to Tacna.

There was an outburst of applause, which nobody bothered to shush. The mood had clearly turned festive. It sounded like several bottles of *pisco* were being passed around and the cloud of cigarette smoke wafting into the hallway became thicker. Then my father's voice rose again: "Let's have a toast, comrades! Long live the Chilean Armed Forces and the Mazorqueros Patriotic League!"

Several toasts followed his; it seemed like each man was taking a turn at proposing one: to Arturo Prat, hero of the War of the Pacific against Peru and Bolivia, to Tacna women, the most beautiful in the world.

By now they were giddy and began to reminisce, to recount anecdotes, to boast. Who had scoffed up the most women in one single night? Let's toast to that!

Who had filched the most valuables? Let's toast to that!

Who had neutralized the most brats? Let's toast to that!

The mood became frenzied. Everybody had something to contribute. Everything was a source of hilarity.

"Remember that filthy *cholo*, Besadro something or other, in his striped pajamas, trying to hold his pants up with one hand and his hair piece straight with the other?"

"And that ugly-as-hell cow of a woman who refused to move and it took three men to pull out of bed?"

"And remember that big house on Freyre Street, when Gómez nabbed a porcelain doll for his daughter and the Major, sounding dead serious, shouted 'Sergeant Gómez, put that doll back right now!' And when Gómez put it back and came to attention, the Major burst out laughing, picked the doll up and announced, 'This valuable belongs to me, Sergeant Gómez'!"

I took it all in. When I heard the story of Laura's doll, I could hardly breathe and felt as if my heart and my stomach were going to jump out of my mouth. I pinched myself, thinking that perhaps I was having a nightmare, but my heart and my stomach stayed in place and the pinching only confirmed that I was wide awake.

Still sitting, I dragged myself to our compartment, sliding my back along the wall. I got up, opened and closed the door in dead silence, climbed onto the top bunk and fell asleep as if someone had clobbered me on the head.

Iquique

THE TRAIN TOOK US to Iquique, a coastal town four hundred and fifty kilometres south of Tacna. I have little recollection of our first few days there as I was stricken with a bout of high fever — a hazy memory of moving from a hotel to our new house, twice the size of the one in Tacna; a doctor coming in to check on me and asking me to stick my tongue out; somebody placing a cold wrap on my forehead... But my dreams and nightmares during that time are still vivid in my mind.

In one of them, I was suspended in the air over the river and saw the corpses rising from the roaring swirl of mud and debris, their eyes open wide in horror, their mouths screaming and their bodies contorting and convulsing. But then the corpses turned into a cloud of butterflies that took flight all around me in the most absolute silence, their colourful wings against white light. The porcelain doll was floating on her back, stiff and stony, oblivious to the fluttering butterflies above her.

In another nightmare, my father didn't have a face, but I knew it was him because of his uniform and his voice. He had the doll in his hands and was pulling her eyes out, but then the doll became Laura and he had her eyes in his hands, blood dripping all over as he laughed like a maniac.

Who was my father? The gentle, adoring man who treated me like a princess? The enraged one who had given me a beating? The funny storyteller? The handsome Chilean patriot? The zealot who had spoken proudly and with glee about murdering Peruvians?

Did I still love him as I had until a few days before? I didn't know. Part of me wanted to love him, wanted to forget everything that had happened since the day of the flood, pretend it had all been a nightmare and that my father was still the same person I had grown up with. But I couldn't. I had seen the corpses in the river and overheard my father's and his cohorts' conversations on the train. I could not pretend that my father was not a cruel, cold-blooded murderer. Whenever the full force of this realization hit me, I hated him. I hated him so much that I wanted him dead. I had no idea how he'd die, but one day he'd just be gone and I wouldn't have to think about him anymore. I'd be free. I'd go back to Tacna, find Mercedes and go live with her. Those kinds of thoughts made me feel light and buoyed, but not for long. When I came to my senses and realized that my wishes were beyond reach, I'd feel completely dejected once again.

While I was still in bed, recovering from my fevers, my "good" father would come into my room and try to cheer me up with his riddles and stories.

"There were two cows in a field. The first cow said 'moo' and the second cow said 'baaaa.' The first cow asked the second cow, 'why did you say baaaa instead of moo'? The second cow answered, 'because I'm learning a foreign language.'"

For a couple of seconds he would make me smile, but then I would remember the murderous man inside him.

One day I mustered the courage to confront him. "What happened to my friend Laura? How did you get her porcelain doll?"

"What are you talking about, my princess? Who's Laura?"

"My friend, my Peruvian friend; she used to come to the river to play. But then she stopped coming... And the doll you gave me was hers," I responded, my heart going wild.

"I don't know what you're talking about, Lucía," he said, getting up and starting to walk towards the door.

I took a deep breath. "She lived on Freyre Street, and on the train your friends said that you'd gone there with them and taken the doll," I said.

"You must've been dreaming," he said, his back to me.

By now, my heart was ready to jump out of my mouth, but I managed to press on: "No, I was wide awake. I was sitting on the floor in the hallway and heard everything you and the other soldiers said about Peruvians and the corpses in the river, the corpses that I saw."

He turned around. His nostrils were flaring and his eyes flashing with surprise, anger and fear. But in no time at all he was smiling again, as he walked up to my bed and caressed my cheek with the back of his hand. He was short of breath. "You were definitely dreaming, my darling, definitely dreaming."

But his eyes had spoken loudly and confirmed what I already knew: that I hadn't imagined anything, that what I had witnessed was real. And now he knew that I knew.

A few days later I also talked to my mother about it, but she refused to believe me.

"My darling, don't say such awful things about your daddy. You had a nightmare, that's all. Don't forget that your fever started on the train, so it's quite likely that you also had hallucinations. Put that ridiculous story out of your mind because I certainly don't want to hear about it again, okay?" she dictated. "Shall we go shopping for new clothes?" she asked then.

Most certainly, my mother was under my father's spell and couldn't bring herself to find any fault with him. He was her hero, her prince charming, her master and guardian. He provided a comfortable house, plenty of food, beautiful clothes, a titillating social life, maids and chauffeurs. After thirteen years of marriage, she still couldn't believe that he had chosen *her* for a wife — a cigarette girl at Apollo Cinema in Santiago — over dozens of "high society" young ladies, like the ones he took to the movies on Sundays.

In Tacna, I had loved to go shopping with my mother, not so much because of the new outfits and shoes I would be getting, but because other than our brief fashion consultations on Sunday mornings, these were the only times I could have her all to myself. As we walked hand in hand, admiring the latest styles at Venus's and Marquesa's, or sat down for high tea at the Tour Eiffel, I would beg her to tell me the stories about her life I had already heard umpteen times but filled me with excitement every time I heard them. She was more than happy to oblige.

"As you know my darling, I grew up in Valparaíso. I was the younger of two girls, *la regalona* in the family, the apple of my parents' and sister's eyes. My dad was a sailor with the merchant marine, so he was hardly ever home. But when he did return from his long journeys, his arms were always loaded with presents from faraway lands — like the jewellery box that you like so much. But those days came to an abrupt end when, after five months at sea, my dad didn't come home."

She would get teary when telling that story, and in no time at all I would be snivelling as well. How not to get sad when picturing the scene — a young woman and her two little girls standing on the docks, expectancy all over their faces, waiting and waiting, witnessing the joy of the reunited families around them and preparing for their own moment of elation, only to realize that their husband and father would not be stepping off that boat?

"The company told my mom that my father had resigned his post voluntarily and jumped ship in Panama. So, there was nothing they could do for her. No more monthly salaries, no severance pay, nothing," my mother would say, taking a handkerchief out of her purse and dabbing at her eyes.

My grandmother and aunt had been quick to write him off, and my mother had also pretended that she didn't care about her father anymore. But deep down she never understood why her beloved *papi* had decided not to come back to them.

"Was it because my sister and I fought too much? Or because our mom's food was not tasty enough? Or our house too small?" she would ask the space in front of her.

They had left their home in Valparaíso and gone to live with my grandmother's mother in Barrio Independencia in Santiago. Surviving had been tough, but they had managed. First, my grandmother had worked as a live-in maid for a wealthy family in the Providencia district and then as a labourer at a garment factory. Encarnación, my mother's sister, had graduated from normal school and then gone back to Valparaíso to be an elementary school teacher. My mother had not finished school.

When she got to this part of the story, she'd say "Encarnación had the smarts, but I had the charm and the looks," as she posed for an invisible camera. So, she had used her beauty and bubbly personality to get ahead. She had worked as a waitress at a couple of downtown cafes and then landed her Sunday job as a cigarette girl at the Apollo.

"The position definitely had its perks," she'd say, a flirtatious smile on her face. "I got to see the latest movies, wore a sexy outfit, got generous tips and met handsome, wealthy men!"

These men took her to the theatre, restaurants and clubs and also showered her with presents. She let them dote on her and thanked the heavens for her good looks and her good fortune. One of those men had been my dad.

"Ernesto fell head over heels in love with me, my darling. After our first date he asked me to stop seeing other boys, and shortly after, he proposed! I was absolutely ecstatic," she'd say, a grin on her face and her flawlessly manicured right hand extended to show me her diamond and ruby engagement ring.

The wedding at the Santiago Cathedral and the reception at Hotel Carrera had been attended by over a hundred guests, among them the country's most esteemed military and civilian leaders, including the president of the Republic! "Don Ramón was such a sweet man, but a terrible dancer, I must say," she would comment then.

In Tacna my mother had continued to rub elbows with the Chilean elite, and in Iquique she was quick to befriend the other officers' wives, as well as ladies from the British community. Her social agenda was busier than ever. If she had stopped for one second to consider that what I had told her about her husband might be true, her whole world would've come tumbling down; her dream-come-true life would've been shattered.

In Iquique we had two maids, and even though they never replaced Mercedes in my heart, I was quick to befriend them and found solace in their company. They doted on me and in no time at all had me hooked on homemade *chumbeques*, which they baked for our daily teatime together. They called me Señorita, which I found hilarious, but as much as I asked them to call me Lucía, they never complied.

Just like in Tacna, my mother continued to listen to *The Right to Live* while my father took his daily nap, so I used the time to escape the house. I felt bad about compromising the maids' jobs and safety — I hadn't forgotten that in Tacna my father had given me *and* Mercedes a beating, but I was desperate to get out of the house. I found it hard to be around my father. Since our conversation about what I had overheard on the train, there was tension between us, which he tried to mask with overly zealous displays of attention.

"Here's a bit of money in case you need to buy anything, my princess. Would you like me to drive you to school this morning? Shall I send a chauffeur to take you home from your dance class?"

Soon after arriving in Iquique, I had started going to music and dance classes at Queen Victoria Cultural Centre. When my father had announced that he'd be driving me there, I had been quick to react: "Oh, no! You don't have to drive me, Dad. The Centre is just a few blocks away and I can walk there and back. Thank you anyway."

He had looked taken aback but had not insisted. My "old" father would have insisted and ultimately imposed his will. My "new" father — the one that knew that *I* knew he was a murderer — had held back.

At first, I was surprised by his reaction, but then I understood that now I had quite a bit of power over him. While this gave me satisfaction, it also made me detest him even more. He was nothing more than a worm in the skin of a lion.

As for my mother, I didn't know how I felt about her. As much as she tried to entice me with offers of new dresses or outings to Petit Paris teashop downtown, I couldn't bring myself to spend time with her. The mere thought of it made me tired. All I really wanted was to be on my own. So, I talked the maids into turning a blind eye to my afternoon escapades and used my short periods of freedom to get to know the city.

Iquique was ugly. Very, very ugly. Not at all like Tacna. A few palm trees here and there, a few green patches here and there, a few flowers here and there, but otherwise no vegetation to speak of, no jacarandas, no tamarind trees, no fruit trees, no shrubs, nothing. Just brown dirt and grey cement.

Two o'clock in the afternoon was siesta time and there was not a soul in the streets. Most likely all the ladies had their ears glued to the radio and all the men were snoring away before going back to work. And the kids? Where were the kids? Definitely not downtown.

I must admit that Plaza Prat was pretty, especially with its Torre Reloj, an imposing clock tower in the middle of the square. It struck the hour, the half hour and the quarter hour with a series of haunting, deep bongs that made me feel like crying for no good reason at all. Right beside the square was the Municipal Theatre, a big building with columns and ornaments that to my mind looked like cake decorations, and around the corner, Baquedano Avenue was lined with huge, beautiful houses sporting front porches and turrets.

One day I was walking along Thompson Street, when I noticed a bulletin board pegged to the wall of an old building brandishing Chilean flags on either side of a red banner which read "FOCH — Federación Obrera de Chile." What caught my eye was a newspaper clipping with a headline in large, bold letters: CHILEAN MILITARY AND PATRIOTIC LEAGUES ACCUSED OF MASSACRE OF PERUVIANS IN TACNA.

My heart started galloping and the ground below me wavered, but I steadied myself and read: "The Peruvian government has made a submission to the League of Nations demanding a full investigation of the systematic murder of Peruvian civilians by the Chilean Armed Forces and paramilitary groups known as 'Patriotic Leagues.'" The piece went on to report on the Caplina River flood and the corpses in the river. What I had known and kept secret for weeks was public knowledge now. Finally, I could stop wondering and doubting myself. What would happen next? Would my father go to jail?

But the article didn't stop at the Tacna massacre:

Our country's Armed Forces have become experts in murdering civilians. Yesterday it was Chilean workers in Punta Arenas, Puerto Natales, Coronel, Lota, Curanilahue, Valparaíso, Antofagasta, Iquique, Santiago and the saltpetre mines. Today it's innocent families in Tacna. Who will be next? We stand in solidarity with our Peruvian brothers and sisters and add our voices to their plight for justice. WORKERS OF THE WORLD, UNITE! LONG LIVE THE PROLETARIAT!

Why had the armed Forces killed people inside our own country? What was the proletariat? Who could I ask? Who could I talk to? Nobody.

From then on, I made a point of reading the bulletin board every day. What if they posted lists of the dead in the river and Laura's name was on it? What if they posted my father's name as one of the murderers?

By then, I had also discovered the beach, so after my daily visit to the FOCH building, I made my way down there and spent the rest of my free time by the ocean. This was where all the kids went to play at siesta time! That's why I had never seen them on the streets.

Well... not *all* the kids went to play at the beach. Only the poor kids. Most likely, the rich kids were playing at home, just as I would've and should've been if I had been like them. But I wasn't, and every afternoon I wished I was one of the poor kids — they seemed so carefree, so happy and full of life, running around barefoot, jumping in the water, waltzing with the waves.

One day, as I watched them, Chopin's "Grande Valse Brillante" came into my head and blended with the sound of the waves. My dance teacher had played it for us the day before and prompted us to improvise, to use classical steps if we wanted to, but also create our own steps and choreographies. Now I could see the kids on the beach dressed in costumes representing sea creatures — dolphins, octopuses, seals, starfish, sea horses, colourful fish, big and small — dancing together without hindrance and liberating their light-hearted spirits as they moved to the beat of the music and the waves.

By now it was early June and nothing new had been posted about Tacna. Every article on the FOCH bulletin board had to do with the saltpetre miners and their families, the abject poverty they lived in, the miners' horrible working conditions and their plight for improvements. There were pictures of hideous towns and dilapidated shacks; of men, women and children dressed in rags standing on a pile of rocks, hoisting Chilean flags and banners that read "General Strike," "Resistance," "Nationalization"; of dirt streets and gigantic machines that looked like monsters from another planet. But what really puzzled me was a picture of something that looked like a coin with a caption that read: "It's 1925 and saltpetre miners' salaries are still not paid in pesos but in tokens that can be used only at the company store." What did that mean? More questions waiting to be answered.

On June 3, everything changed. I remember the exact date because that evening the music students, including me, were to offer a recital at Queen Victoria Cultural Centre. I had been practising Schubert's "Musical Moment Number 3" on the piano for weeks, and the day before my mom had taken me to Pretty Lady's to get a whole new outfit. But there was no recital because that afternoon the city was paralyzed by a general strike.

At lunch time, the radio announced that workers were walking off their jobs and the city was shutting down. "Bolshevik agitators are causing havoc in the region," the reporter said.

That afternoon, the streets of Iquique were full of people. Mostly poor people but also some who looked better off. There were men, women and children holding Chilean flags and chanting: "We want justice!" "General strike!" "Long live the proletariat!" Those words again: "strike," "proletariat." Maybe I could approach a woman holding a banner that read "Teachers' Union" and ask her what those words meant? But I was too shy to ask. Besides, I was much too aware of the way I looked, of my fair skin, my expensive dress and good shoes, so different from what everybody else was wearing. So, I made myself as small and see-through as I could and kept on walking towards the FOCH building. When I got there, I noticed that for the first time ever, the front door was open. From a balcony on the second floor, a man was shouting into a megaphone.

There were too many people in front of the bulletin board, so I just stood to the side and listened to him. He was announcing that the saltpetre miners were on strike and that the Iquique workers had also gone on strike to demand justice for the miners.

After a few minutes, I mustered the courage to walk into the building. There was a large courtyard in the middle and doors all around it, which opened onto a covered verandah. Each room had a sign over the door — "Transportation Workers' Union," "Seamstresses' Union," "Packing Workers' Union," "Longshoremen's Union," "Teachers' Union." Then I saw a sign that read "Women's National Council."

With shaky knees and a galloping heart, I went in that door. Why that door? I'm not sure but most likely because the sign had the word "women" in it and I thought that it'd be easier for me to talk to a woman than to a man. There were several ladies in the room, some engrossed in conversation with one another, and others at desks, typing away. Nobody paid any attention to me. I looked around for a while, discounting the few talking groups, and then settled on a small, older lady with a silver bun on top of her head and round, thick Bakelite glasses on her nose.

I walked to the front of her desk and blurted out: "Excuse me, could you please tell me what 'general strike,' 'proletariat,' 'token' and 'Bolshevik agitators' mean?"

At first, she kept on typing, but then her hands went still, she tilted her head, took her glasses off and looked up at me. "What did you say, dear?"

"Could you please tell me what 'general strike,' 'proletariat,' 'token' and 'Bolshevik agitators' mean?" I repeated, expectantly.

She looked at me, puzzled, but then a big smile crossed her face. She pulled a chair beside her and, with a few taps on the seat, prompted me to sit down.

Then, as if this was the most natural thing in the world — a girl coming into the FOCH building at siesta time and asking the first

person she saw fit to explain the meaning of a few words to her —
she proceeded to give me a sprightly lecture on the class system and
the process of turning the capitalist state into one run by workers, all
in a brand of Spanish that I had never heard before.

Rich people owned the factories and the mines, hired poor
people to do all the work, then sold the minerals and the stuff the
poor people made, paid the workers hardly anything and kept most
of the money for themselves. So, the rich people became richer and
richer, and the poor people were stuck being poor. In the case of the
saltpetre miners, they weren't even paid with real money but with
these coins called tokens, which they had no choice but spend in the
rich owners' stores.

So, the miners and all the workers in the region had stopped
working; they had gone on a general strike because it was the only
way to show the rich people that without the poor people's work
there would be no minerals and no products to sell. Then, the rich
people would come around and realize that they'd better start paying
the workers better and with real money.

I didn't quite understand the next part, about the time when
there wouldn't be rich or poor people anymore. We hadn't got to the
words "proletariat" and "Bolshevik agitators" either, so I thought I'd
have to come back so that this kind lady could explain them to me.

"Thank you, I have to go now," I said, getting up to leave.

"Not so fast, dear, not so fast," she responded, signalling for me
to sit down again. She extended her right hand and said: "We were
so busy talking about all those important things, that we forgot to
introduce ourselves! I'm Asunta. What's your name?"

"Lucía," I replied, shaking her hand.

"How old are you, Lucía?" she asked now, examining my face.

"Fourteen," I lied, feeling my cheeks go red and perspiration
start trickling down my back. I feared that if I had said "twelve," she
would've asked me where I lived, whether my mom and dad knew
where I was, if an adult had come to the FOCH headquarters with

me, et cetera, et cetera. Everybody was always quick to point out how tall I was for my age, so I thought that it wasn't at all farfetched to pass myself off as a fourteen-year-old.

"So, you're in grade eight," she told herself, before pressing on.

"What school do you go to, Lucía?"

"Saint George's," I replied, lowering my gaze and looking at my shoes, knowing that if my clothes hadn't given me away already, this would be the definite tell-tale on my plush background.

"I guess they don't teach you about strikes and the proletariat at Saint George's," Miss Asunta said, offering me a wink and a crooked smile as she continued.

"I'll tell you what. Why don't you come here every day at this time in the afternoon, and we can talk about all those things you want to know, the issues that your teachers and your parents haven't explained to you?"

I nodded and smiled. For the first time in ages, I felt excited about something.

"It's a deal. I'll make sure to be here," Miss Asunta said, getting up, extending her hand again, shaking mine and then giving me a hug and a kiss goodbye.

"See you tomorrow, Lucía," she sang, as I crossed the threshold on my way out.

"See you tomorrow, Miss Asunta," I responded, turning my head and waving my hand.

But there was no tomorrow. I was too afraid. What if I blurted out all about Tacna? Even if I didn't tell her about Tacna, what if she found out who my father was? So, I never went back. Little did I know then that I would run into Miss Asunta a couple of months later, but under very different circumstances.

ONE DAY, WHEN I got to the beach, I saw a large group of kids standing around one of the wooden arches where the fishermen hung their catch and repaired their nets. Right in the middle, dangling from the crossbeam and upside down, there was a boy. A dead boy. His eyes were closed and his face as white as a ghost's. A fisherman kept squeezing the boy's body with his hands, while another one dealt him slaps on the face. Then, all of a sudden, a spurt of water shot out of the boy's mouth and he began to cough. He opened his eyes, looked around, closed them again and began to scream and wail.

The fishermen untied him, took him down and stood him up on the sand. At the beginning, the boy was a bit wobbly, but soon he was able to stand on his own. He stopped crying, his face lit up, and he offered the two fishermen a big smile. All the kids clapped and laughed and repeated his name with glee: "Manuel, Manuel, Manuel!"

Then, they rolled a big, wooden barrel towards him. This time Manuel broke into an even bigger smile.

After that, I kept seeing Manuel at the beach — perched on a rock, harvesting sea urchins and mussels, searching for octopus or digging for clams. He was short and thin but looked strong and wiry. What set him apart was that he was a loner, like me, and instead of scavenging for food in a group, like the other kids, he did it by himself. A few little boys liked to follow him around and Manuel didn't mind — he joked with them for a minute or two — but never strayed for long from his task.

One day, on my way to the beach, I turned the corner onto O'Higgins Avenue and there he was, on *his* way to the beach. I thought of crossing the street, but then I heard: "What's your name?"

"Lucía," I responded, looking at my feet and then his — mine clad in a pair of sandals and his, bare and dirty.

"I'm Manuel," he said then, also looking down at our feet.

"I know, I heard your name the other day, when you almost drowned," I answered.

He laughed.

"Why did you want to get that barrel?" I asked.

"For my mama. She needed a good washing trough. Now she's got two, because we cut the barrel in half," he answered.

"Do you sell what you scavenge at the beach?" I wanted to know.

"No, I take it home and my aunt and my mama cook it. Sometimes, if I find enough, we share it with the neighbours," he responded, swinging his empty burlap bag. Then he stopped and turned to face me. I stopped too. He looked at me inquisitively and then asked: "Why do you go to the beach?"

I hesitated and felt my face blush, but I held his gaze. "Because I like it," I responded finally.

"But you're a rich kid and rich kids don't come to this beach. Aren't you afraid you'll get your dress dirty and your shoes wet? And you always come alone and keep to yourself," he pressed on.

"I like being alone," I said this time, ignoring the part about the rich kid, the dress and the shoes. I started to walk again, and he followed suit.

"I like being alone too. Then I can think about my papa and my sister, and about La Coruña," he was saying now.

"La Coruña?" I asked.

"Yes, the saltpetre mine where I used to live; up there, in the *pampa*," he answered, pointing up and beyond the mountain that wedges Iquique against the ocean.

Then I remembered the articles on the bulletin board about the unrest in the mines.

"Your dad and your sister are there?" I wanted to know.

"Kind of," he mumbled.

"I used to live somewhere else too," I blurted out, before I could stop myself.

"Where?" he countered.

"Never mind, that was a long time ago," I managed to respond, feeling short of breath.

By then we had got to the beach, so he went on to the rocks to catch his food and I took my sandals off and started walking along the shore in the frothy water. I wished I had asked him about the *pampa* and life in the mines, about why he had moved to Iquique. But then I felt relieved that there hadn't been any more time for conversation, because obviously, he was also curious about me.

If he had wanted to know where I used to live and why I had moved to Iquique, what would I have told him? Most likely, the official version that my mom offered her friends: my father had been promoted to lieutenant colonel and assigned a very important portfolio in Iquique. But I didn't want Manuel or anybody I met on my own to know that my father was a military man. He was a murderer and I was ashamed to be his daughter.

Every afternoon, when I got to the beach, I would search for Manuel and sure enough, there he was, on the rocks, filling his bag with food.

Why hadn't his dad and sister come to Iquique with the rest of the family? When I had asked him if they lived up in the *pampa*, he had said "kind of." What did he mean? Did he have other brothers and sisters?

Then, one day curiosity got the better of me and I followed Manuel home. It turned out that he lived just a block up from Bellavista Beach, in a small row house. I hid behind a lamp post, watched him turn the corner, get to his door and walk inside. Then I walked up and knocked. Right away I changed my mind and decided to turn back and run, but my legs had turned to jelly. The door opened, and Manuel was standing there staring at me as if he had seen a ghost.

"Lucía?!"

"I followed you," I responded, feeling very stupid.

And as Manuel kept staring at me and still wasn't saying anything, I added, turning and pointing down the street: "From the beach."

Then, I heard a familiar voice: "Lucía?? Lucía!!"

It was Miss Asunta.

By now Manuel had moved to the side and she was asking me to come in. "What a pleasant surprise, my dear! I've been wondering about you!" she said, as she gave me a hug and a peck on the cheek, took my hand, led me to the kitchen table and prompted me to sit down.

"That's Flora, Manuel's mother," she said then, pointing to a lady who was typing furiously at the other end of the table.

The lady stopped typing, got up, walked over, extended her hand and shook mine.

"Moncho, Manuel's brother is playing outside, and Rufina, the baby, is having a nap," added Miss Asunta.

Manuel was still at the door, trying to figure out what was going on, when Miss Asunta asked: "So, Manuel and Lucía? How do you two know each other?"

"From the beach," we both answered at the same time, as Manuel closed the door.

"But... how do *you two* know each other?" Manuel asked then, a puzzled look on his face, as he walked up to the table and sat down.

"Oh, Lucía came into the Women's Council office the afternoon that the general strike broke out. She wanted to know the meaning of a few words, so I explained them to her," Miss Asunta answered matter-of-factly.

"What words?" Manuel wanted to know.

"Proletariat, general strike, token and Bolshevik agitator," I shot out, counting them with my fingers.

Manuel laughed as if he'd heard the funniest joke ever.

I sprang off the chair and stumbled towards the door, feeling like a fool. But Miss Asunta's voice stopped me.

"Lucía, come back here and sit down. Don't pay any attention to Manuel. He's just being arrogant and disrespectful," she said.

"Manuel, you may have learned those words when you were very young, but Lucía didn't. So, apologize to her right now," she ordered.

I was still frozen by the door, my back to the room, when I heard Manuel get up from the table and walk towards me. "Sorry, Lucía, I didn't..." he mumbled.

"Don't mumble! Speak like an honourable man," Miss Asunta ordered him.

Manuel cleared his throat, took a good, deep breath and said in a clear, loud voice: "Sorry Lucía. That was disrespectful and ignorant of me."

Satisfied, Miss Asunta uttered her last order, as she filled the kettle and set it on the stove: "Good. Now, both of you, come and sit down. We're going to have a cup of tea."

MANUEL
· · · · · · · · · · · · · · ·

October – November 1925

Iquique

FOLLOWING THAT INITIAL SURPRISE visit, Lucía started to come to our house every day. She said she couldn't stay long, but there was always enough time for Aunt Asunta to give her a lesson on the struggles of the proletariat and for my mama and I to tell her a story about La Coruña.

She hardly ever said anything, and my mama and Aunt Asunta didn't ask her any questions either. I did, but her answers were evasive to say the least.

"Where do you live?"

"Over there," she responded, pointing her chin in the general direction of the door.

"What does your father do?"

"Nothing."

"And your mom?"

"Nothing."

"Where did you live before coming to Iquique?"

"Far away."

"Something very disturbing must've happened to that girl," Aunt Asunta declared the afternoon of Lucía's first visit.

"Well, she is a rich girl... She wears expensive dresses and shoes. And have you looked at her hands? White and smooth like calla lilies — hasn't used them for anything other than smoothing her blonde curls. But rich people have their dramas too. Maybe she saw something she wasn't supposed to see, or perhaps she was taken advantage of by somebody, you know what I mean.... a man?" my mama added from behind the typewriter, raising her eyebrows.

"Well, it obviously has to do with her family. That's why she doesn't want to say anything about it, and she doesn't want us to know who her parents are," continued Aunt Asunta.

"We shouldn't force her to say anything," my mama concluded.

"Tomorrow I'll follow her when she leaves the house. At least we'll find out where she lives," I said.

"No, Manuel, you won't follow her. If she happens to see you, she'll never come back. And you won't ask her any more questions either. When she's ready, she'll start to talk," Aunt Asunta commanded.

But I couldn't stop wondering. Another thing that really puzzled me was Lucía's desire to know about us and our way of thinking. She was a rich girl after all, so why was she so interested in our lives and our movement? Besides, she seemed to agree with the ideas that she heard at our house. Aunt Asunta told us that Lucía used to read the bulletin board outside the FOCH building. Why? Why was she interested in reading news about unions and strikes?

It was all a big mystery to me, even though my mama and Aunt Asunta reminded me that many leaders of the movement in Europe were not working-class people but well-to-do young men and women who had renounced their social class and joined the struggles of the proletariat.

"Take Rosa Luxemburg, for example," Aunt Asunta stated.

"Or Louise Michel," my mama added.

"Or Karl Marx and Frederic Engels," Aunt Asunta went on.

"Or Clara Zetkin," my mama said.

"I know, I know!" I said, frustrated. "Lucía may very well end up being a revolutionary leader, but that doesn't explain *why* she comes to our house *now* and refuses to tell us who she is!" I countered.

"She'll come around, you'll see," Aunt Asunta said.

I wasn't so sure. The one thing the three of us agreed on was that Lucía should not tell anybody about her visits to our house or repeat what she heard. When my mama gave her that directive, all Lucía said was: "I know how to keep things to myself."

"That's an understatement if I ever heard one," I thought.

As it turned out, she didn't have to tell us anything because a few days later we figured out who she was all on our own.

Shanty towns had been sprouting like mushrooms all over the north, not just because of the repression in the *pampa* but also because of the invention of synthetic nitrate. This meant that the demand for Chilean saltpetre was dwindling rapidly and many mines were closing down. Thousands of miners were out of work.

One of those shanty towns was Pampa Nueva, erected by the survivors of La Coruña. In a sandy field near the ocean, south of the city, they had built their shacks with whatever materials they could lay their hands on — flattened cardboard boxes, sheets of tin, planks, rocks, mud, fabric. While a few men and women had found work in the city, the great majority were unemployed, so they survived on what they could get from the ocean, the few coins the kids collected panhandling in town and what people like us could contribute.

Aunt Asunta had already been going to Pampa Nueva for a few months — a bag of food in one hand and a bundle of reading materials in the other — when my mama decided to join her. She was feeling better and, as she put it, if Aunt Asunta hadn't welcomed us into her home, most likely we would've ended up there ourselves.

"The least I can do is help Asunta and our poor neighbours," she said.

On one of those afternoons they asked me to come along as they had a lot of material to carry, including two extra bundles of the FOCH newsletter, hot off the press.

We had hardly got there when a military truck, a jeep and a black car drove up and parked by the encampment. The military had raided Pampa Nueva before, looking for "Bolshevik agitators" and "subversive" materials, so we buried our bundles behind a shack as fast as we could. We were figuring out the best way to leave unnoticed when we heard music over a loudspeaker. It was a military march.

By now, everybody had come running to see what was going on, so we slid in behind the crowd, keeping to the back to allow for a quick escape. Soldiers were unloading the truck and piling boxes and bags by the road. Also, two rich women and a girl, plus a *gringo* man had got out of the car and four military men, out of the jeep.

As the soldiers finished unloading the truck, other cars drove up and men with cameras and notebooks jumped out. Then, one of the military men climbed on top of a small platform and started to talk into a megaphone: "Ladies and gentlemen. Good afternoon to you all. Knowing of your difficult circumstances, these generous ladies, my wife, Señora Antonia de Céspedes, and Señora Margaret de Inglis, a distinguished member of the Iquique British community, took it upon themselves to collect goods, all in excellent condition and of the highest quality, which we bring to you today in a mission of compassion and good will.

"Our Chilean Armed Forces, which I proudly represent, were happy to help with the transportation of the goods, and Mr. Robert Brown, representative of King George V in our city, was also kind enough to help the ladies with logistical support and a contribution of fine merchandise imported from England.

"I take this opportunity to relay my warmest greetings on behalf of myself, my wife and my beautiful daughter Lucía and to assure you that our glorious Armed Forces will continue to work tirelessly for the honour and grandeur of our beloved fatherland."

It was the pig who had led the troops that had killed more than two thousand people at La Coruña, including my sister Eva. The pig who had ordered my papa's execution at the slaughterhouse. The pig who had shipped us off to Iquique on a cargo train, as if we had been cattle and not human beings. The pig who had held us at the barracks. The pig who had turned his nose up as he told us to watch out, because he was going to keep on killing us. Lucía was his daughter. A murderer's daughter. The daughter of the murderer of my papa and my sister. The same surge of fury I had felt at the barracks took over my body, but this time I knew better than yell at the pig.

We took off as surreptitiously as we could and practically ran home. My mind was racing. Was Lucía her father's informer, a squealer, a spy? Were her "innocent" questions about the meaning of words, her interest in learning about La Coruña and our movement mere excuses to get information out of us so that she could pass it on to her father? Any time now, once the pig had heard enough, would the military raid our house and take my auntie and my mama?

My mama was furious too. She believed that Lucía was indeed a cunning, insincere girl who had led us on. Aunt Asunta was of a different mind. She thought that Lucía was just confused and lonely and that her interest in the movement was real. Something had happened to her, she claimed, something that had made her walk into the FOCH building that day in early June and then follow me home.

After much discussion, it was agreed that we couldn't take any chances and had to leave the house immediately. Aunt Asunta summoned a horse-drawn cart, we piled onto it our mattresses and bedding, clothes, books, the Underwood, kitchenware and the little food we had, and left for Grandma Rosa's place.

Grandma Rosa, my mama's mother, lived in a little house very similar to Aunt Asunta's, but in Barrio El Colorado, farther from the centre of town. When she opened the door, she looked at us as if we were complete strangers. Then I realized that she hadn't seen my mama since she had left for the *pampa*.

"Hello mom, it's me, Flora, and these are my children. Remember Miss Asunta, my teacher?" my mama said, putting a hand on my aunt's shoulder.

My grandmother looked at us with a blank face. Then she glared at my mama. "You told me you'd be gone for a month. It's been almost fourteen years since you took off and now you come here with a bunch of kids and your friend as if you'd left yesterday."

At first, my mama didn't respond. She just looked at her shoes. Then she said: "I did send you a letter telling you what'd happened, but you never wrote back. I thought you were angry with me because I wouldn't be bringing money home anymore."

"Your daughter met a very good man in La Coruña and married him. That's why she stayed there. But just a few months ago... he died... as did her little girl. When she came back to Iquique she wanted to come and see you, but she was too... distraught... and ill, actually," Aunt Asunta said.

"Grandma, can we come in?" I asked.

"We are in dire circumstances. Please let us explain," Aunt Asunta added.

My grandma frowned, looked at her hands and moved her mouth as if she was chewing on something. Then she opened the door and invited us in. We unloaded the cart in a jiffy, piled our stuff on the sidewalk and walked in.

Over tea, my mama, Aunt Asunta and I took turns telling her our story from beginning to end.

When we were finished, Grandma Rosa did her thing with her hands and her mouth again, and then said: "You can stay here, but there's not enough money to feed everyone."

Relief brought a smile to our faces.

"That's not a problem, Grandma! Every day I will bring food from the ocean!" I promised.

"My salary was enough to sustain us all at my place, so it should be enough here as well!" Aunt Asunta said, stretching her hands across the table and squeezing my grandma's.

My mama got up, walked around the table and hugged her mother.

We settled in the best we could, and by the next day we had resumed our routine. I went to school, Aunt Asunta went to work, and Mama stayed home with Grandma, Moncho and Rufina. In the afternoon, I took off for the beach. Lucía was nowhere to be seen. Of course she'd do a vanishing act! As I worked away, I went over her visits and our conversations in my mind, trying to figure out if the motivation behind them could've been something other than informing her father. I couldn't find any.

The following day, Aunt Asunta didn't come home from work at the usual time. We waited for a good hour before I went looking for her. At her school, the afternoon shift had just started, and everything was quiet and appeared normal — kids and teachers in their classrooms and a P.E. class doing push-ups in the schoolyard. I walked up to the office and asked the woman sitting at the front desk about my aunt.

First, she just looked up at me without saying a word. Then, with tears in her eyes, she said: "The morning staff told us that the military took her away, son."

I walked out of the school and sat on the curb. I was trying to figure out what to do next when the custodian came out, sat beside me and began to speak: "They parked right here, where we're sitting. Three soldiers got out and went looking for your aunt. There was screaming and shouting — the kids were scared, the teachers too. When I heard the kerfuffle, I came running out. The soldiers were dragging Miss Asunta out of the school. The principal tried to stop them, but they shoved her aside. Your aunt cursed them, kicked them, spat on them, and then she yelled her name out really loud as they were forcing her into the jeep," he said.

He smiled a sad smile as he went on: "'My name is Asunta Vila and these bastards are arresting me because I'm an anarchist! My name is Asunta Vila, my name is Asunta Vila!' is what she hollered at the top of her lungs."

I could see my aunt fighting back, hear her voice swearing at the soldiers and shouting her name. She was tough and strong-minded, but she was so small... and she was old. I sat at the curb for a while, a flood of sadness washing over me. But then the sadness turned into rage. I cursed Lucía with all my might, her pretty face, her fancy clothes, her stupid questions, her mousy voice, all about her. And I cursed her father, the assassin, the pig. If Aunt Asunta hadn't been so candid and kind, Lucía would not have become a fixture at our house and none of this would've happened!

I ran to the barracks to ask about my aunt, but the soldiers at the gate sent me packing. I went to the FOCH building to see if any of her comrades had heard anything, but they hadn't. My mama was afraid that if I kept trying to find my aunt, the soldiers would follow me to our house and take *her* away. At the shanty town, the reporters had probably snapped plenty of photos of us. And, even more important, if Lucía had squealed on us and was to blame for my aunt's arrest, she would've already identified my mama in the pictures.

So, all we could do was hope that Aunt Asunta would be released and when we were least expecting it, walk in the door and start condemning the capitalist state and its mercenary armed forces. She'd be scrawny, dirty, black and blue all over, her hair in knots, but her eyes would be as blue and fiery as ever. But more than a week went by and Aunt Asunta didn't come back.

Now, without her salary, we didn't have an income and Grandma Rosa's pension was not enough to support us all. For a moment my mama considered looking for a job at a factory or a packing plant, but my grandma talked her out of it: "You said it yourself, Flora. You can't run the risk of getting arrested."

After talking about it for a while, it was decided that I'd go back to Aunt Asunta's house, get the furniture and sell it at the flea market by the port. Also, I'd bring back the two halves of the barrel, which we had left in the backyard. Grandma Rosa would offer Mama's laundry services in the well-to-do houses on the other side of the square. And finally, I'd stop going to school and look for a job.

This sent my mama into a crying fit, and in no time, Grandma was sobbing and Moncho and Rufina were wailing. So, before *I* broke down and joined the chorus, I left the house.

The beach was deserted. I sat on a rock and watched the sun — a blazing red ball hanging over the tenuous, quivering line that separates day from night. The sky and the ocean were smeared with blood and the clouds seemed to be made of copper and ash. I had heard the word "torture" whispered when my papa was being taken out of the tripe room. I knew what it meant. I had heard it a couple of years before, when a few FOCH leaders had been arrested in Iquique.

"Most likely they're torturing them," my mama had said to my papa. "They'll want to know where the clandestine printshop is, who writes the articles for *The Voice of the Proletariat*."

"Hopefully they'll be able to resist long enough for our comrades to move the shop and go into hiding," my papa had said.

"What's 'torture'?" I had asked.

My mama and papa had looked at each other. Finally, my mama had responded: "Torture is hurting somebody on purpose, just to make them suffer or to get information out of them," she'd said.

Where was Aunt Asunta now? Was she being tortured as I watched the sun sink below the horizon, the shadows of night begin to shroud the ocean and the stars speckle the sky with silver? Why was I enjoying the onset of night while most likely Aunt Asunta was suffering or already dead? Why was I still alive in the midst of so much tragedy? Was it only so that I could support my family or was there another reason as well? That evening I wondered about God and understood why people believed in him — to find solace, to get answers to questions they couldn't answer. But I decided that I would find my answers within myself and in the world around me — the world I lived in. Eventually, I would understand why I had been spared and what the purpose of my life was.

Before leaving for Grandma Rosa's, I had made sure to slip Aunt Asunta's "revolutionary tool," her battery-run flashlight into my pocket. Now I used it to make my way along the beach and onto the street.

When I got to the house, the neighbours were quick to come out and tell me what had happened since we'd left. The "rich girl" had come to visit the day after we'd moved out and late that same evening the house had been raided by the military. They took the letter the rich girl had slid under the door.

"What letter?!" I asked, puzzled.

"We saw her through the window," the mother replied. "She didn't knock, she just slid a letter under the door and turned to leave. That's when I came out and told her that you all had moved out the day before. Then, when the military came later on that day, I saw one of them put the letter in his pocket."

"What did the girl say?" I asked, feeling my heart go wild.

"Nothing, really. She wanted to know where you'd gone, that's all. But we didn't know," she responded, offering me a coy smile and fishing for an answer. She'd always been a nosy woman, but for the first time now I was thankful for it. If she'd been minding her own business, she wouldn't have seen Lucía slide a letter under the door. Then, she asked outright: "Where are you staying?"

I responded with another question: "Did the military ask you where we'd gone?"

"Yeah. They did, but we didn't know."

"What else did they ask you?"

"Oh, nothing much. If a lot of people came to your house. That kind of thing."

"What did you say?"

"I said 'No, just friends of your auntie's.'"

"Did they show you pictures?"

"Yeah, but I didn't recognize anybody. The only people I knew were Miss Asunta and your mommy — they were standing side by side and Señora Flora was holding Rufina in her arms."

I thanked her for filling me in and went into the house. I didn't need the key, as the lock had been forced and the door was ajar. The kids next door helped me load everything onto a horse-drawn cart and I left for the port.

The market was swarming with people, and it didn't take long to get rid of the furniture. After about an hour I had a wad of bills in my pocket. I bought a rickety wheelbarrow from an old man — thought that it might come in handy, depending on the kind of job I got — loaded the two troughs onto it and started on my way to Grandma's. The wheelbarrow kept tipping over, but eventually I got the hang of it. When I made it home, set the contraptions on the floor and the wad of bills on the table, my brother and sister clapped, my mama offered me a big smile, and Grandma Rosa planted a kiss on my cheek.

The next day, I started looking for a job. It took me three days to find one.

The longshoremen laughed at me when I told them I wanted to work at the docks. "You want to work at the docks?" one fellow shouted, crimping his face and pointing at me with his index finger as if I was a circus freak. "Hey, guys! What do you think?! This shrimp here wants to work the docks!" he announced to the other men who were trotting up and down a ramp with sacks on their shoulders. They all turned, sized me up and burst out laughing. "Sorry kid, but you're too young and too small for this kind of work," the clown said then, as he picked up a sack.

I was so embarrassed I ran out of there as fast as I could.

Then I tried a few tanneries, a packing plant, a clothing factory and several blacksmith's shops. Nobody wanted me. They either didn't need anyone or I was too young and too small for the job.

On the third day I went to the beach and talked to the fishermen who had saved my life a few months before. They offered to take me out to sea with them but explained that they couldn't pay me. The best they could do was let me have a few fish which I could sell at the market. By then I was getting desperate, so I almost said "Yes," but decided to think about it instead. I thanked them and went to sit on the rock where I used to search for sea urchins and mussels. I thought and thought about what else I could do, what kinds of things I *knew* how to do other than cleaning crushers, and then it dawned on me: I was a good reader and a good writer.

I walked to the news stand on Plaza Pratt and asked the woman which papers and magazines were published in Iquique. She thought about it for a bit and then picked up *El Nortino — The Northerner*.

"This is a very good magazine son, and it's fairly new," she explained, while leafing through its pages. "Started to come out just a couple of months ago. It has very informative articles about all kinds of things, national and international news, interviews, book reviews, true stories, funny stories and even poems! I love reading it myself. Are you going to buy it?" she asked then, closing the magazine and holding it close to her chest.

"I wish I could, because my mama would just love it and actually, me too," I replied coyly. "But my papa died, my auntie died, and now I'm the only breadwinner in our household," I went on, lowering my eyes and letting out a big sigh. I knew that a sad story would soften the woman's heart and I really needed to get my hands on that magazine no matter what.

"I'll tell you what," I continued, looking at her in the eye. "Let me have it and I promise to come back and pay you... let's say next Wednesday evening." I figured by then I would've pinched a few coins from the grocery money and who knows, I might even have a job! "Please?" I pleaded.

The woman tilted her head, pressed her lips together, gave me a sideways look, blinked a few times and finally handed me the magazine.

I offered her my best smile, thanked her profusely and ran to the other side of the square. I sat on a bench and read *The Northerner* from cover to cover. By then, I had concocted a plan. I went home, washed myself, changed into clean clothes, polished my shoes, slicked my hair down, pulled my notebook out of my schoolbag and then took my time walking to 347 Patricio Lynch Street, the address on the magazine's masthead.

A couple of weeks after starting school in Iquique, the teacher had asked us to write a composition about our family. I went through my journal, picked out some passages that I could insert into my story and started to write. I talked about how our family of six had turned into a family of four in less than twenty-four hours, only to change again to a family of five when my mama's friend Asunta had opened her home to us and become our auntie. I described the *pampa* and life at La Coruña, explained our movement, the strike and the attack by the army. I talked about all the people who had been killed, including my sister Eva, my papa's execution and the train ride to Iquique. I poured my heart out, but I didn't whine. I didn't want the teacher to feel sorry for us. I just wanted her to know the truth.

A couple of days later, she asked me to stay after class. With teary eyes, she told me that mine was the best composition she had read by any of her students, ever.

"What happened to your family and the people of La Coruña is nothing less than a tragedy, Manuel. You write about it very eloquently and convincingly, but not only that; your descriptions of the *pampa* are beautiful, and the portraits you paint of the *pampinos* are so vivid. You bring it all to life, son. The way you tell it is clear and compelling... and moving. So sorry about your father and your sister. That's absolutely... revolting. You're very strong, Manuel, and so is your mom."

By the time she had finished, tears were rolling down her cheeks and mine as well. I grabbed my notebook off the desk and ran out of the room.

Now, I had a plan. I would show my composition to the boss of *The Northerner*, or rather the "editor" — a word I had learned by studying the magazine's masthead.

When I told the receptionist that I was there to see Mr. Hector

Bacic, she looked puzzled. "It's about business," I clarified. "It's important," I added.

"But what's the specific purpose of your visit?" she wanted to know.

"That's something I would rather discuss with him directly," I responded, doing my best not to fidget with the notebook and the magazine and to look calm and collected.

"Wait a minute," she replied then. She left her desk for a few moments, and when she came back, directed me to go through the door to her left and knock on the first door on the right.

While in the reception area I had heard the din coming out of that door, but when I crossed the threshold, I couldn't believe my eyes and my ears — through a cloud of cigarette smoke, I could discern at least a dozen men and women sitting at desks, all typing away as if there was no tomorrow. As I took the scene in, I knocked on the first door on the right.

"Come in!" a raspy voice commanded.

Behind mountains of papers, books and magazines sat a big, rosy-cheeked man with a cigarillo dangling out of the corner of his mouth and a pair of wire-rimmed glasses perched on the tip of his nose.

"What can I do for you, son?" he hollered, banging the desk with the palms of his hands.

I cleared my throat and responded: "My name is Manuel Garay and I would like to show you a composition I wrote and that my teacher at Boys' School Number 2 found... interesting and... compelling."

"Mmmm. I'm a busy man, Manuel," he responded, looking at me over the rim of his glasses while holding on to the desk and balancing his chair on its back legs. Then he brought the chair to rest on its four legs and took a long, deep drag on his now very short cigarillo.

"Why would a busy man like me want to read your composition, son?" he asked, putting the cigarillo out in an already half full ashtray.

I cleared my throat again, collected my thoughts, pulled the issue of *The Northerner* from under my arm and replied: "With all due respect, sir, I have read this issue of the magazine, and while I'm very impressed with all the interesting articles, I would like to say that in my opinion *The Northerner* would benefit from a story like mine — a true story that can really grab a reader's attention and leave him begging for more."

I had been practising this speech since I had devised my plan and was quite pleased with the way it came out.

All this time I had been standing in front of Mr. Bacic's desk, so when he motioned for me to sit down and asked me to hand him my notebook, I knew I had won my first battle.

It took him an eternity to read it. At the beginning, he kept moving his eyes from the page to me, but after a while, his eyes stayed lowered and fixed on the writing. I had won my second battle.

When he finally finished, he took a white handkerchief out of his pants' pocket and mopped his brow. He put the kerchief back in his pocket, opened a drawer and took out a bottle of *pisco* and a glass. He poured himself a good two inches and took a long swig. Then he pulled a cigarillo out of his shirt pocket, reached for a box of matches on his desk, struck a match, lit the cigarillo, took a few slow drags and nodded his head a few times.

I was doing my best to stay still, but my right leg wasn't. It kept twitching, no matter how much I wanted it to stop.

"Yes," Mr. Bacic said finally. "Yes, I see what you mean," he added, leafing through my notebook.

"How old are you Manuel?" he asked.

I knew that at some point he'd ask me that question and I had already decided to say that I was thirteen, which wasn't really a lie because in a few months I would turn thirteen.

"Thirteen," I replied.

"And who taught you how to write?" he went on.

"My mama and my teacher at La Coruña," I responded.

"Son, what I mean is who taught you how to compose a story,

to tell a story, not just how to form the letters and the words," he explained.

"Nobody, sir," I said. "I just told my story, that's all."

"Mmmm. You have a very good story here, Manuel. It needs some work... Any writer needs years to hone his skills and so will you, son, but this is a very good start," he said, waving my notebook.

"Thank you, sir."

"And it's a true story?"

"Yes sir. All true. Not a lie in it."

"Mmmm... Listen to me son. Your story is not quite ready for publication, but we can work on that. But even if it were, I couldn't publish it now — the magazine would be shut down by the government and I would go to jail. But at some point, when this situation is over and we have our freedoms back, I will publish it in installments. One page per week. Do you know what I mean?"

I nodded.

"In the meantime, here's what I want you to do. I want you to write short compositions about Iquique — your impressions, what you see, little stories, anecdotes, minor events that you've witnessed or that have happened to you. I will be your editor, guide you through the process, teach you what you don't already know. Is there a pen name you want to use?" he went on to ask.

"Tamarugo," I shot out, my heart racing and my head buzzing with ideas.

He laughed. "Tamarugo," he repeated. "Yes. I like it. Tamarugo. That's good," he added, lighting another cigarillo and pouring himself another shot of pisco.

"Sir," I pleaded then, in my most persuasive of voices. "I'm the man of the family now and I need to make a living."

Mr. Bacic crimped his face and stared at me for what felt like forever. Then he nodded and pronounced the most beautiful words I had heard in a long, long time: "I understand. You're in luck, Manuel. I do need an office boy, a smart, hard-working boy like you — somebody who will do errands, deliver the magazines to the newsstands, that sort of thing. I will pay you fifty-five pesos a week for that job and our standard fifteen for your chronicles."

He jotted down the numbers on a sheet of paper, did the addition and went on. "That'll be a total of seventy a week. What do you say?"

I had already arrived at the same figure in my head — about half of Aunt Asunta's salary, which meant that between my wages, my grandma's pension and my mom's washing gigs, we could make it work.

I could feel the grin on my face get wider and wider and a surge of excitement ordering me to whoop and jump around the room, but I contained myself the best I could, stood up and replied: "I say yes, sir. Yes. When can I start? Can I start right away?"

"Yes, Manuel. You can start at this very moment. Welcome to *The Northerner*," Mr. Bacic responded, getting up, walking around the desk and shaking my hand.

LUCÍA

. . . .

October – November 1925

Iquique and Valparaíso

A FEW WEEKS AFTER I'd started going to Manuel's house, just as we were finishing lunch, my mother told my father about the latest charity she and her friend Mrs. Inglis had been working on — collecting goods for the dwellers of Pampa Nueva, a new shanty town at the south end of the city.

"Isn't it wonderful that the Officers' Wives Club and the British Ladies Club have come together to work on this? *And* as wonderful that the British consul himself has donated tons of imported tea and biscuits?" she commented, a beatific smile on her face. "So, now we have a room full of bedding, clothing and groceries at the British Club to take to Pampa Nueva!"

Then she got up, walked around the table and put her arms around my dad, while asking in a child-like voice: "Darling, could you please help with the transportation?"

"Why would I want to help a bunch of dirty, stinky agitators from the saltpetre mines? They're all Bolsheviks, you know," he answered bitterly.

"If we help them, they'll understand that the Chilean Armed Forces and the British community want the best for them," she countered, massaging his shoulders. "This is a great opportunity for you to show them that you are on their side."

After mulling it over for a few moments, my father agreed. I guess he also realized that this was a golden opportunity for him and his cohorts to take a good look at the encampment and at the people who lived there.

"Yes. You're right, sweetheart. It's important to show them that we want the best for them and that we're on their side. Yes, an army truck will take the goods to them. And I will come along as well. Just let me know when you want to go."

My mom hugged and kissed him effusively. "Thank you, my love, thank you, thank you!"

That's when I blurted out: "Can I come too, please?"

An opportunity to meet more *pampa* families had been presented to me on a golden platter. How could I pass it by? Not only that, I would be helping them, doing a good deed for people in need.

"Yes, my love. That's a very good idea. Then you can start learning about charity work," my mom responded.

So, a few days later, off we went to Pampa Nueva. My mom and Mrs. Inglis wouldn't stop talking about all the long hours of work they had put into this project and how, finally, it was now coming to a happy ending. I thought that Mr. Brown, the British consul, looked hilarious in a white linen suit and Panama hat, but he was nice enough — kept cracking jokes and taking swigs from his pocket flask. I just kept quiet, trying to imagine what the encampment would look like and thinking about how happy the *pampinos* would be with our gifts.

As soon as we got out of the car though, I knew that I shouldn't have come. A group of poorly dressed, barefoot people stood across the road, taking in the truck, the boxes, the bags, the cars, us — a look of contempt in their eyes. There was a collection of carboard and tin shacks behind them: the camp, their homes. I saw myself through their eyes: a clean, well-fed girl wearing expensive, fashionable clothes; a girl who clearly lived in a big, comfortable house without having to worry about where her next meal would come from. My family was on the side of the "bourgeoisie," the social class that "exploited" poor people, as Miss Asunta had explained. My father and mother may not have owned mines or factories, but my father was at the service of the wealthy: whenever the workers stood up for themselves, he and his soldiers attacked and killed them. As for my mother, she was nothing more than a stupid woman who went along with whatever my father said or did. And what did all that make me? I hated myself then and I hated my parents with all my might.

By the time my dad got up on the platform to deliver his speech, all I wanted was for the earth to swallow me up — Miss Asunta, Señora Flora, Manuel, Moncho and Rufina were among the crowd and were staring at me with wide eyes. I lowered mine for a few moments and when I looked again, they were gone.

My mom and Mrs. Inglis were very upset because nobody from the shanty town clapped when my father finished speaking. Not only that, they hadn't even come up to thank them for all the goods they had collected and delivered. On the way back, they went on and on about how they had put their hearts and souls into this charity, and for what? For a bunch of unappreciative, thankless and very rude squatters. The whole affair had been a total waste of time and energy. They claimed that the only good thing was that they had learned their lesson and now knew better than trying to help these low-class, ill-mannered, ignorant, illiterate clods.

I was snivelling. I was furious and I was sad. My friends had found me out and I didn't know what I was going to do about it.

Next thing I knew, my mom had snuggled up to me, put her arm around my shoulders and started to apologize between sniffles and hiccups: "Sorry, my darling, for taking you to such a horrible place. I shouldn't have. But not all of them are like that, my sweetheart. Promise. All the other poor people we have helped are very, very nice. Isn't that right, Margaret?"

I wanted to scream at her and her friend — what did they know about what had happened to those people? Did they know that they were survivors of a massacre my father had orchestrated and led? Of course not! They didn't *want* to know. All they wanted was to feel good about themselves for "helping" the poor. But instead of yelling at them, my anger and frustration came out in the form of loud sobbing, which alarmed the consul and prompted him to ask the chauffeur to take us home as quickly as possible.

I turned down my mom's offer of a Bilz soda and cookies and locked myself in my bedroom. After a while she got tired of knocking and asking me to come out. I could hear her whimpering as she walked down the hallway, but I didn't care. I was finally left in peace.

I wrote a long letter to Miss Asunta, Señora Flora and Manuel. I told them about Tacna, the dead in the river, the train, my father, all of it. The next afternoon, I walked to their house and slid it surreptitiously under the door. I'd decided that I'd give them a day to read it and go back for a visit the following day — that is, if they let me in. But just as I started to walk away, the neighbours came out and told me that my friends had left the night before.

"Where did they go?! When are they coming back?!" I asked, but they just shook their heads. My friends hadn't said. They'd just upped and left. Clearly, they had left because they had seen me at the shanty town and believed that I would tell my father who they were and where they lived.

The next day, when I came home from school, my father was waiting for me in the hallway. As soon as I stepped in, he grabbed me by the chin and forced me to look at sheets of paper he was dangling in front of my eyes as he yelled: "How did you meet these people??!! Why did you tell them all these lies??!!"

It was my letter to Miss Asunta, Señora Flora and Manuel. I felt a ball of fire rush from the pit of my stomach up into my chest and then out of my mouth. Before I knew it, I had spat in my father's face.

He slapped me hard.

The next day, as soon as he went for his nap and my mother disappeared to the living room, I left the house. I walked to the FOCH building looking for Miss Asunta, but somebody else was sitting behind her desk.

"Where's Miss Asunta?" I asked.

The woman just looked at me.

"I'm looking for Miss Asunta," I said.

She kept staring at me as she got up and walked around the desk.

"You're that girl that came here a few months ago. And then you started visiting Asunta at home. She told us about you — the "mysterious visitor," she called you. Well, now we know all about you, don't we?! You're Ernesto Céspedes' daughter!" she said, grabbing me by the shoulder and opening her eyes wide. "And we know that because of you, the military abducted Asunta and she's nowhere to be found! How do you feel about that, eh?!" she yelled.

I wiggled my shoulder out of her grip, turned around and ran. Ran out of the building, around the corner and down the street as fast as I could. Where was I going? It didn't matter. I just had to get away. Finally, I found myself completely out of breath in the middle of the square. I sat on a bench.

Not only my friends, but my friends' friends had found me out. And now they all believed I was my father's spy. And Miss Asunta had gone missing. I heard the bell clock strike two-thirty, two forty-five, three o'clock, but I didn't move. Home was the last place I wanted to go. But where could I go instead?

Miss Mireya, my dance teacher. She would hear me out.

In Tacna, I had loved dancing and creating ballet performances in my head. In Iquique, this love had turned into a passion and a refuge. If I'd had it my way, I would've danced and dreamed up choreographies all day long. Miss Mireya was classically trained, but she was also an ardent admirer and follower of Isadora Duncan's new approach to dance. So, while she insisted on good posture and technical excellence, she also encouraged us to move freely and express ourselves through our bodies. This took me to new heights. As we danced to Tchaikovsky's "Waltz of the Flowers," I'd forget about my worries and let my body soar while I envisioned dozens of dancers rise and blossom as nature would with the coming of spring. Trees, flowers and animals would wake up, sway in the breeze and dance with one another under the cupola of a blue sky.

One day I mustered up the courage to talk to Miss Mireya about the choreographies in my head. She was fascinated. The following class she called me aside and handed me a notebook with a supple leather cover, the words "My Choreographies Journal" engraved on it. "Keep this notebook with you at all times and make sure to jot down and sketch your ideas before they go fuzzy in your head," she said. From that day, that journal had become a faithful companion.

I would tell Miss Mireya my story. She would listen to me and she'd believe me.

I sprang to my feet and started walking towards Queen Victoria Cultural Centre but I didn't make it very far. A military jeep came to a screeching halt right beside me, a soldier jumped out, scooped me up and plonked me in the back seat. Next thing I knew, I was punching him on the back of the head and hollering for him to stop.

"I'm just following your father's orders, miss," he kept saying, as he drove on and tried to fend off my blows with his free arm.

My father was waiting at the front gate. He dismissed the soldier and ordered me to step in. I had already decided that if he made any attempts at slapping or thrashing me, I would defend myself. I would kick him and punch him, and bite him, and... But he just showed me into the living room and ordered me to sit down. I stayed standing by the door.

My mom was sitting on the couch, her eyes trained on her lap.

"The day after tomorrow you will leave Iquique and go live with your mother's sister in Valparaíso," my father announced. "She's a devout Catholic and a teacher at Sacred Heart School for Young Ladies. She will know how to keep you in line," he added.

I had never met Aunt Encarnación — all I knew was that she was smart and had studied to be a teacher. Maybe she had turned into a bitter spinster who enjoyed mistreating children? But what other choices did I have? My friends were gone; Miss Asunta had been taken and it was all my fault. Besides, nothing could be worse than living in Ernesto Céspedes' house. So, I didn't protest.

I was putting the last few things in my trunk when my father came into my room, closed the door quietly behind him and motioned for me to sit on the bed. I remained where I was as he started to pace.

"Lucía, I cannot put into words the immense love I feel for you. You are the most important person in my life. I must say that I was deeply hurt by what you said in that letter, but I have forgiven you. You're just an innocent little girl and that's why those people were able to mislead you the way they did. Forget about whatever they told you because it's all lies. They're agitators, Bolsheviks! They're ignorant, they're dirty and they're violent! All they want is total anarchy, complete chaos! They refuse to obey the laws of the land and have no respect for our fatherland!! But you don't have to worry now because you will never see them again. Your Aunt Encarnación will take good care of you. I will make sure of that, and, as usual, you'll have everything you need. One request though: do not tell your aunt any of the lies you talked about in that letter. It's the least I can ask of you, Lucía. You're leaving all this Bolshevik nonsense behind now. Forget about it all and enjoy your new life in Valparaíso. It's a beautiful place — I know you'll like it. Also, Sacred Heart for Young Ladies is a fine school, and I'm sure you will continue to make us proud by being an excellent student, just like you've been all along."

As he opened the door to leave, I called out, "Father!"

He turned around and looked at me, expectantly. I knew that he was hoping for an "I love you too," but that was not something I would ever say to him again. I just wanted to know: "In Valparaiso, will I have a chance to dance?"

My father swallowed hard. "Yes, Lucía, in Valparaíso you will carry on with your dance lessons," he responded, as he turned around and walked out of the room.

MY MOTHER AND I made the trip on a Navy boat called *Arturo Prat*. Captain Gallardo was a friend of my dad's and offered to take us as his guests.

The minute we stepped in I fell in love with our cabin. Everything fit the small space perfectly — the two narrow beds, the wardrobe with a section for hang-up clothes and a vertical row of drawers, the small desk. I had great fun putting all my clothes away, even if it was just for five days. The bathroom was tiny, but it had everything: a toilet, a basin, a small bathtub and a bidet. To me, staying in this cabin felt like playing in an oversized doll's house.

The boat had a large dining room with several tables, all bolted to the floor — a beautiful, round table with plush, green velvet chairs for the officers, and several long tables with benches for the crew. A couple of hours after leaving Iquique, my mom got terribly seasick and didn't recover until we got to Valparaíso, so I ended up being the only female guest at the officers' table.

I was assigned the chair to the right of Captain Gallardo's, which made me nervous; after all, he was my dad's friend. Also, what if he was nosy and started asking me indiscreet questions? But all my concerns were for naught because he turned out to be quite the storyteller. I didn't have to say a word about anything for the duration of the trip, because he took up the whole time at the table with accounts of his worldwide travels.

I also spent a lot of time sitting on a high stool in the galley, watching and talking to Rolo, the cook. It was the first time I had seen a man cook, so I was intrigued. When I asked him why there wasn't a woman cook, he explained that women weren't allowed in the Navy, so men had to learn how to do everything themselves — from cooking and cleaning to doing laundry and ironing, and even sewing and knitting! At first, I didn't believe him about the sewing and knitting, but that same afternoon he showed me a pair of plaid stockings he was making with a circular knitting needle, and the day after, I saw him fastening the buttons on a shirt and mending a bed sheet.

Rolo's cooking was wonderful, and apparently the ocean breeze had awoken my appetite because I ended up eating enough for both me and my mom. My favourite dishes were his *chupe de pulpo* — octopus stew — and *caldillo de congrio* — conger chowder. He also baked delicious bread. As the stove was like an open hearth and didn't have an oven, he had devised a makeshift oven with an empty ten-litre olive-oil can, which he accommodated on top of the boiler. He baked fresh bread for breakfast and teatime; I've never eaten so much hot bread and butter in my whole life.

On that boat, for the first time in months, I felt free and unburdened of worries — Tacna and Iquique were behind me now. And to top it all off, my mom didn't leave our cabin so, during the day, I could do practically anything I wanted. I stayed on deck for hours, watching the ocean, breathing the fresh air and just feeling the sun and wind on my face.

Nighttime was a different story. As I lay in my berth, I thought about Manuel and his family. Part of me was glad to be going away — I was so ashamed! But another part of me, actually most of me, longed to re-live our moments together. I had loved going to their place every afternoon. But that would never happen again. Miss Asunta had been taken by my father's goons and who knows where the rest of the family was living now. Maybe they had gone back to the *pampa*.

On those nights I also continued to mull over what had happened in Tacna. A few weeks before, at one of my parents' dinner parties in our Iquique home, the topic of the plebiscite had come up and my father had said that it had been called off until the Peruvian government finished investigating the issue of the corpses in the river. He said it matter-of-factly, as if he'd had nothing to do with it.

"But plebiscite or not, investigation or not," he'd said, "let's not forget that our superior brand has already been stamped on the city of Tacna, my friends." Then he offered his usual toast: "Long live Chile, our beloved fatherland!"

By now I had come to comprehend how powerful he was. His arrogance was well founded. He worked for the bourgeoisie and he was above everybody and everything because he commanded a whole regiment of soldiers and could kill people whenever and wherever he wanted. He would never be punished for his crimes.

The second or third day I'd visited Miss Asunta's house, Manuel had explained how his father and sister had been killed in La Coruña. I'd gone numb. From the way Manuel described the army officer who had ordered his papa's execution and then harangued the survivors at the Iquique barracks, I couldn't but conclude that he was my father. He couldn't kill Peruvians anymore, so now he was killing poor Chileans.

After five days at sea, we got to Valparaíso. By then my mom was feeling better, so she joined Captain Gallardo and me on deck. The rocks at the entrance to the bay were alive with hundreds of sea lions, seals and penguins. The sea lions mooed like cows, the seals laughed and clapped, and the penguins walked like clowns, while hundreds of seagulls screeched and squealed as they fluttered their wings up above.

All around the crescent bay, the hills of Valparaíso rose up like gigantic quilts. From our spot at the mouth of the harbour, it seemed as if each house was a colourful patch sewn to those around it and to the earth by an invisible thread. These quilts were the perfect backdrop to the scene around us, and in no time at all, the animals had become dancers. The birds were dressed in flowy powder-puff tutus, the seals and sea lions in shiny chocolate brown and grey bodysuits, and the penguins in white outfits and long black vests. And the music? Mmmm... Mozart's "Eine Kleine Nachtmusik," of course!

The *Arturo Prat* docked at the Navy pier, and from there we were taken to the public wharf in a jeep. I was sad that the journey had come to an end, quite nervous about meeting Aunt Encarnación and even more nervous about the new life I was embarking on. What if she was mean to me? What if she didn't let me do the things I liked? What if, what if? But my misgivings evaporated when my aunt opened her arms, gave me a tight bear hug and whispered in my ear: "I'm so happy you've come to live with me. We're going to have a lot of fun together!"

The two sisters couldn't have looked any more different if they'd tried. My mom was dressed in the latest fashion — a short, fitted blue coat over a white flapper dress of the same length, her face all made up and her hair sporting a cropped and wavy style à la Gloria Swanson. My aunt, on the other hand, was wearing a long brown coat, had no make-up on and her hair was combed straight back and gathered in a knot on the crown of her head.

My mom wanted to take a taxi home, but my aunt explained that cars couldn't make it up her steep street, so she had already arranged for a donkey to carry our luggage and...

"What about us! Are we riding donkeys as well?" my mom interrupted, a grin on her face. I was hoping that my aunt would say "Yes," but it turned out that we'd be taking the streetcar across downtown and then the Espíritu Santo funicular, the cable car up Bellavista Hill.

Bellavista Hill? I was going to live on a hill with the same name as my friends' neighbourhood in Iquique?! I wondered if there was a hidden meaning to that coincidence.

My mom's panicky voice interrupted my thoughts. Could the owner of this beast of burden be entrusted with our luggage? Would she be able to walk the two blocks from the cable car stop to the house in high heels? My aunt assured her that she had known the donkey's owner for years and that there was nothing to fear. As for the walk... did my mom have a pair of flat shoes in her suitcase that she could change into? She didn't.

I had never ridden on a funicular before — there weren't such things in Tacna or Iquique; according to my mom and Aunt Encarnación, they were exclusive to Valparaíso. When I saw the nearly vertical drop we would be climbing and the small box we would be riding up in, I got butterflies in my stomach. But once we were on our way, I enjoyed watching the bay and trying to figure out which of all the boats was the *Arturo Prat*.

The five-minute walk from the cable car stop to my aunt's took fifteen as my mom kept twisting her ankles and slipping and sliding on the uneven sidewalk. When we finally made it, Don José and the donkey were waiting outside. Our luggage was safe and sound, which made my mom happy.

What didn't make her happy was my Aunt Encarnación's place — the bottom half of a small, two-storey, aqua-blue house on Ferrari Street. What did she expect? A house as big and fancy as ours in Iquique? Didn't she know that her sister was an elementary school teacher? Compared to ours, my aunt's house did look like a shack, but if you were to put it next to Miss Asunta's, it was a mansion. It had a large front room, a separate kitchen, a bathroom *inside* the house and two small bedrooms. It was outfitted simply and mod-estly — no rugs, no velvet living room set or rosewood dining room set, no chandeliers, no English china and silverware — just pine and wicker furniture and sturdy dishes and cutlery.

My mom wanted to help pay for a nicer place or at least to get better looking furniture for the front room, but my aunt declined her offer. She said that she liked her place just the way it was. I liked it too; it felt right — not too big and not too small, bright and cozy at the same time.

During the week that my mom stayed in Valparaíso, she acted in her usual busy-bee manner and ended up buying half the town, including a beautiful upright Baumann piano from a friend of my aunt's. She also acquired a whole new wardrobe for herself — "This style hasn't made it to Iquique yet!" she would call out from the dressing room as she tried on yet another outfit.

She insisted on getting my aunt and myself the latest fashions as well, but my aunt was adamant: "Antonia, I will never wear those kinds of clothes and actually, Lucía won't either. So, how about you get us a good coat and a pair of sturdy boots each? Winters can be cold here in Valparaíso."

Aunt Encarnación and I did get new coats and boots, and also shoes, skirts and blouses, dresses and cardigan sweaters, gloves and hats, all chosen by my aunt and myself. In the blink of an eye my expertise in fashion changed from classy upper-class to classy working-class.

"Auntie, I think that the navy-blue skirt you set aside would go better with that ivory piqué blouse, not the black poplin one you picked," I advised. "Black is too close to blue, while the ivory blouse will contrast nicely with the skirt and if you complete the outfit with a pair of simple pearl earrings, you will look perfect."

My aunt was impressed. It turned out that Aunt Encarnación was not an austere, mean spinster and a devout Catholic after all. She did not teach at Sacred Heart School for Young Ladies either. She was warm and sociable and taught at a Montessori school.

How could my father have been so wrong about her? I didn't have to wait long for an answer: my mom had bamboozled him.

The afternoon I hadn't come home on time, and my father had sent a soldier out to find me, he had stormed into the living room and announced to my mom that he was sending me off to Santiago to live with his parents.

"Oh, no, Ernesto!" she had said. "My sister Encarnación would be a much, much better choice. She's always been deeply religious and don't forget that she is a teacher, so she'll know how to keep Lucía on the straight and narrow. Besides, she lives alone, so our girl will have her full and exclusive attention. Besides, my love, do you want to send your daughter to Santiago? I don't — it's such a large, dangerous and mean city compared to Valparaíso. I must say that I always loved Valparaíso; it's such a pretty place and the people are so warm and friendly.

"Encarnación will love to have Lucía's company and a bit of extra cash coming in each month. Most importantly though, she is just the person to keep our girl out of trouble. In her letters she often tells me about her 'problem' students and how rewarding it is when she manages to get them to drop their rebellious ways and start behaving like proper ladies."

My father hadn't seen Aunt Encarnación since the day he had married my mom, so he had no idea what had become of her. He knew that the two women kept a correspondence but had never bothered to find out anything whatsoever about his sister-in-law's life. So, he'd yielded to my mom's convincing arguments and agreed that living with Aunt Encarnación would be more beneficial to my education and overall upbringing. After all, my rebelliousness needed to be stemmed at the roots and, from what he could gather, a good dose of religion and a strict guardian would serve that purpose very well.

By this point in the story my mom and my aunt were in stitches, but it didn't take long for my mom's glee to turn into tears. "You will take good care of my baby, won't you, Encarnación?" she was saying now. "You know what Ernesto's like — there's no way he would've agreed to keep Lucía in Iquique. He was bent on sending her away. Can you imagine the poor girl living with his parents? A pair of stuck-up, decrepit geezers in that huge, dark dungeon of a house? She would've died! If she can't be with me, at least she will be with you. And I know that you will love her and treat her as if she were your own daughter, right?"

I felt fuzzy inside.

As there were only a couple of weeks left in the school year, it was decided that I would study on my own and take my final exams as a home-schooled student. So, I started spending my mornings at Aunt Encarnación's school, studying and doing homework in a corner of her classroom. After lunch, we sat at the dining room table together and she tutored me.

The late afternoons and evenings were busy with my piano lessons and dance classes, and my aunt's meetings. The first time we went to one, she made me promise that I wouldn't tell anybody or write to my mom about it. It was a Teachers' Union meeting. When we went to the second one, she made me promise all over again. It was a Communist Party meeting. The third one was a reading circle in a shanty town up our hill. I couldn't believe it. My aunt was a younger version of Miss Asunta! No wonder both their neighbourhoods were called Bellavista!

After that third meeting, I told Aunt Encarnación my whole story. She listened attentively. She paced the room. She swore. She cried. Every now and then, she interjected comments: "I knew there was something fishy behind your father's urgency to get you out of Iquique. All my sister said was that you'd become extremely rebellious and she couldn't control you; that she was too busy to keep track of everything you did.

"You're right. Your father has got your mother by the short and curlies! I love her very much, but... she's so fucking stupid! Sorry Lucía. No, I shouldn't say that. She's not stupid. She never finished school. All she had going for her was her looks. So, marrying Ernesto was like a fairy tale come true. I guess she's still living the fairy tale and from the sound of it, she'll never wake up.

"Yes. We heard about the massacre of Peruvians through the Party and the FOCH. I knew that fascist brother-in-law of mine must've been involved! I knew it! But from what you tell me, he wasn't only involved, he was in charge!

"Yes, the La Coruña massacre. We did hear about it through the Party *and* the Teacher's Union *and* the FOCH. Horrible, horrible stuff... And you met the family of the leader who was executed. Wow! What an experience, Lucía. And how sad about the little girl... Eva? It hadn't occurred to me that Ernesto would've been at the helm of that massacre too, but it makes sense.

"Manuel sounds smart. You must've been *so* lonely, Lucía. And his mom, poor woman. And Miss Asunta? What a character! I wish I could meet her.

"Yes, you're right. Your friends must've been very disappointed when they saw you at Pampa Nueva.

"Some of the 'reporters' there must've been your father's agents — don't forget that his mandate — his desire — is to destroy the movement and he needs pictures of those involved so that he can 'neutralize' them. My guess is that Miss Asunta must've stood out like a sore thumb among the shanty town dwellers. So, when Ernesto saw her picture, he concluded that she was a "Bolshevik agitator." Obviously, it didn't take long for his assistants to find the school where she worked and figure out where she lived. That explains the house raid after you slid your letter under the door. That's how the letter got to your father.

"I hope Miss Asunta is still alive, but I don't know. Don't forget that your father read your letter. That must've made him very, very angry."

When I finished my story, Aunt Encarnación enfolded me in her arms and rocked me for a long time. I hadn't felt that safe since Mercedes was my Loly and I was her Lovely. My aunt promised that through the Teachers' Union she would inquire into Miss Asunta's fate. Then, Aunt Encarnación offered to take on Miss Asunta's role as my "political studies" instructor, that is, if I was interested.

"Yes! I am, I am!" I cried out.

"Okay. Lesson number one," she responded. "While Miss Asunta and I agree on most issues, we disagree on a fundamental one: how our society will be organized after we crush the capitalist state. You told me she's an anarcho-syndicalist, right? Well, as you now know, I'm a communist. Miss Asunta believes that after the revolution, there will not be a state because unions and other community organizations will become strong enough to govern. I believe that we will form a workers' state," she explained and then added, a sparkle in her eye and a big grin in her face, "As we go along with our studies, you'll have to make up your own mind, Lucía, but maybe this piece of information will help you in your decision: Isadora Duncan is a communist."

I gasped and then felt my face open into a wide smile; I had always known Isadora was on our side.

PART II

1926–1948

LUCÍA

. . . .

August – September 1938

Valparaíso

SHORTLY AFTER GETTING TO Valparaíso, I had started attending Madame Giselle Moreau's Académie de Danse Moderne. Madame Moreau was a petite, middle-aged woman with the eyes of an owl and a sulky, blood-red mouth. She claimed that she had come to Chile from her native Paris as the governess of a wealthy family, fallen in love with a taciturn Chilean violinist and never gone back. She took great pride in hailing from "The City of Light" — nothing to do with "lights" but rather with "enlightenment," she'd explain.

"I carry within me a millenary, sophisticated culture and I am proud to be the native speaker of the most sensuous language in the world," she'd declare, standing in her favourite "teapot" pose — her left hand resting on her hip, while her right dangled from the end of a slightly bent arm. She would say this in grammatically perfect Spanish imbued with a thick French accent. When she got excited though, her brain would forget about her sensuous native tongue, drop the French accent and give way to pure Chilean Spanish.

"¡Nooo pu' cabrita, así no! ¡Bien, mijita, bien! ¡Muy bien!"— "Nooo, kiddie, not like that! That a girl, good! Very good!"

One day, we were in the middle of practising "arabesques" when a mouse materialized in the corner of the room and started to run along the edge of the wall, under the barre and right next to our feet. All hell broke loose. Everyone jumped out of the way and started to

scream, including Madame Moreau. But then her voice soared, as
she commanded us stupid kids to stop making such a fuss and get rid
of the filthy creature instead: *"¡Ay, cabritas hue'onas, déjense de hacer
tanta alharaca y saquen a ese bicho asqueroso de aquí!"* It took a while
for the racket to end and for the mouse to disappear, but in no time
at all Madame Moreau had regained her composure, together with
her French accent.

Madame Moreau boasted that she had studied under Isadora
Duncan and Loie Fuller at the prestigious École du Ballet de l'Opéra
de Paris, "created in 1661, by Louis XIV," she would explain, as she
opened her heavily outlined eyes wide. "Paris always attracts the best,
only the best," she would add, with a couple of nods and a fluttering
of heavy eyelashes.

Most likely Madame Moreau had never set foot in Paris and was
a *santiaguina* putting on airs, but I liked her regardless. I sensed that
behind the accent and the heavy makeup, there was a sensitive and
lonely human being in need of attention. Most importantly though,
she was a good teacher and believed in my talent. She dedicated
hours of her time to work with me one-on-one and show me everything she knew. Also, she championed my choreographic ideas.

1928, the year I turned fifteen, was a momentous one for me. I
joined the Communist Youth, fell in love, and had my first choreography performed by the students of the Académie de Danse Moderne
at the Teatro Victoria.

I hadn't forgotten that Miss Asunta and Señora Flora were
staunch anarchists, but I also remembered that one day, as Miss
Asunta was explaining the principles of anarchism to me, Manuel
had interjected that his dad had been a communist.

"Oh, yes, we had our political differences," Señora Flora had said.
"But we agreed on the main issue: the need to overthrow the capitalist state. The way I saw it, we had plenty of time to keep on discussing
what would come next."

"From what I've heard, clearly he was a smart man and a good leader. But couldn't he see that the problem lies with the state? After the revolution, the last thing we need is yet another state!" Miss Asunta had said.

But I had to agree with Manuel's dad and all communists: following the revolution, we would need a state run by the proletariat to ensure a well-organized transition towards our ultimate goal: a stateless, truly egalitarian society. My admiration for Alexandra Kollontai had also helped me reach a decision. For years she had been speaking up for women's sexual liberation and championing the rights of working-class women.

Every Wednesday evening, Aunt Encarnación and I glued our ears to the weekly Radio Moscow Spanish language, shortwave radio broadcast. In between creaks and squeaks we'd listen to the news and the issues being debated in the Soviet Union. On one of those evenings, Alexandra Kollontai addressed working women:

For many centuries, women were oppressed and had no rights.
For many centuries, women were just an appendage to men, their
shadow. The husband provided for his wife so long as she obeyed
his will and endured her powerlessness — her domestic slavery.
The October Revolution liberated women. Now the woman
peasant has the same rights as the man peasant and the woman
worker has the same rights as a male worker. Everywhere, women
can vote and everywhere we can become members of a soviet or
a commissar. A woman can even become a people's commissar
herself. But while according to the law a woman has the same
rights as a man, in real life women have not been liberated. The
woman worker, the woman peasant is still a slave inside her own
house! So, the task of all workers now is to make the changes that
will take the burden of housework and childrearing off of women's
shoulders. The working class has to liberate women from these
tasks. Without equality, there is no communism!
Working women: Let's build nurseries and maternity houses

together! Let's make sure that the soviets set up public canteens so that you don't have to be a slave to your kitchen! Liberate yourselves by helping the Communist Party build a new happy life for all!

That evening my aunt and I talked endlessly about how working women would liberate themselves from the kind of slavery that Kollontai talked about. Passing laws that guaranteed women's equality was an important first step. But as she had said, that didn't mean that in practice women were indeed equal, because on top of working in factories and farms, they still had to take care of their children, cook, clean and do all the household chores.

"The family as we know it perpetuates this form of slavery," my aunt said. "So, Kollontai also argues that the communist economy will do away with the family."

How could that be? Personally, I felt like I had no family other than my Aunt Encarnación. Sure, I had a mother and a father, but I didn't consider them to be my family anymore. So, what was a family, after all? And why would communism "do away" with the family?

At our next Communist Youth meeting I posed the question to our leader, but she redirected it to the group. Pilar Castillo, a girl from Spain who had just joined, stepped up to the challenge. She and her family had fled the Primo de Rivera dictatorship and arrived in Valparaíso a few weeks before. She was tall and voluptuous, had smooth, olive skin, eyes so dark they seemed to have enlarged pupils instead of irises and a full head of unruly, black hair. She also had a fiery personality to match her looks.

"Kollontai is not talking about the family as a group of people connected by blood and love, but as an economic unit," Pilar said in a husky voice and in the same kind of Spanish that Miss Asunta spoke. My heart started to beat fast.

"Go on," our leader said.

"Well, Marx and Engels had already said it — the nuclear family is a product of capitalism, not a 'natural' thing. Before capitalism there were other kinds of families, but capitalism needed a unit that would ensure optimum production and consumption of goods: the man goes to work, the woman takes care of all his needs and the children so he doesn't have to worry about that, and so on — the cycle continues. The way I understand it is that in communism both men and women will be workers and generate wealth, and everyday tasks will be shared by everybody in the neighbourhood. There will be communal kitchens and laundry houses, care centres for the children... And as important," Pilar said, a smile on her face and a twinkle in her eye, "women will be free to fall in love with whomever they want because they won't depend on one man anymore." She was beautiful and she was magnetic.

When the meeting was over, I invited her to go to the square with me. My heart was dancing flamenco inside my chest and my cheeks were on fire, but I did manage to open my mouth and utter "How about a stroll at Plaza Victoria?"

"*Sí, sí! Vamos, mujer!*" — "Yes, yes! Let's go, woman!" she responded enthusiastically, locking arms with me and steering me out of the building.

It was a balmy, spring evening and the square was bubbling with people. The air was laced with the aroma of jasmine and honeysuckle, and the almond trees were puffed up with creamy pink flowers. Kids played tag and hide-and-go-seek, teenage boys horsed around and called out to hip-swaying, giggly girls, and adults socialized and watched the scene from their comfortable vantage points on park benches.

I was telling Pilar about my dance classes when all of a sudden she turned to me and said, as she ran her fingers through my hair, "I love those blonde waves! You also have mesmerizing eyes, Lucía! I wish I could steal just a tiny bit of that sky-blue sparkle. Mine are so dark!"

"Oh no!" I reacted, feeling a surge of blood flood my face. "Your eyes are gorgeous! And your hair too, and the colour of your skin..."

Pilar burst out laughing.

"How about that! You find me beautiful and I find you beautiful! Good, because I wouldn't want to be friends with an ugly girl, particularly if that girl didn't think I was a pretty sight myself!" She chuckled, grabbing my hand and starting to walk again.

After that first stroll, Pilar and I became inseparable. We signed up to do literacy work at the Cerro Barón neighbourhood and continued to debate all kinds of issues, particularly related to women and our liberation from capitalist patriarchy.

I told her all about the choreographies in my head and showed her my notes and amateurish sketches. It turned out that she was a wonderful artist, so she offered to draw my ideas as I told them to her. It was magical — her drawings depicted exactly what I had envisioned. This gave me the courage to ask Madame Moreau to consider staging one of my choreographies at the Victoria.

That's how *Valparaíso Bay* became my *opera prima*. Pilar brought to life my vision of the Valparaíso hills as colourful quilts. She went to every sewing shop in Valparaíso, collected remnants of cloth and cut them into pieces, which she then plastered onto a backdrop where she had drawn the hills of the city. The floor of the stage was flooded with blue light and dozens of dancers impersonated the sea lions, seals, penguins and seagulls that I had seen when the *Arturo Prat* entered the bay.

The story was loosely based on my own: a girl was coming to Valparaíso on board a beautiful boat to meet her estranged mother for the first time. She was leaving behind a life of sorrow and loneliness, and even though she was apprehensive about the future, she welcomed the opportunity for a brand new start. The lead character expressed her trepidations and expectations through her dancing to the crescendos and decrescendos of the "Dance of the Sugar Plum Fairy" from Tchaikovsky's *Nutcracker Ballet*. Towards the end of this piece, she shed the travel clothes she had been wearing and emerged as a new person, dressed in a flowy tulle tunic. Then, enchanted by the sight of the hills of Valparaíso and all the animals welcoming her at the entrance to the bay, she joined them in a joyous dance to Mozart's "Eine Kleine Nachtmusik." Finally, the encounter of the girl and her mother, hesitant at first, but emotional and jubilant soon after, was danced as a duet to Tchaikovsky's "Waltz of the Flowers."

The production was a huge success and from then on, every year Madame Moreau, Pilar and I teamed up to put on a new ballet.

A few months after our first stroll at the square, Pilar and I vowed to love each other forever. For me, those were years of healing and joy — I had a friend, a confidant, a companion, a colleague, a comrade in arms and a lover, all wrapped in one. We'd explore each other's naked bodies for hours — hers, dark and voluptuous; mine, fair and slim — as we recounted our respective lives to each other and made a thousand plans for the future. When the revolution triumphed in Spain, we would go to Madrid. When the revolution triumphed in Chile, we would go to Iquique and the Atacama Desert. Like Alexandra Kollontai, we would fight for the rights of women. We would go to the Soviet Union and meet Kollontai!

But it wasn't meant to be. Not only because the revolution did not triumph either in Spain or Chile, but because Pilar fell in love with a man when, seven years later, she went to Santiago to study at the Camilo Mori Institute of Art and Design.

During our first few weeks apart, we wrote to each other every day. But then, her letters stopped coming. Desperate to know what was going on, I made my way to her parents' bakery on Cordillera Hill. They knew we were best friends, but not that we were also lovers, so I did my best to appear cool and collected.

"I'm surprised she hasn't written to you with the good news! She's in love!" her mother announced, a wide smile opening on her usually stern face, while she weighed a dozen *hayuyas* for one of her clients. "His name is Marcos and he's studying to be an architect. And can you believe it? He's the son of Spanish immigrants!"

I was speechless.

"Wow! That's great news!" I finally managed, as I stumbled towards the door. I don't even remember how I made it back home.

When Aunt Encarnación noticed that Pilar's letters had stopped coming, she'd encouraged me to stay calm: "Most likely she's got a whole load of exams to study for and projects to finish," she'd said. But she had also been quick to add: "However, don't forget that when it comes to love, nothing is written in stone. Besides, love hardly ever lasts forever."

Shortly after starting her first teaching job, Aunt Encarnación had fallen in love. "His name was Jorge and I met him at the Teachers' Union office. I was ecstatic. We were both teachers and union members and got along beautifully. Then, one day, when we were collating the Union's newsletter together, a short, plump woman walked into the office, slapped me across the face, turned around and walked out," my aunt said. "I was still trying to figure out what had happened, when Jorge bolted out of the office, and I heard his panicky voice calling: 'Carmelita, my love, wait, it's not what you think... Darling... Carmelita... Wait...'"

Aunt Encarnación laughed when she told that story now, but she must've been devastated at the time. Now I knew how she'd felt.

Eventually, Pilar did write: "I'm sorry, Lucía. I never thought that I would fall in love with somebody else, but I did. I will always cherish our time together and would love for us to stay friends."

But we didn't stay friends — I couldn't do it. The loss of Pilar from my life pushed me into an abyss. By then Madame Moreau had hired me as an instructor, a job I loved, but every morning I had to drag myself out of bed and off to work. For weeks I lived in a fog, punctured by crying spells and outbursts of anger. How could Pilar's love have vanished so quickly? What had I done to deserve her betrayal? I lost my appetite. When I looked in the mirror now, I saw a scrawny scarecrow of a woman instead of the slender, spirited dancer I had been.

While my aunt was supportive and affectionate throughout my

ordeal, after a while she started to lose patience with me: "Pull your-self together, Lucía! Enough is enough! I understand that you feel like the world has come to an end, but it hasn't. Life goes on. What about your work, your choreographies, your dancing? Are you going to give it all up because your heart is broken?"

A few days later, on a Sunday morning, Madame Moreau showed up at our door. I was taken aback. What had brought her to our house?

Over tea, she explained: "Lucía, I have a proposal for you. As you know, we've had to turn prospective students away because we don't have the space to accommodate them, which is a real shame. But, if you opened your own academy, we'd be able to accept them all! You could take the more advanced students with you and I'd keep the beginners and low intermediates. Since my knees started bother-ing me, that's how we've been divvying up the work anyway. And of course, we'd keep on working together on our yearly productions. I have some savings which I can pass on to you... as a loan. What do you say?"

A window opened in my foggy brain. I could see myself running my own academy, creating my own teaching methods, trying my choreographic ideas with my own students... Would I be capable of pulling it off?

"I don't know..." I started, but my aunt didn't let me go on.

"Yes, you know that you can do it, Lucía! Madame Moreau is serving you a wonderful opportunity on a platter and she's doing so because she knows that you're ready to run your own academy."

"Your work will pull you out of the pits, Lucía. Many years ago it did it for me and I know that now it'll do it for you. Besides, your aunt is right. You are ready to fly on your own. You deserve to have a space where you can do as you see fit — experiment with your teach-ing approaches and break new ground with your choreographies," Madame Moreau added.

She was right. While I still felt sad and even bitter about my breakup with Pilar, I did pull myself together, looked for a place, got organized and finally established the Academia de Danza Contemporánea Lucía Céspedes, the Lucía Céspedes Academy of Contemporary Dance, which opened its doors on September 1, 1935. It didn't take long for new students to start enrolling and for my schedule to fill up. It took a long time for my heart to heal, but eventually I relegated Pilar to the back of my mind and was able to pour all my energy into my work.

A couple of years later, as Aunt Encarnación and I were having a cup of tea and listening to *Tango en el crepúsculo* — *Tango in the Twilight* on Radio Nuevomundo, there was a loud knock on the door. Who could it be at that late hour?

I got up, walked to the door and asked hesitantly: "Who is it?"

"Telegram!" a baritone voice sang.

My aunt and I were puzzled. Who had sent us a telegram? And why?

It was from my father:

Antonia critical condition Military Hospital Stop Captain Edmundo Ramírez Chilean Navy Headquarters Valparaíso will arrange passage to Iquique Stop Sent money transfer your name State Bank Colon Avenue Stop Encarnación not welcome Stop Papá Stop

I felt weak in the knees. What was wrong with my mom? Her weekly letters hadn't mentioned anything about her health being compromised. What if she was okay and my father was just trying to trick me into going back to Iquique? For quite a while now, he had known "the truth" about Aunt Encarnación and had written a few times cursing her and demanding that I go back "home."

The next day my aunt got in touch with her colleagues in Iquique and asked them to find out if Antonia González de Céspedes was indeed at the Military Hospital. Their response was prompt: Yes.

We decided that, welcome or not, Aunt Encarnación would go with me and we'd stay at a pension. We arrived at six in the morning on August 31. The bay and the city were shrouded in *camanchaca*, a thick blanket of fog that had turned Iquique into a land of apparitions — miniscule silver droplets floating in the air, blurred shapes and loud, disembodied sounds. My recollections of the seven months I had lived there didn't include *camanchaca* — perhaps I had never been outdoors that early in the day. Or perhaps today the surreal scenery had been concocted by higher powers just to match my state of mind: hazy but pierced by blaring memories and feelings.

Twelve years earlier, I had left Iquique with a broken heart — Manuel and his family believed I had betrayed them, I felt like a stranger in my own home, and I didn't know what my life in Valparaíso would be like. Now, I was back, my mother was in critical condition, and I didn't know how I felt about that or how I felt about her. Would it help her recovery if I lied and said, "I love you, Mom?"

I didn't have a chance to try. When we got to the hospital, we were informed that Mrs. Antonia González de Céspedes had gone into septic shock and passed away just half an hour earlier. Her records showed that she had been in and out of hospital for the last month, due to an infection in her internal organs. Unfortunately, the infection had spread and become more aggressive, so she had finally been admitted into the Intensive Care Unit six days before. Doctors had done everything in their power to save her but had been unsuccessful. In the end, her blood had become poisoned and her whole system, compromised. This had led to her unfortunate and untimely death. They were very sorry indeed. My father had been notified and should be arriving any minute now. In the meantime, we were welcome to go to my mother's room and keep her company.

I don't remember getting there, but I can still smell the mix of rot, urine, wilted flowers and iodoform, all interlaced with Shalimar — my mom's signature perfume — that hit me like a slap in the face when I opened the door to her room. In the middle of the all-white space and against the back wall stood a white metal bed — and a surprisingly large mound covered with a white coverlet taking most of its breadth.

Gagging from the stench, I just stood at the door, but Aunt Encarnación stormed in, drew the curtains and opened the windows, which let in a welcomed waft of fresh air and a flood of bright daylight. Resting on a white pillow, my mother's head was a puffed up, blotchy balloon capped by a clump of gooey hair and studded with a pair of wide-open eyes looking straight up at the ceiling.

Next thing I knew, I was on the floor, a splash of vomit next to my face. I must've regained consciousness right away, because I heard my aunt scream and run to my side. I tried to get up, but the whole room was going around in circles.

A troop of nurses came running and surrounded me. I was picked up off the floor and made to sit on a chair: "It's her daughter... poor thing. Couldn't bear the sight of her dead mommy. Just got here from Santiago... No, no — from Valparaíso... It's okay, darling. It is a horrible thing, we know. Such a lovely lady, your mom. And so young... But we have to accept God's will..."

I tried to get up, but a heavy hand pushed me down: "Rest, my dear, rest. No rush to get up. Here, take a sip of water."

But I had to get out of there. I used all the strength I could muster, scrambled to my feet and ran. When I got to the street, a black Mercedes Benz followed by two military jeeps were turning the corner. By then, my aunt had caught up with me and linked her arm with mine. We walked briskly away from the hospital door, crossed the street and in the next block found a café that was just opening for the day.

"The head nurse explained that your father had asked that Antonia's eyes be left open if she died when he wasn't there; he wanted to close them himself," she said, taking my hand across the table.

I was shivering and my head was pounding. I was also feeling like a worm; I hadn't even managed to go near my mother's body to pay my respects.

My aunt must've been reading my mind: "The scene was hard to take; she had swollen up because of the infection. The stench was bad too. My poor sister... so obsessed with her beauty and she ends up like this," she said, wiping tears off her face.

The funeral was a couple of days later, but I couldn't bring myself to go. Just the thought of it made me choke with anxiety.

My aunt did her best to change my mind: "Believing that you don't love your mother is not a good enough reason not to go to her funeral, Lucía! You must pull yourself together and go! If you don't, you will regret it later. We can stay at the very back of the crowd — Ernesto doesn't even have to see us. I brought a couple of veils to wear at the church. If you cover your hair and part of your face, nobody will recognize you, not even your father," she said.

But I couldn't do it. I stayed at the pension instead, tuned into Radio Europa, the local classical music station and was fortunate to be soothed by my favourite opera, Bizet's *Carmen*. I thought about walking to the square or to the beach where I had met Manuel but couldn't muster the energy or the desire to do anything other than listen to Pia Tassinari's luscious voice and imagine her as a fiery flamenco dancer.

My aunt described the grandiose funeral to me — the horse-drawn black-and-gold hearse, the dozens of wreaths and flower arrangements and the military band. The cathedral had been bursting at the seams and the bishop himself had officiated the mass. The crowd had not only included the Iquique upper crust — the British ladies and the officers' wives clad in black outfits and veiled hats — but also a good number of working-class people, most likely beneficiaries of my mother's charitable work. My father couldn't have been any more conspicuous in his stately uniform and cape, a score of medals pinned to his chest.

Mrs. Inglis had given the eulogy. She had spoken of Antonia de Céspedes' beauty, her tireless work for the poor, the beautiful roses she grew in her garden — a true symbol of her generosity of spirit and *joie de vivre* and her devotion to her family. I guess she meant "her devotion to her husband."

I asked my aunt if anybody had mentioned my absence.

"Well, the British lady did mention your name in the eulogy but didn't say anything about your absence. I did see people looking around though, whispering your name, probably wondering where you were," she responded.

At the church, she had sat at the very back and, on the way to the cemetery, had walked among the crowd — away from my father. But when the procession finally got to my mother's grave, the group had shuffled and she had ended up quite close to Ernesto Céspedes.

"He turned his head several times, but I don't think he recognized me — after all, we only met once and that was more than twenty-five years ago," my aunt said. "I think he was looking for you. He knows that we came to Iquique — the captain who made our travel arrangements must have told him, so yes, I'm sure he was trying to find you in the crowd."

Before taking the boat back to Valparaíso, my aunt insisted that we go visit my mother's grave. "Lucía! Get a grip on yourself! You refused to go to her funeral, so the least you can do is visit your mother's grave!" she shouted, shaking her head.

I had to agree. I gathered myself and we made our way to the cemetery. The mausoleum where my mother was buried looked like a miniature palace — an ornate, white marble building with two pillars in the front, a mahogany door between them, "Céspedes" inscribed in Gothic script above it, and enough space inside to house a small living family, never mind a dead one. It even had a manicured garden all around displaying beautiful rose bushes, most likely transplanted from my mom's collection at home. Obviously, my father had made preparations well in advance for his own and the family's hereafter.

Also in Gothic script, my mother's name and biographical data had been inscribed on the wall to the left of the door, followed by an epitaph that read: "Say not in grief she is no more, but in gratitude that she was."

I felt neither grief nor gratitude. I felt nothing — other than astonishment at the mausoleum's display of opulence.

"I should've guessed that my father would want to leave this kind of legacy behind. This mausoleum reads 'Ernesto Céspedes' all over," I noted, feeling the smooth marble with my hand.

But my aunt didn't respond. When I turned around, I saw that she had fallen on her knees and was sobbing, her hands on her face and her body quivering with heartache. At first, I was paralyzed by the sight, never having seen my aunt cry like that before. But next thing I knew, I was hugging her and crying with her, feeling her pain and through it, the tragedy of my mother's untimely death. I welcomed this outburst of emotion. I was not the heartless creature I feared I had become; I *was* able to feel, and what I felt for my mother that evening was profound and genuine pity.

We arrived back in Valparaíso at the end of September, the beginning of spring, and the city was in bloom. My aunt went back to work right away, but I stayed home for a few more days. Since bursting into tears at the Iquique cemetery, I had been crying about everything and anything — recollections of Mercedes and our family's life in Tacna, before everything had been turned upside down; memories of my lonely days in Iquique; flashes of my mother's smile, of her fashionable outfits and hairdos, of my desire to be like her when I was growing up; thoughts of Miss Asunta and Manuel. I hated feeling like that — actually, it made me furious, but I couldn't help it.

I didn't want to burden my aunt with my woes — my mother's passing had hit her hard, but none of my friends knew my whole story, so I didn't have anybody to talk to. It was time to reconnect with Pilar.

Through the grapevine I'd heard that Marcos had turned out to be an asshole — had left her when she got pregnant, so she'd come back to Valparaíso and was living with her parents and working at the bakery. My aunt had urged me to go visit her, meet the child, become friends again. But my heart had stopped me. As much as I had wanted to believe that I was over our breakup, the mere thought of seeing Pilar again turned me into a nervous wreck. What if I was still in love with her? What if she had changed so much that my cherished memories of our time together were ruined? What if she gave me the cold shoulder? Now I was ready to take the risk.

ON A WARM, SUNNY afternoon, I made my way to Panadería Castillo. The shop was overflowing with customers and Pilar was working the counter. It was teatime and the four o'clock batch of *pan batido, hayuyas, alfajores* and apple *kuchen* had just come out.

I stood by the back wall and watched her. I felt weak in the knees and my face was burning. If Pilar had changed at all, it was for the better. She was more beautiful than ever and as bubbly and warm as I remembered. She knew her customers' names and was familiar not only with their choice of bread but also with their everyday lives.

"The usual Señora Elena?" "Is your mom feeling better today Señorita Yoli?" "Did Miguelito pass that math test that had you in a knot yesterday, Señora Adela?"

There were only a couple of customers left when Pilar noticed me. While taking her apron off and undoing her hair net, she called to the back of the shop for someone to replace her. Her unruly mane burst free and tumbled down her back and all around her face. Then she opened the counter's flap door and walked out to meet me, a wide smile on her face and tears in her eyes.

We lingered in a warm embrace.

"Let's have a cup of tea," she finally suggested, pointing to the stairs that went up to the Castillo family home.

Pilar's daughter Alexandra was out with her grandparents, so we had the whole flat to ourselves. The first few moments were awkward, but it didn't take long for us to go past the small talk. She told me all about fucking Marcos and how stupid she'd been. I told her about my mom's death, my aunt and my dance academy.

"What about your love life?" she asked, out of the blue.

"I don't have one," I responded, blushing.

"What do you mean you don't have one?! Don't tell me that in all these years nobody has fallen for you," she joked.

"Well, I have had a couple of... *pololeos* — flings, you know, with men," I muttered. "But I haven't really fallen in love again."

She looked at me in silence for a while. "I'm sorry about what happened, Lucía. I was so... immature, I guess you'd call it, so fucking stupid, really. Many times I've been on the verge of coming to your place for a visit. But I've been embarrassed, ashamed, really. Sorry," she repeated.

"There's nothing to be sorry or ashamed about, Pilar," I responded. "You fell in love with somebody else and, as my aunt says, 'love hardly ever lasts forever.'"

"But I should've written to you, Lucía. Confided in you. Talked to you the way we always had. You shouldn't have found out about Marcos from my mother!" she exclaimed, getting up and shaking her head.

"I need your help, Pilar. That's why I came to see you," I confessed.

"Of course! Tell me what's going on and I'll do my best to help," she responded, sitting down again.

"I think that my childhood ordeals are finally catching up with me. I can't stop crying. Everything makes me cry. I feel so weak, and stupid... But I remember those ordeals well — they're part of my conscious self," I said. "Is there something that my unconscious is hiding from me? Am I suffering from some kind of neurosis or hysteria? What do you think, Pilar?" I asked. I had read Freud and Reich and their theories made sense to me.

"Can't help you there, kiddo. I know fuck all about conscious selves and unconscious selves. What I do know is that you've been carrying a lot of pain from a very young age," she said, getting up and placing her open palm on my chest and looking me in the eye. "Anybody would be 'neurotic' and 'hysterical' if they'd been through what you've been through, Freud and Reich included!" she went on, starting to pace and throwing her arms up in the air.

I couldn't help but smile. She hadn't changed a bit. She was still as passionate and dramatic as before. She paced some more and finally sat down next to me.

"Lucía, my guess is that your mother's death and your trip to Iquique stirred the stew of feelings that has been simmering inside you for all these years. In my humble opinion, all you need is somebody to talk to, hear you out, understand you. Somebody other than your aunt. You need a friend." Her eyes were moist. "I'm here and I would love to be your friend again," she said then, her voice low and raspy.

"I would love to be your friend too," I whispered back.

MANUEL
. . . .

September 1938

Iquique and Valparaíso

IN 1926, ARMY GENERAL Carlos Ibáñez del Campo, the Mussolini-admiring, populist scumbag and power-monger who had been minister of defence at the time of the La Coruña massacre, had weaseled his way into the country's presidency. Then, the covert war he had been waging on workers and their organizations turned into a full-on attack against anyone who didn't agree with his fascistic ideology. Many communist and anarchist leaders were imprisoned and banished to barren islands off the coast.

A few years later, Mr. Bacic called me into his office and said: "Time to become a real journalist, Tamarugo. Can't do without your chronicles — they help with the sales — but you're ready to move on and add a whole new set of tools to your reporter's bag."

Fascism and Nazism were on the rise in Western Europe, while the Soviet Union consolidated its grip on Eastern Europe and dictated what Communist Parties in every corner of the globe should think and do. I started to read everything I could put my hands on and listened to shortwave radio broadcasts from around the world. As for my writing, I had become an expert in circuitous ways to say what I wanted without betraying the truth or skirting the issues. I tried hard to do my job with integrity, just like Mr. Bacic had taught me, while making sure I didn't cut my own throat.

Ernesto Céspedes was in the news often — every time he went

up in the military ranks, the bourgeois media would run a flattering interview in which he unabashedly talked about his role in keeping the Bolsheviks at bay and the fatherland "clean and pure." His wife was in the social section of the newspapers practically every week — having drinks with the British consul, organizing fashion shows, collecting goods for a girls' orphanage. Lucía never showed up in any of those photographs.

Shortly after the Pampa Nueva incident and Aunt Asunta's disappearance, I had made my way to Saint George's and watched the girls walk out at the end of the school day, but Lucía was not among them. I didn't muster the courage to ask anyone about her — I was a poor, brown boy in "off-limits" territory, and most likely somebody would've called the cops. I also went looking for her at the beach, but she was nowhere to be seen; when I asked the fishermen and the other boys, they said that she had stopped coming quite a while back.

I'm not sure why I'd gone looking for her. While discovering that she was Ernesto Céspedes' daughter had made me very angry, I had come to the conclusion that she was not responsible for Aunt Asunta's disappearance. After much consideration, my mama and I had surmised that most likely the pictures that the so-called reporters had taken at Pampa Nueva had led Céspedes to my aunt's place and then to her school. She must've stood out like a beacon with her white skin and blue eyes among us *pampinos*. Back then I'd told myself that I wanted to find Lucía so that I could beat the crap out of her for being so deceitful. But that was just my juvenile bravado. Actually, I had been driven by curiosity; I wanted to uncover her secrets, find out what she had said in the letter she'd slid under our door, why she'd wanted to befriend us. But I never found her.

Carlos Ibáñez del Campo's government only lasted for a few years. As the economy crumbled, he began to lose popular support, and large sectors of the Armed Forces also turned their back on him, including now Brigadier General Ernesto Céspedes. Ibáñez del Campo was forced to resign. Political chaos ensued until finally

Arturo Alessandri, the candidate of the Chilean traditional right, was elected president and Céspedes was promoted to division general. Now he was just a few steps from the very top of the military echelons. The prediction was that within five years he would become general in chief of the Chilean Armed Forces as a whole.

El Mercurio, the national daily owned by and at the service of the bourgeoisie and the oligarchy, ran an extensive article on Céspedes and his meteoric career. They praised his intelligence and poise, his unwavering loyalty to our country's superior values and above all, his capacity to defend Chilean democracy and counteract the forces of international communism and anarchism.

Until then, every newspaper article and radio program about him had implied that in 1925 he had been transferred to Iquique from his native Santiago. But the *El Mercurio* story mentioned Céspedes' "service to the fatherland" in Tacna, a city that had been under Chilean occupation for forty-four years before being returned to Peru in the late 1920s.

The tabloid *El Bocón* dug into his past and brought out plenty of dirt. They claimed that he'd had a Peruvian lover in Tacna, that his wife had been a high-end prostitute in Santiago and that his daughter had turned into a commie and an eccentric dancer. They even published an ancient, blurry picture of Antonia Céspedes dressed in a scanty outfit and a recent one of Lucía Céspedes coming out of a building in downtown Valparaíso, where, allegedly, she ran a dance academy.

What had he been doing in Tacna?

"My guess is that Ernesto Céspedes was involved in the 1925 massacre of Peruvians in Tacna," Mr. Bacic said, matter-of-factly.

"What massacre?!" I demanded, starting to pace.

Mr. Bacic put his cigarillo butt out in his already full ashtray, pulled another one out of his shirt pocket, reached for a box of matches on his desk, lit it, drew a couple of drags, poured himself another shot of pisco and took a sip.

"Sit down, Tamarugo," he said, pointing to the chair in front of him. "No need to get so excited. There was going to be a plebiscite for the citizens of Tacna to decide whether they wanted their town to remain in Chile or go back to Peru. It was one of the conditions in the peace treaty the two countries signed at the end of the War of the Pacific. So, the Chilean Army and the so-called 'Patriotic Leagues' proceeded to kill over a thousand Peruvians to make sure that they couldn't vote in the plebiscite — the plebiscite that never happened."

"I never knew anything about that," I admitted, sitting down and shaking my head.

"I'm not surprised. Hardly anybody knows. I was working for the *Iquique Sun* back then and got a letter from a Peruvian journalist in Lima. He had come across my name as somebody who might be willing to publish a story about the Tacna events. Entire families had been disappearing, but the official word from the Chilean 'authorities' was that they had left town. It turned out that they had been massacred. Nobody would've known for sure had it not been for the mountain rains, which caused the Caplina River to swell and rush down the canyon where the bodies had been buried. The river waters exhumed the bodies and carried them down all the way to Tacna.

"I wrote the article, but I was gagged. My boss wouldn't publish it, and when I submitted it to newspapers and magazines in Santiago under a pen name, nobody dared pick it up. Only a couple of friends at the FOCH read it and wrote a little blurb for their bulletin board. That's all they could do. Back then, they had their hands full with the general strike and the La Coruña massacre," Mr. Bacic explained.

My mind was racing. That's what Lucía knew about: her father's involvement in the massacre.

"We have to interview Lucía Céspedes," I said, jumping to my feet. "This is the time to expose the son-of-a-bitch. He's a mass murderer. That's what he is!"

"His daughter? Why would you interview his daughter?!" Mr. Bacic asked.

I told him the Lucía story.

"Mmmm... interesting. Why didn't you talk to me about it years ago, Tamarugo?" he asked, looking at me over his eye glasses and holding my gaze.

I had to think about it. "I guess I was ashamed. I didn't want anyone to know that Ernesto Céspedes' daughter had befriended me and my family," I answered.

"Fair enough," Mr. Bacic said, pushing his glasses up his nose.

I asked a colleague in Valparaíso to find Lucía's academy and send me the address. A few days later, I managed to get passage on a cargo boat in exchange for stevedoring along the way. This time I was hired on the spot and nobody questioned my ability to load and unload cargo.

Following stops in Tocopilla, Antofagasta, Chañaral and Coquimbo, we docked in Valparaíso in the early evening of a rainy, windy day. I made my way to Academia de Danza Contemporánea Lucía Céspedes on Pedro Montt Avenue, and sure enough, there she was, dancing away with a troupe of young women, all enveloped in white, gauzy tunics.

She still looked like the rich girl I'd known in Iquique — tall, slender, a sculpted face, a pair of wide blue eyes and a mane of honey-coloured waves cascading down her back. Certainly, she was the perfect example of angelical beauty.

Her commands — "Sway in the crystalline air like a falling, golden leaf," "Open up your petals — you're a velvety white rose," and other such phrases sounded ridiculous to me, but the girls and Lucía herself did look rather nice floating around the room in their white tunics. Obviously, this was what the experts called "contemporary dance." I decided that it looked interesting — a lot better than a bunch of stiff-legged, ostrich-like women tip-toeing their way across a stage.

Lucía didn't notice me until the class was over. It took her a few moments to recognize me, but when she did, she was clearly taken aback — opened her eyes wide and blushed. I was a bit nervous myself, but by the time I'd walked over to greet her, we had both regained our composure. When she extended her hand and held my gaze, I finally let my guard down. Part of me had still felt dubious about her actions back in 1925, but when I looked into those celestial eyes of hers, all I saw was truthfulness — as clear as the *pampa* sky.

We walked down Pedro Montt Avenue in silence. Around us, umbrellas fought valiantly against the wind, children shrieked as they broke away from their mothers' hands and jumped into puddles, office workers made unsuccessful attempts to protect their precious suits by holding a newspaper over their shoulders, and young secretaries scampered by in their sloshy high heels and sodden tailored overcoats.

"How did you find me?" she asked finally.

"A colleague of mine here in Valparaíso got me the address for your academy," I responded.

"What do you mean 'a colleague'?" she asked.

"A journalist. I'm a journalist," I answered.

"That's interesting," she commented. "I thought you and the family had gone back to La Coruña."

"No, we stayed in Iquique."

"How did you know I had an academy?" she pressed on.

"From *El Bocón*," I responded.

"Who's *el bocón*?" she asked, obviously believing that I was referring to a person with a big mouth.

I laughed. She looked at me, puzzled and amused.

I explained that *El Bocón* was a gossip rag. She'd never heard of it. "They dug out some dirt about your... father... and published it a couple of weeks ago," I told her.

I wanted to tread lightly, so I withheld the information about her being a communist and her mother having been a call girl when she was young.

"What do you mean 'dirt'?" she asked.

"Oh! About your father's lovers, that kind of thing..." I said, matter-of-factly.

"And about me having a dance academy in Valparaíso," she said.

"How did you end up in Valparaíso, anyway?" I interjected, before she could ask me more about the *El Bocón* article.

"My father wanted me out of Iquique," she said. "I had written you a letter..."

"I know about the letter," I said. "The neighbours told me that you'd slid it under our door."

"I was mortified about what had happened at Pampa Nueva. I felt like a traitor, which I guess I was. In the letter I explained why I hadn't told you who I was... what my father had done before we'd moved to Iquique... in Tacna... where we lived."

"I also know about Tacna," I said.

She stopped in her tracks and held my gaze. Her eyes welled up and overflowed.

"Is that why you're here, to talk about Tacna?" she asked, wiping her face with the back of her hands. Her voice was hoarse.

"Yes," I answered. "I want to expose your father for who he is. But more important than that, I want to help bring Ernesto Céspedes to justice."

By then we had got to the Marco Polo on Las Heras Street, Lucía's suggestion. It was bustling with diners. We had already decided to go look for a quieter place when the owner showed us to a corner table that she quickly turned into a private cubicle by closing a flowery curtain on its two exposed sides. We had a chuckle about that.

I ordered a bottle of Undurraga Viejo Roble and *paila marina* — seafood stew. She asked for *caldillo de congrio* — conger chowder, telling me that it reminded her of her voyage between Iquique and Valparaíso in 1925. I told her that all I'd been fed during *my* voyage was *porotos con riendas* — bean and spaghetti noodle stew. We had a chuckle about that as well.

We sat in silence for a while. Finally, she asked: "What do you mean 'bring Ernesto Céspedes to justice'?"

"The Peruvian government has shown an interest in having him extradited to Peru so that he can be tried for the 1925 massacre in Tacna. But for that to happen, they need as much evidence as possible to present to the Chilean justice system because your father would have to go through an extradition trial here first," I answered. "As we speak, Mr. Bacic, my boss, and his Peruvian colleagues are talking to the authorities."

"Wouldn't that be something," she said.

The wine came. We toasted to our reunion. I offered my condolences on her mother's passing, told her that I had gone to the funeral looking for her, but she wasn't there.

"I was in Iquique but didn't go to the funeral," she said, shaking her head. "Just couldn't bring myself to walk on the Iquique streets again, or to see my father. He had let me know that my mother was critically ill, but I arrived too late, got to the hospital half an hour after she'd died."

I took her hand across the table. "That must've been heartbreaking," I said.

"Yes and no," she sighed.

I squeezed her hand. She smiled a sad smile.

"I didn't really love my mother, Manuel. I felt sorry for her, but I didn't love her," she said. Her eyes were moist.

"How's *your* mom, Manuel?" she asked then, a smile on her face.

"My mama died three years ago... of consumption. She had just turned forty-two," I answered, feeling my throat tighten. It was still hard for me to talk about it. The memories of her long illness were not pretty.

"Oh, no!" she said.

"She never really recovered from the La Coruña events. Well, when you met her, she had already lost a lot of weight *and* her desire to live. Consumption pounces on the weak, so she was a prime candidate."

"I'm so sorry, Manuel. I have such fond memories of her. But your brother and sister are okay?" she asked.

"Oh yes, they're just fine, and so is my grandma, even though she's pushing seventy. We went to live with her when we left Aunt Asunta's place. You haven't asked about her, so I guess you know that she disappeared, right?" I said.

She nodded. "I do. The women at the FOCH building let me know about it when I went looking for her. They actually accused me of having informed on her. Then my aunt's colleagues in Iquique confirmed it. My aunt Encarnación. That's who I live with here in Valparaíso. She's a teacher as well. Poor Miss Asunta... another victim of my father's crimes," she said, sorrow in her voice.

"How do you feel about your father, Lucía?" I asked then.

She came back with a quick and loud "I hate him," as she pulled her hand away. "You know as well as I do that he's nothing but a murderer."

By then we had finished eating.

"Let's go home, Manuel. We can talk more freely there. Also, I want you to meet my aunt."

I picked up the bill from the table and was getting ready to pay, when I heard her say to the waitress: "This will cover my portion. He'll pay for his."

"Lucía," I managed.

"It's okay, Manuel. You don't have to play 'gentleman' with me. I'm used to paying my own way," she said and started to walk out of the restaurant.

I put a few bills on the table and followed her. Most certainly, she had turned into a self-assured and independent woman.

As we walked up the hill, she asked: "Are you an anarchist, like your Aunt Asunta and your mom?"

"Yes, of course! And are you a communist?" I asked.

She stopped walking and looked at me with suspicion.

"Yes. How do you know?" she asked, as she started to walk again.

"Sounds like *El Bocón*'s sources are reliable," I said.

"What?! They also mentioned that I'm a communist? That's scary!" She sounded alarmed.

"It is. But I wouldn't get too worried about it," I said. "The thing about those tabloids is that they go where the wind blows. Their focus changes by the minute and they're always looking for their next story. Your father stopped being news the same day they published that piece of trash, and he won't get their attention again until he climbs another step up the ladder and becomes the army general for the whole country."

Her aunt couldn't believe her eyes when Lucía showed up with me at her door. "What?! This is Manuel?! Iquique Manuel?!"

Over a cup of tea, I told them about Aunt Asunta's disappearance and how I had landed my job at *The Northener*; they were pleased to hear that Moncho was a union leader at the Iquique docks, and Rufina, an exemplary student in her last year of high school.

Finally, I explained the purpose of my visit: "Lucía, I think I know why you were so secretive when we met in Iquique. My suspicion is that you witnessed something having to do with the massacre of Peruvians."

She nodded and began to speak. I took notes, asked questions, pressed her on every detail. Her testimony of the events at the river and on the train was solid. As much as I tried to trick her and make her doubt her memory, she didn't budge and her story didn't change.

"This is very valuable testimony, Lucía. Very valuable," I said. "It will be impossible to get the Chilean courts to try Céspedes for the La Coruña massacre. There he was acting on behalf of the Chilean government, which had declared a state of siege a couple of days before. So, he was protected by martial law. But Tacna is a different story. Even though he was also acting on behalf of the Chilean state, there he was killing foreigners, not Chileans," I said.

"If we succeed in getting Céspedes extradited to Peru, I will die in peace," Mr. Bacic had said before I left.

"Boss — why don't you retire instead of dying?" I'd said, half-jok-ingly, half-seriously. Mr. Bacic had been suffering from chest pains and his doctor had ordered him to stay home and rest. It would've helped if he had also stopped smoking and drinking so much but, as expected, he hadn't paid any heed to the doctor's orders and kept on working like a dog, smoking like a chimney and drinking like a fish.

"Yes, Manuel, Yes. I know. I'm getting too old for this, aren't I? But first, I have to make sure that Céspedes gets extradited to Peru. Then, I'll retire. Promise," he'd said. Now it was Lucía's and my turn to do our part in making it happen.

"Lucía, can you travel to Lima with me?" I asked her, point blank. "Your testimony will be crucial. They need to hear it firsthand."

She opened her eyes wide. "I don't know... What about... what about the academy?" she said then, looking at her aunt.

"You can hire one of your graduates to take over your classes. Manuel is right. Your testimony is crucial to the case," Aunt Encarnación responded.

Two days later, we were on board the *Siete Mares* on our way to Lima.

LUCÍA
. . . .

September – October 1938

Valparaíso and Lima

I TOLD HIM THAT I wanted to make love to him. A deep yearning had come upon me the moment I'd seen him, leaning against the door jamb at the entrance to the studio, drenched to the core with rain.

He was still short and thin — just a bigger version of the Manuel I'd known in Iquique. His rugged, brown face looked older than his age, but his eyes were young — piercing and playful, exactly the way I remembered them. And when he'd walked across the floor with that springy gait that I'd found so peculiar and beguiling when we were kids, I'd felt the urge to run up to him and greet him with a loving hug.

It wasn't lust. That much I knew. What was it then?

For thirteen years I had done my best to forget about Manuel and my past. Now, he had shown up at my door and made me realize that all along I had carried him inside me, entangled with my memories of Tacna, Mercedes, the Caplina River, the train, Iquique, Miss Asunta, the beach, his family. What had he done with *his* memories? How had he moved on after all the horror he had endured?

I wanted to know. I wanted to find the answers under his skin and in the nooks and crannies of his body. It was the evening of our first day at sea; we had just finished dessert and were sitting at the end of a long, communal table, across from each other. I leaned forward, cupped my hands around my mouth and whispered: "Manuel, I want to make love to you."

He stared at his empty bowl and smiled a crooked smile. "I don't think it's a good idea, Lucía," he said finally, looking me in the eye. "Don't take me wrong. I think you're beautiful and... but we can't let our... this... distract us from our work. If the Peruvian authorities realize that we're lovers, our credibility will suffer. Mine as an investigative journalist, and yours as a key witness," he added.

"So, you're no longer the impetuous boy that jumped into the ocean to get his mother a washing trough," I countered.

He chuckled. "I guess not, Lucía. I guess I've learned my lesson."

The air between us thickened. "Are you married Manuel?" I blurted out then. Why hadn't I thought of that possibility until now?

This time he laughed outright. "I don't believe in bourgeois institutions, Lucía."

"Okay, then, do you have a companion, a girlfriend? Are you in love?" I asked.

He became pensive and took a while to respond. "No, I'm not in love. To tell you the truth, I don't think I've ever been in love. A long time ago I thought I was in love, but I don't think I was because my broken heart mended in no time at all," he said, a wide grin on his face.

"Who was she?" I asked.

"A prostitute," he replied.

His response took me by surprise. "A prostitute?!"

"Yeah, her name was Minerva. She was fifteen, the same age as me at the time — basically a slave to the madam who had taken her in after she'd run away from home. The mere thought of Minerva having sex with other men made me sick with despair, so I talked her into running away with me. I told my mama and grandma that I wanted her to come live with us and, after much coaxing and cajoling, they gave in; after all, Minerva was a poor girl, a victim of society's evils, I was infatuated with her and she could always help with the housework and my mom's laundry gigs. In the end, Minerva snitched on me to her *mamita* — that's what she called the madam, and the night I went to get her, the security guard beat the shit out of me while Minerva and the old witch watched the spectacle impassively. That was the last time I set foot in a bordello," he explained with a chuckle.

"And the last time you were in love," I added.

"The only time I was in love... maybe." He chuckled some more. "What about you, Lucía? I know you're not married, but are you in love? Do you have a boyfriend?" he asked.

"No, I don't," I said. "About being in love... mmmm... I don't know. I may be in love with the same person I was in love with three, four years ago. Maybe," I responded.

Pilar and I had been spending a lot of time together since the day I had gone to the bakery. It was so easy to be in her company! She knew me, she understood me. And she was strong... and smart... and beautiful. "She's so beautiful!" I said out loud.

"She?!" he pounced.

I smiled. Of course, he'd be taken aback.

"Yes. She. Her name is Pilar Castillo — a Spaniard, like your Aunt Asunta, but not a Catalonian. She's from Madrid and came to Valparaíso with her parents many years ago, fleeing the Primo de Rivera dictatorship," I explained.

It took a while for Manuel to speak again. "I don't understand," he said finally, clearly uncomfortable. "If you... like women, why do you want to make love to me?" He looked truly puzzled.

"I don't know, Manuel. It's not that I 'like' women. I fell in love with Pilar when I was fifteen years old. Then she left me — for a man. Now we renewed our friendship and I *may* be falling in love with her all over again. That's all," I said.

"Oh! So, you do like men as well," he concluded.

"Well, after Pilar and I broke up, I did have a couple of *pololeos* with men, but I didn't fall in love with them," I said.

"What do you mean? How do you know?" Manuel asked.

His questions baffled me. Didn't this grown man know what falling in love felt like? What was he fishing for? But then I realized that his questions were genuine.

"I knew because my connection to these men didn't even come close to what I'd felt for Pilar. Pilar and I had been friends, confidants, lovers. Nobody was as beautiful as she was. And she felt the same way about me. Our bodies were a source of pleasure, comfort, intimacy. We were so close. We could talk for hours on end... I felt safe with her. Other than my aunt, she was the only person I told about my past."

I was still immersed in nostalgia, when I heard Manuel's voice: "I've never been with anyone like that. I've just had... I don't know... what you called 'flings,' I guess. But nobody to confide in. Nobody to trust, really trust, to call my true friend."

"Why Manuel? Why do you think you've never been in love?" I asked.

He took his time. "I don't know. Perhaps because I don't think there's anybody out there that would understand what I've been through."

"I think I know what you mean... and I think that the reason I want to get close to you, make love to you, is because I want to get inside you. I want to know how you've been able to survive so much pain," I said. "How have you done it, Manuel?"

"I don't know, Lucía. I've just forged ahead. That's all," he said.

We got up at the same time and met halfway. I rested my chin on the top of his head and he buried his face in my shoulder, as we encircled each other with our arms. I felt my body melt. We had found each other after all these years of absences — a man and a woman of disparate backgrounds linked by pain and a common enemy: my father and everything he represented.

"I looked and looked for you at the beach and around town. I waited for you outside your school, but I never saw you again. I told myself that I would find your house but was too scared to go near the military housing complex," he whispered in my ear. "I told myself that I wanted to find you so that I could beat the shit out of you, but the truth is that I just wanted to see you, talk to you, sort out the confusion that was driving me nuts after the Pampa Nueva episode," he added, kissing my head.

"I missed you too, Manuel; you and your mom, and Miss Asunta, and Moncho and Rufina, and the beach, and your house, and... After everything that happened, I felt like a traitor, even though I'd never told anyone about you and your family," I responded, taking a step back and looking at him.

"I know, I know," he said.

That night we didn't go to bed. We talked all night over a bottle of wine. He wanted to know everything about my childhood, and I wanted to know everything about his. Our respective mothers came into the conversation. What were their stories? What were they like?

Dawn caught us on the deck, wrapped in thick, wool blankets Manuel had retrieved from the cabin we were sharing with two young men.

"We're lucky to be out here. Clearly, those guys have been farting away all night — the place stinks!" he said with a chuckle, while holding his nose with his index finger and thumb.

The next day, after a few hours of sleep, we began to talk again. This time, it didn't take us long to start arguing about politics. I asked him if he was going to vote for the Popular Front in the upcoming presidential elections.

"I don't believe in bourgeois elections," he responded. "And the Popular Front? That's just another hall of mirrors set up by the powers-that-be to confuse the working class."

His cynicism irked me. "What's wrong with the Popular Front's program?! Don't you believe in labour laws that favour the working class? Don't you believe in universal health care and free education for all?" I asked.

"Of course, I believe in all that! But getting in bed with the bourgeoisie and trusting that they will serve the interests of the proletariat is definitely not one of the things I believe in!" he responded.

"It's a tactical decision. We haven't forgotten about the revolution, but right now we need to form alliances with the democratic sectors of the bourgeoisie so that we can defeat fascism," I countered.

"Lucía, Lucía, you're just repeating Comrade Stalin's words," he said, in a condescending voice that irked me even more.

"Well, Comrade Stalin happens to be right. At this political juncture, fascism is the enemy!" I shot back.

"And are Soviet people the enemy as well? While he claims that the proletarian revolution in other parts of the world must wait, he's slaughtering peasants, workers and intellectuals in his own country. He's a traitor. That's what he is," he said.

"Stalin is not slaughtering anybody. I can't believe that you, you of all people, would repeat the rumours spread by Yankee imperialism!" I countered.

He took his time to respond. "Stalin is killing thousands, hundreds of thousands of people, Lucía. It's not a rumour. It's a fact," he said in a conciliatory tone. "But the massacres are not only happening inside the Soviet Union. Just last year, following on their 'father's' footsteps — or shall I say their 'god's' footsteps — pro-Stalinist communists in Spain killed hundreds of anarchists. Yes, they killed their comrades in arms against Franco."

"How do you know?" I asked.

"The killing of anarchists in Spain is common knowledge. As for what's happening inside the Soviet Union, my contacts in Europe tell me that some intellectuals have been able to leave and are speaking out," he responded.

"How do you know they're telling the truth? Maybe they're just agents of imperialism," I countered.

"No Lucía. They're not agents of imperialism. They're

revolutionaries, but they're not Stalinists because Stalin has turned his back on the Revolution and become a brutal dictator," he said.

I didn't know how to respond. I didn't want to believe him. I was a communist, not an anarchist, and the Soviet Union represented the kind of society we communists wanted to build in our own countries. It would take many years for me to finally concede that he'd been right and I'd been wrong. Yes, when working-class organizations make alliances with the bourgeoisie, they're bound to be betrayed. And yes, Stalin had murdered hundreds of thousands of people and had committed treason against the Revolution.

The rest of the week at sea went by fast. We decided not to talk about politics anymore, but anything else was a valid topic of conversation. It turned out that the stories of our own lives were enough to fill the hours.

My desire to make love to him had melted away. Through his stories and ruminations about life I had been able to see him up close, to appreciate his extraordinary spirit and understand the subversive nature of his life. His fate was to die with the rest of them: his father, his sister, the many others who had been killed in La Coruña, and the millions who over the centuries had succumbed and continued to succumb to the wretched working and living conditions imposed by the conquerors, the imperialists, the mining companies, the land owners, the money-makers, the exploiters, the oppressors. He was meant to die, but he had dared to live.

Our business in Lima went well. We met with government officials, and I offered my testimony in front of a judge. We were thanked profusely and assured that matters were developing well and expeditiously. If everything stayed on course, an extradition trial would take place in the next few months in Santiago.

On our last evening there, Manuel and I celebrated over a few *pisco sours* and heavenly dishes of *ají de gallina* and *cau-cau*. As we were enjoying our dessert — *suspiro limeño* — he dropped a bomb: he wasn't going back to Chile with me.

"I heard this news the day after we got to Lima but didn't want it to distract us from our business," he said. "Mr. Bacic had a heart attack; he's recovering but has decided that it's time to close down *The Northerner* and retire. Fortunately for me, *Rebelión* has hired me to cover the Civil War in Spain."

Rebelión was an internationally renowned, leftist weekly out of Santiago.

"Congratulations, Manuel!" I managed, even though I was trying to figure out how I'd get through my father's extradition trial without him there.

"I'm so sorry, Lucía. I really wanted to be there for Céspedes' trial — to offer you support and to cover it," he said.

I swallowed hard. "It'll be okay, Manuel. You'll be doing very important work and I'll have plenty of support as it is," I said, thinking of my aunt and Pilar. "You just take care and make sure to come back in one piece, okay?"

MANUEL
· · · · · · · · · · · · · · ·

November 1938

Barcelona

AFTER TWENTY-SEVEN DAYS OF travel aboard the *Rimac*, a rickety cargo boat loaded with humongous tubs filled with iron ore, I made my way from the port of Arcachon on the French Atlantic coast to Perpignan on the Mediterranean, and then down to Barcelona.

Rebelión was paying for my expenses, and Mr. Carrasco, its editor in chief, had directed me to check in at Barcelona's Hotel Palace, "the safest place in town and where most international reporters are staying," he'd said. So, that's where I went.

From the outside, the hotel looked unassuming, but when I stepped in, I found myself in a true palace. "Holy crap! No wonder there's a civil war going on," I said to myself. Clearly, the bourgeoisie wouldn't want to let go of this kind of riches: golden, ornate trimmings all over the walls and around the windows, crystal chandeliers galore (maybe they were cheaper by the dozen), plush sofas and armchairs. If Mr. Carrasco hadn't already reserved a room and commanded me to stay there, I would've turned around and walked right out.

The other reason I didn't walk out was because I saw her. I was standing at the entrance to the lobby, feeling like a train wreck and stinking to high heaven, my canvas bag slung over my shoulder, most likely with my mouth open as I took the place in, thirsty as hell and ready to collapse, when I saw her, sitting close by at a small round table, fiddling with a camera. Her mouth was curled up just a bit and she was giving me a sardonic look through the gauze of her cigarette smoke, as if to say, "Here comes another poor bastard."

She was dressed in black pants, a black shirt and combat boots. Her dark hair was cropped close to her head, and a bushy unibrow, which crossed the upper half of her face like an angry statement, contrasted sharply with a pair of delicious, honey-coloured eyes. The lower half of her face was occupied by a longish, straight nose and a fleshy mouth, which she had painted blood-red.

I don't know what came over me, but I heard these words spill out of my mouth: "Can I kiss you?"

"Only if it's urgent," she responded, her eyes trained on the camera.

I laughed.

Then, while taking a drag from her cigarette, she turned her head towards me and said: "For your information, we're in the middle of a war. Nobody knows if they're going to be alive tomorrow or not. A bomb could fall on this very building right now and kill us all. So, if you really need to kiss me, go ahead."

Was she serious? Was she being sarcastic?

"I stink," I managed to whisper, feeling more and more self-conscious by the second.

"I know. But I've smelled worse, believe me," she answered, crushing her cigarette stub in an ashtray and going back to inspecting her camera.

I dropped my bag and approached her hesitantly. I kneeled beside her and reached out for her chin. She looked at me with those ambrosial eyes of hers and I saw a sparkle grow towards me. Perhaps she was also in need of an urgent kiss.

We took the stairs up to her room and fell on the bed in a tangle of arms and legs. When I woke up, it was nighttime. I could hear the sounds of Las Ramblas on the other side of the window, but the heavy curtains let little light in.

Everything hurt: my head, my back, my feet, even my hair. When I turned the light on, I found myself in a small version of the hotel lobby, a room with golden rococo trimming all over and a chandelier hanging from the centre of the ceiling.

There I was, stark naked, standing in the middle of this room, the last few hours of my life slowly returning to my consciousness, when the door stormed open and the honey-eyed woman came in.

"You're awake!" she exclaimed, shooting her right hand towards me, as she swallowed the distance between us in two decisive steps. "I'm Rosa Fromm," she said.

Hesitantly, I lifted my right hand off my crotch; I had placed it there on top of my left one, in an attempt to hide my private parts.

"And you are?" she asked, looking at me in the eye.

"Manuel Garay."

She was still shaking my hand as if it were a fruit tree, while I attempted, unsuccessfully, to cover my private parts with my lonely left hand.

"I'm a photojournalist originally from Germany, but since 1933, from Paris, France," she said.

"I'm a journalist from Chile," I said.

She let go of my hand, which sprang back to my crotch.

"All right then, Manolito, why don't you get yourself cleaned up and join us for a meal and a drink downstairs? Food is rationed, but the cook managed to get a hold of some beef kidneys and prepared them in a scrumptious sherry sauce, *a la catalana*," she said, as she retreated walking backwards, turned around and went out the door.

I've never been as aware of my size and the brownness of my skin as during those few moments. Rosa was a good five inches taller than me and her skin was the colour of those Greek statues that you see in history books.

She had called me Manolito. Manolito! Little Manuel. Nobody had ever called me that, not even my mama. Who did she think she was? She did tower over me, but did that give her the right to call me Manolito?

"We" turned out to be a group of foreign correspondents who had converged in Barcelona, Spain's anarchist capital and one of the last Republican bastions in the country.

When I walked into the dining-room they all exclaimed "Manolito!" in unison and got up to slap my back relentlessly. They were all sky-high and as fair as Rosa. I felt like a shrimp, a brown shrimp, a battered brown shrimp. They were all over me. Had they never seen a small, brown man before? Weren't there plenty of Spaniards that looked somewhat similar to me? What was going on?

"Sit down, please!"

"Rosa tells us you're from Chile!"

"You're the first Chilean journalist we've met!"

"Welcome, welcome!"

"How long did it take you to get here?"

"Hope you like kidneys. It took me a while to get used to the... pungent flavour."

"Make yourself at home."

"You must know that we're losing the war, right?"

I did know that Prime Minister Juan Negrín had pulled the international brigades from the combat zones in an act of diplomacy that had resulted in nothing more than reducing the Republican Army by a good twenty thousand men. In his naiveté — not to say stupidity — he'd thought that if he sent the foreigners home, the Nationalists would do the same. Of course, Nazi Germany and fascist Italy did nothing of the sort. Their armies stayed firmly put in Spain, and they continued to send weapons and provide logistical support.

I also knew that just a few days before, the long-drawn-out Battle of the Ebro had been won by the fascists. It was becoming more and more clear that the Republicans would lose the war and a humanitarian crisis of gigantic proportions would ensue. Actually, it was already in progress. Thousands of people were already flocking to the Spanish side of the Pyrenees. Obviously, they and many more would try to walk across the mountains when the fascists took over Catalonia.

"Yes, I know. Unfortunately, the ugly side, the evil side is winning," I said, letting myself taste the bitterness of those words in my mouth. "And the outcome of this war will have dire consequences everywhere," I added.

When I had left Chile, the Battle of the Ebro was raging, and there was great hope that the Republicans would be victorious. But, after three months of combat, the Nationalists' military superiority had prevailed. Now, it was unlikely that the Republicans would manage to gather the strength and the resources to turn things around. Short of a miracle, the Nationalists would win the war and set the stage for the spread of Nazism and fascism not only all over Europe, but also in the rest of the world.

"And if the fascists have acted like beasts up to now, just wait and see what the next few weeks and months will be like," Rosa said.

"That's why we need to act as witnesses until the end," George, a lanky man from London, said.

"Yes. Until the bitter end," Rosa added.

Rosa was the only woman in the group, but she could as well have been another man — everybody treated her like a comrade in arms, which I gathered she was. Most of the men had served on the international brigades, and so had she. While joining the fight, they had also been covering the war as foreign correspondents and they were not about to stop now.

"It is true that what Manolito calls 'the evil side' is winning, but there are more than two sides in this war," Jean-Louis, a correspondent from Lyon, was saying now. "Our side is bitterly divided and that's one of the reasons we'll lose to the fascists."

There were nods of agreement around the table.

I told them I knew about the killings of anarchists by Stalinist communists the year before but wasn't aware of how deep and wide the schism ran.

"Very wide and very deep," Rosa said. "Personally, I refuse to fight alongside a man who hates anarchists even more than he hates fascists."

"That's exactly what I'm talking about. At times like this it's absolutely necessary to come together, to fight as one. The ideological differences can be sorted out later, after we win, which needless to say, we won't," Jean-Louis argued, raising his voice.

"Well, go talk to your Stalinist 'friends' then, Jean Louis. Tell *them* to stop killing anarchists!" Rosa shouted.

"Rosa, Rosa... You know that I don't have any Stalinist 'friends,'" Jean-Louis responded.

Rosa smiled a sad smile.

"Well, while I agree with Jean-Louis, I think it's unfair to paint the divisions within the Republican forces as the reason for losing the war," Helmut, a reporter from Munich, said.

"*One* of the reasons," Jean-Louis interjected.

"We're losing the war because the Nationalists have the full support of Nazi Germany and fascist Italy, plus the Moroccan Corps, while Britain and France refuse to put their weight behind the Republic. They have declared themselves 'neutral.' Neutral my ass. Their position is nothing more than disguised support for the Nationalists," Helmut went on.

"I agree. And, as we all know, Germany sent another huge shipment of arms and tanks to the fascists — just now, a few days ago," George added.

"To be honest, we have to admit that the only material aid we've had has come from the Soviet Union, and it doesn't even start to compare to the German and Italian involvement, which in fact is straightforward military intervention. Stalin is an asshole, not doubt about that, but he *has* helped us," Jean-Louis continued.

"Selectively, Jean-Louis, selectively. The weapons he's sent have been earmarked for the communist organizations within the Republican side, so let's not get carried away with our praise for fucking Stalin," Rosa countered.

Everybody went silent and, for a few seconds, all eyes were fixed on the table. George cut through the tension when he turned to me and asked, a big grin on his face:

"I hope *you*'re not a fucking Stalinist, Manolito?!"

Everyone burst out laughing, but I knew that the question was serious.

"No, comrades. I'm not a fucking Stalinist. I'm not a communist, period. I've been an anarchist since I was a little boy," I stated proudly.

Clapping and cheering erupted. Then, Rosa proposed a toast: "To our anarchist comrade, Chilean journalist Manolito Garay. *Salud*!"

The bombardment of questions began before we had even put our glasses down: "How come you say that you've been an anarchist since you were a little boy?" "Where did you grow up?" "What do your parents do?"

So, I spent the rest of the evening telling them everything about La Coruña and Iquique. They reacted with a plethora of ohs, ahs, huhs and ughs, ha-has, hee-hees and olés! They dabbed their eyes with their hankies, banged on the table with their fists, rubbed their tummies from laughing so hard and drank inordinate amounts of wine.

LUCÍA
· · · · · · · · · · ·

November 1938 – January 1939

Valparaíso

SOON AFTER RETURNING FROM Lima, Pilar and I started seeing each other almost daily, and it didn't take long for us to get close again. I was hesitant at first, but as time went by it became clear that she did want to stick around this time. We were in love again. So, when she proposed it, I agreed to move in together.

I told my aunt about it, but she didn't quite get it.

"But you are together. You've been back together since you came back from Lima, no?" she half said, half asked.

"Well... yes, but now we want to live together," I answered.

"Oh! That makes sense. Are her parents okay with it? I guess we could all move to a place that will accommodate everyone... or, I could share my room with Alexandra, if that's okay with her and Pilar," my aunt offered, a smile spreading across her face.

Clearly, my aunt was not ready to let me go. I couldn't stand the expectant look in her eyes, so I averted mine and took a deep breath before I answered.

"Aunt Encarnación, we're not going to live here. We found a flat on Rudolph Street, right across from funicular Espíritu Santo, just a few blocks up from here. It's small, but very, very nice — it has two bedrooms, one for me and Pilar and the other one for Alexandra, a cute little kitchen, a bathroom, a living-dining room and here's the best part: because it's on the ground floor, it has a backyard with a peach tree and a swing and a clothesline and..."

"You're moving out?! You're moving out and you haven't had the decency to tell me until now, when you've already got a place and it's a done deal? What do you think I am? Chopped liver? Why didn't you talk to me about this? Is this the way you pay me back for all the years I've taken care of you as if you were my own daughter... all the sacrifices..."

By now she was crying, and I was furious.

"This is exactly why I didn't say anything about it before. Because you get all worked up and instead of talking like a rational human being, which, by the way, you believe you're a model of — yeah, you do, you think that you are *so, so* rational, but instead you start acting like a *canuto*, one of those Christian preachers at the square, laying your guilt trips on me... 'Sacrifices'... 'Sacrifices'... 'Pay you back,' 'Pay you back'... I never knew you had made so many sacrifices. And pay you back? How are you going to pay *me* back, because I have loved *you* like a mother..."

Now I was the one crying my eyes out and, in spite of all my efforts, feeling guilty as shit, which made me even angrier. I turned around, ready to stomp out of the room, when I felt my aunt's arms engulf me.

"No, my darling, no, of course you don't have to pay me back. That was a stupid thing to say. I don't know why those things come out of my mouth. I understand, I understand. It's just that..."

I nuzzled my way into my aunt's shoulder and let myself melt in her arms, as I had done so many times before. When I finally regained my composure, I wiped off my tears, looked at her in the eye and asked: "Where did you learn that guilt-tripping shit, Auntie?"

She chuckled. "The Catholic religion for sure. You think you've left all that crap behind, but it's worse than a hungry mutt — no matter how much you kick it, it still follows you around."

"I'll miss you, Aunt Encarnación, but we'll be very close by. We'll come to visit all the time, promise, and you'll come to visit too," I offered now.

"I know, I know, Lucía. I understand. I knew this day would come... You need your own home," she said, letting go of me. "The three of you will be very happy."

As it turned out, Pilar had had to endure an even worse scene with her parents, who were not only flabbergasted because she would be "stripping them of their right to live with their granddaughter, their own flesh and blood" but also because for the first time, Pilar told them that we were not only friends, but also lovers, that we wanted to have our own home and live as a family.

"How can you do this to us?!" her mother had yelled, running out of the room and locking herself in the bathroom.

"Hope you're happy with what you've done — inflicting this kind of pain on your mother," her father had hissed.

As for our "thing," as Pilar's mother had called it — wrinkling her nose and flapping her hand as if chasing a fly away — the mere thought of two women living together as "husband and wife" revolted her.

"What kind of example are you giving your daughter?!" her mother had cried out, literally pulling her hair.

"The best possible example, mother — a home founded on love," Pilar had answered.

"You two women are sick," her father had added in a low, hoarse voice. "Sick, sick, sick."

Pilar told me about the scene with full details, chapter and verse — every word, every facial expression and tone of voice. It all sounded so melodramatic that I couldn't restrain myself and started laughing. Soon enough we were both bent over, laughing like lunatics, while we pointed at each other and cried out, over and over: "Sick woman, sick woman, sick woman!"

But, of course, the situation was no laughing matter, and it would take a long time for Pilar's parents to come around. If it hadn't been for Alexandra, their beloved grandchild, perhaps they never would've accepted our relationship. But Alexandra became the conduit between their household and ours — they couldn't, wouldn't turn their back on her, and slowly but surely, they came to realize that we would not back down. Furthermore, Alexandra continued to be the cheerful, well-adjusted little girl they had helped to bring up. We must've been doing something right, after all.

A few neighbours were surprised to see me leave my aunt's and even more surprised to hear that I'd be living with Pilar and Alexandra.

"You're abandoning Miss Encarnación?"

"Doesn't your friend want to live with her parents anymore?"

"I'm only moving a few blocks away, so I'll be seeing my aunt all the time, and Pilar's parents are getting old and need a well-deserved break," I responded. "But Pilar still needs help with Alexandra, so I offered to move in with them."

"Let them talk," was Pilar's answer when I told her about it.

But it was more complicated than that. We needed to warn Alexandra about possible "questions" and "comments," not only from the neighbours but from her teachers and classmates as well.

"I know that you love each other very much and like to kiss and hug and sleep in the same bed and stuff like that, but that will be our own secret because other people's heads are too small and don't have room for those kinds of thoughts. So, if anybody asks me anything, I'll say that you two are very good friends," she said matter-of-factly when we brought the issue up. Then she went back to doing her homework at the dining-room table.

Summer arrived with its blue days and ocean breezes, and life took its course. We settled in our little house and started our new life together. After much discussion, we decided to give our place a name: *Las tres lunas* — The Three Moons, and Alexandra painted three creamy, full moons surrounded by a constellation of silver stars over our indigo front door.

Our girl was on summer holidays, so Pilar would take her to work at the bakery, while I attended to the academy and put the finishing touches on my latest choreography. In the last few years I had been moving from classical to popular music, or a combination of both. So, in this latest choreography I was using Sergei Rachmaninoff's "Rhapsody on a Theme of Paganini's," the Mexican boleros of María Grever and Agustín Lara, and two legendary tangos: "El choclo" and "La cumparsita." For the final scene, I had decided on Ary Barroso's Brazilian *samba* "Anoiteceu" — "Nightfall."

I created a character called Amapola, the title of one of Grever's songs, as the ballet's centrepiece. Amapola was a young, gifted seamstress who had the ability to sew beautiful outfits that made her customers forget about their worries and find joy in their otherwise dull lives. One day, a sullen, disgruntled young man by the name of Francisco comes into her shop and orders a pair of pants and a matching vest. None of Amapola's suggestions seems to please him, but at long last he grudgingly agrees to a design and choice of fabric.

When he comes back to pick up the outfit and tries it on, a surge of happiness fills his chest. He forgets about his woes and leaves the shop feeling light-hearted and optimistic about life. He keeps coming back to order more outfits, and it doesn't take long for Amapola and Francisco to fall in love. After a short courtship they get married.

When they return from their honeymoon, Francisco decides that now that Amapola is a married woman, she must forget about her work as a seamstress and he forbids her to go into her shop. Amapola languishes at home, bored and despondent, while Francisco goes back to acting in his sullen and disgruntled old ways. The whole town also begins to fall into the depths of despair.

When Amapola learns that she's pregnant, she decides that no matter what, she has to start sewing again because it's the only way to ensure that her baby is born into a happy family and community. Francisco tries to stop her, but the town rallies around her and he has no choice but to give in. Amapola goes back to creating her magical apparels and joy returns to her home and the whole town. The final scene finds everyone at the square celebrating the baby's birth.

Madame Moreau was more than enthusiastic about this production; she was ecstatic. *"Merveilleux, ma chérie, merveilleux,"* she would repeat over and over again.

"What inspired you to create such a beautiful character and compelling story?" she wanted to know.

I was more than happy to tell her: "Oh! You know how much I love creating costumes, and how those costumes add so much magic to a character and a choreography! So, for sure that was one source of inspiration. Also, many years ago I heard Alexandra Kolontai speak on the radio and she talked about how women must stop being slaves to their kitchens and children, how that kind of work must be done collectively so that women can do other things as well, contribute to society, work outside the home. And that's the case with Amapola! Cooped up at home, her spirit starts to shrivel, but when she breaks free and returns to work, she thrives and her joy spreads to the whole town!"

"Yes! So true, so true!" Madame Moreau responded, nodding vigorously.

I had a wonderful time creating the whole choreography, but just like Amapola, designing the wardrobe was particularly gratifying — colourful everyday summer dresses printed with sunflowers and roses, tailored suits appropriate for work at the office, coveralls for factory workers, skirts, blouses, hats and coats, you name it — after all, I did have to dress a whole town! And, of course, I also had to outfit the dancers for the final celebration — sparkling costumes and splashy head pieces to create a carnival-like feeling while they danced to Barroso's Brazilian *samba*.

Our yearly productions had become legendary in the Valparaíso region, and we'd had to expand the run to a whole week so as to accommodate our large audiences. People would come from neighbouring Viña del Mar and the numerous towns up the Aconcagua

Valley. All in all, these were exciting times; I loved my work and was grateful for the success Madame Moreau's and my company enjoyed. As for our family life, Sundays were the best. In the morning, Alexandra would climb into our bed and the three of us would cuddle until our stomachs started to growl. After breakfast we'd take off for Plaza Victoria, which was pulsating with the sound of music and children playing. This was Valparaíso, bursting with infectious vitality and joy. Life was good.

My happy heart had relegated my trip to Lima to the depths of my mind. But one day, a telegram came letting me know that Ernesto Céspedes' extradition trial was due to begin the following week in Santiago.

By the next day, the story was all over the news — "Chilean Sovereignty under Attack!" claimed the front page of *El Mercurio*; "Chilean Armed Forces Killed Thousands of Peruvians," accused the cover of leftist *Rebelión; Las* últimas *noticias* ran a tribute to my father and his illustrious career, accompanied by a photograph that highlighted his good looks and haughty demeanor. Radio Nuevo Mundo did an interview with the Chilean government's representative to the League of Nations, while *Universo* invited Lieutenant Colonel Something-or-Other to convey the Armed Forces' position on the matter. Every media outlet in the country was on the issue. Some reports claimed that repentant members of the Patriotic Leagues had come forward. Others, that there were Peruvian witnesses ready to testify, that forensic experts had determined that the bullet wounds found in the corpses unearthed by the surge of the Caplina River matched the ammunition used by the Chilean Armed Forces in Tacna at the time. And so on and so forth.

In a matter of days, I had to drop everything and travel to Santiago to testify at the trial. The production of *Amapola, the Prodigious Seamstress* would have to wait for my return.

MANUEL
. . . .

December 1938

Segre Front

IN NO TIME, ROSA became my best friend and lover. We could talk for hours and then make passionate love wherever we happened to be — under a bridge, behind a tree, in the bushes. Or we could just keep each other silent company as she reviewed her photographs and wrote in her journal and I worked on my submissions to *Rebelión*.

Rosa's parents were intellectuals, she told me; her father had taught philosophy and her mother, literature, both at the University of Leipzig. The family had had a privileged life in Germany, so, as an only child, Rosa had been afforded many opportunities.

"My parents sent me to music lessons, dance lessons, painting lessons, you name it," she said. "But what really changed my life was the Leica they gave me for my thirteenth birthday."

Her art teacher had told her about a little camera that would revolutionize the world of photography — the man was a friend of a friend of Oskar Barnack, the inventor, and had heard that Leitz, the camera manufacturers, would be launching Barnack's newest creation at the Leipzig Spring Fair.

"I did own a camera, a box Brownie, and had been taking pictures for a couple of years already. But hearing about this little machine that could capture images in quick succession and be carried around in the palm of your hand got me really excited. I talked to my parents about it and voilà, they got me one for my birthday," she explained.

The family had left Nazi Germany in 1933 and settled in Paris. There, Rosa's parents had opened a cultural centre called Rosa Luxemburg, after the Polish-German revolutionary — a kind of hub for writers and artists on the left, a place to meet and present their work.

"Now you know why they named me 'Rosa,'" she said, as she smiled away.

I grew increasingly fond of her. Finally, I had met somebody I could talk to about my life *and* make love to. I especially appreciated her honesty and openness, not to mention her eyes, her supple, milky skin and hairy legs. Besides, she was fearless, and that pushed me to be a bit braver myself, to take more risks than I would have otherwise.

By all accounts, the Catalonia Nationalist Offensive was supposed to start in mid-December, so we made our way to the Segre River, about a hundred and fifty kilometres west of Barcelona. Thousands of *milicianos* were leaving for the front, so we jumped in one of their trucks.

Rosa was wearing a thick black coat over her *miliciana* outfit and a slightly tilted red beret on her head. A battered leather bag was slung over her shoulder and she was holding her beloved Leica in her right hand. Her eyes radiated a mix of excitement and sadness. Excitement for the impending action, sadness for the inevitable deaths we'd certainly witness.

In spite of the circumstances — the *milicianos* were poorly dressed, shod and armed, and everybody knew that the Republican Army had lost most of its armament and experienced units at the Battle of the Ebro — spirits were high. A young woman had brought her guitar along and in no time we were all singing "*A las barricadas, En la plaza de mi pueblo, Arroja la bomba, Ay Carmela, El gallo rojo y el gallo negro, Hijos del pueblo...*"

An abandoned, one-room stone house with a dirt floor just outside Artesa de Segre became our crash pad. There were seven of us — Helmut, George and Jean-Louis from Hotel Palace, two Catalonians, Rosa and me.

Rosa and I slept on a narrow mat in a corner of the room. On our first night there, we discovered that it was best to take turns being on top of each other — the mat wasn't wide enough to accommodate both of us and the ground was frigid. This way, at least the person on top could catch a wink for ten or fifteen minutes at a time — until the one at the bottom announced that they were turning into an icicle.

To say that after a few nights of this turn-over-like-a-pancake sleeping arrangement we were wasted would be an understatement. But adrenalin is a powerful thing. It keeps you going whether your body and mind want to or not, whether you're cold, hungry, thirsty or terror-stricken — like a mouse who's been under the paw of a feral cat for days on end. Like us.

On December 23, at the confluence of the Segre and the Ebro, south of us, the fascists crossed the river and broke the Republican lines. Their forces were composed of the Navarrese Army and the Cuerpo Legionario Italiano. Yes, Mussolini had sent over fifty thousand men to fight for the Nationalists. They advanced a few kilometres, but Enrique Lister's Republican forces stopped them in their tracks. When this news reached us, we cheered and wrote away, sending the good news to the world. But it didn't take long for our hopes to be shattered. After a couple of days, the fascists broke the Republican lines again and kept tramping their way to Barcelona, leaving a trail of rape, torture and death behind.

A few days later, west of Artesa de Segre, the Nationalists were stopped by the Twenty-Sixth Division, the army that our anarchist hero Buenaventura Durruti had originally formed in 1936 and that the Barcelona *milicianos* had come to join. Now, the Division was awaiting a new Nationalist attack. This time the men had planned to position themselves within the town, protected by the stone walls and buildings, and inside irrigation channels they'd turned into trenches. The heavy artillery had already been placed on top of the hills that flank the town.

The night before the battle began, a group of *milicianos* found shelter in a dilapidated stable across the field from our shack, so we made our way there with all the food and drink we could put our hands on. The rain was coming down in buckets — as it had been for days, and the ground was a soup of thick, slimy mud. It was pitch dark and our only point of reference was the men's muffled voices, which the gusts of wind kept blowing away. By the time we made it to the barn, we were soaked to the bone and our shoes were oozing muck.

The *milicianos* had managed to get a small fire going and the place had turned into a fetid Turkish bath — everybody's clothes and shoes were steaming, giving out a melange of bodily odours — urine, sweat, stale breath and smelly feet. Our shack must've smelled the same — only we didn't notice it.

They were thankful for the food and drinks — a bottle of *pisco* I had brought all the way from home and saved for a special occasion was passed around until it ran empty. Plenty of mmmm's and lip-smacking were heard in the semidarkness, together with the urgent slurps.

The men's spirits were high, in spite of being drenched, exhausted, hungry and perhaps terrified?

"Let your people know that we'll defend the Revolution with our lives," one of them shouted.

"This is where we stop the fascists!" another voice called out.

There were cheers all around, followed by the first verses of *"Hijos del pueblo,"* sung in a deep, baritone voice. A few seconds later, everybody had joined in and were on their feet, fists held high.

Hijos del pueblo te oprimen cadenas
La injusticia se apodera de ti
Si vivir es un mundo de penas
Antes que esclavo prefiero morir

Estos burgueses asaz egoístas
Que discriminan la humanidad
Serán barridos por los anarquistas
Al fuerte grito de "¡Libertad!"

Offspring of the people, you are oppressed by chains
Injustice controls you
If living becomes a world of sorrows
I'd rather die than be a slave

These infinitely egotistic bourgeois
Who discriminate against humanity
Will be swept away by the anarchists
As a resounding call for "Freedom!" is heard.

I don't know exactly when we went back to our shack, but the light of dawn was just beginning to seep in between the uneven slats when we were awoken by a series of explosions. Rosa sprang up — she was lying on top of me — and ran out the door as she shouted, "The fascists are here!"

Cannon balls were hitting the ground just a few hundred metres from us. All of a sudden, I was in the La Coruña soccer field again, surrounded by women and children, my mama a few steps ahead of me, Eva and Moncho by my side, the soldiers advancing relentlessly towards us, our chants turning into screams... I reached into my pocket, but there were no hand bombs there, like the ones my papa had given me to hurl at the soldiers. Only a damp, small notebook and a pen. "*These* are my weapons now," I said to myself.

Our troops began to return the enemy fire and the noise was deafening. The rain had relented, but the ground was still sodden and the air laden with moisture — the smoke of the explosions hanging on to it like a thick curtain. Men were running across the field — their footwear heavy with mud, climbing the hills — slipping and falling, slipping and falling. The staccato machine-gun fire coming from the rooftops of Artesa punctured the din, and the muzzle flash lit the grey sky above us with furry balls of flames.

Rosa had found cover behind a tree and motioned for me to join her. I ran for my life, hoping that a cannon ball wouldn't hit the ground in the minute or so that it'd take me to reach her. She was sitting against the trunk, covered in mud.

"I fell down a couple of times and lost a boot in the sludge," she said, "but my Leica is still as clean as a whistle," she added, her amber eyes twinkling and her teeth looking very white in the middle of her now brown face.

"Let's climb that hill! I must get some shots from the top!" she yelled, jumping to her feet and starting to run.

"Rosa! Wait!" I shouted after her, but she didn't heed me.

For a few seconds I was paralyzed, but then I ran after her.

We made it to the top almost at the same time. We sat in between the bushes, catching our breath. Along the ridge, farther up, our artillery was pummelling the fascists on the other side. Enemy machine-gun fire flew over our heads. Then we heard a beast-like groan. One of our men had been hit.

"I have to get up there," Rosa yelled, as she began to crawl towards the ridge.

Next thing I knew, she was falling backwards, tumbling down the hill.

"Rosa! I'm coming!" I yelled, as I turned around and began to drag my ass down to where she now lay on her back, against a shrub.

She had lost her beret. Her coat had come unbuttoned. Her Leica was standing on end beside her right hand. Her eyes were wide open and there was a big, gaping hole in her forehead.

"Eva, wake up!" I heard myself shout, as I shook her.

LUCÍA

· · · · · · · · · · ·

January 1939

Santiago

AS I STEPPED OUT of the morning train, dry, warm air kissed my face — a promise of the summer heat that would envelop the city later in the day. The snow-capped Andes rose majestically as a backdrop to the madness in the streets — honking buses, horse-drawn carts loaded with fruit and veggies on their way to market, vendors pushing their buggies and calling out their goods, streetcars coming to a screeching halt, people walking hurriedly in every direction.

I snaked my way across Rozas Street and miraculously made it to the other side unscathed. The address I had jotted down in my notebook was only six blocks away: "Palacio de los Tribunales de Justicia, 1140 Compañía de Jesús Street." I quickened my step and got there just in time to squeeze into the public gallery.

The place was full to the brim and the air heavy with cigarette smoke. The press gallery bustled with men in suits and fedoras, their cameras' flashes sending darts of light across the room. All around me, mostly men, but also a few women — all dressed in their Sunday outfits — smiled and talked excitedly, as if they were at the stadium awaiting the beginning of a soccer game or at the tracks anticipating the victory of their favourite horse.

The merriment fizzled when a small group of young men and women unfurled a banner that read "Justice for Massacred Peruvians" while they shouted the slogan of the Communist Youth. I felt a surge of pride grow from my gut to my face but was quick to nip my budding smile. I had to be as inconspicuous as possible. A few people clapped, but most booed and hissed. Soon enough, guards removed the youth from the gallery.

Then, a loud whisper arose from the crowd — "He's here, he's here." A side door opened, and my father walked in clad in his formal summer uniform: a black peaked cap with red and gold trim, black pants and a white jacket with red and gold epaulettes and a gold belt. A handful of medals adorned his chest and he was carrying a dress sword in his hand. He looked striking. As if he were a royal dignitary, he was surrounded by a large retinue — other men in uniform and his team of lawyers, all dressed to the hilt.

The place erupted in applause. Calls of *"Viva Chile!"* *"Viva el Ejército de Chile!"* — "Long live the Chilean Army" — *"Viva el General Ernesto Céspedes!"* echoed across the courtroom. Every time, the crowd responded with a fervent *"Viva!"* The displays of patriotic fervour stopped when the arrival of Judge Mauricio Morris was announced.

A tall, balding man cloaked in a black gown walked towards the bench with his head buried in his chest. He sat down and struck the block with the gavel. He had a narrow, pale face, bulging eyes and a long nose; his thin mouth was turned down and his brow, knitted. He was not a pretty sight. Was he angry? Who was he angry with? The Peruvian government? My father? Life? Was he a "patriot"? Was he a fair judge? Hard to tell, as he didn't give anything away — not a glance in the direction of my father, the defence, the prosecution or the public. His eyes remained trained on his sheaf of papers as he explained the case and the proceedings in a loud, staccato voice.

In summary, the prosecution had to prove that there were sufficient grounds to extradite Ernesto Céspedes to Peru, where he was accused of master-minding, directing and participating in the killing of over a thousand Peruvian civilians — men, women and children — in or near the city of Tacna in the year 1925.

Several times the judge was interrupted by boos and hisses, which he attempted to stop by hammering the block with the gavel, while shouting "Order in the court, order in the court." The bailiff just sat and stared at dead air as if nothing were happening. Clearly, if it hadn't been illegal, he would've joined the crowd. The end of the judge's presentation was greeted with another eruption of whistling, booing and hissing, which went on and on to the point that Judge Morris's pale face turned red and then purple, while he kept hammering the block like a madman. Finally, he shouted something to the bailiff. The bailiff got up slowly and walked towards the bar as if he'd been going for a stroll in the park. He stood there until the racket subsided.

In the preceding week, the mainstream media had abandoned all pretence of objectivity and shown its true colours. "President Pedro Aguirre Cerda is a Traitor," had read the front page of *El Mercurio* the day before. The heading jumped out of the newsstands with the authority of a proven fact. Only if you bothered to get closer, you were able to discern the miniscule sub-heading: "The Armed Forces and the Right Claim." The article went on to explain that President Aguirre Cerda and his "Bolshevik" Popular Front had paved the way for Peru, one of Chile's most bitter enemies, to smear the country's reputation with false accusations rooted in nothing but their shame and resentment at having lost the War of the Pacific.

The cover of *Revista Ercilla* sported a photograph of my father with a caption that read: "General Ernesto Céspedes – Chilean Hero," while *Topaze's*, the weekly satirical magazine, featured a cartoon of President Pedro Aguirre Cerda as a caricature of a Peruvian indigenous woman — long black braids, layered circle skirts and a bowler hat — a Peruvian flag emblazoned on his chest.

Rebelión had also weighed in. A couple of days earlier, it had run an article denouncing my father and the Chilean Armed Forces not only for the massacre of Peruvians but also for the slaying of thousands of Chilean workers and peasants along the years. Dozens of incidents were mentioned, among them La Coruña. My heart stopped. Had Manuel authored the piece? Of course not. He was still away. I had been devouring his weekly chronicles of the Spanish Civil War — factual accounts of the events interlaced with deeply moving stories about the effects of the war on the civilian population.

The first day of the trial was taken up by the prosecution's and the defence's opening statements, expert lectures on international law and reports on forensic research that proved that the Chilean Armed Forces had indeed shot and killed thousands of Peruvian civilians. On the second day, Peruvians began to take the witness stand.

A young man talked about how at age five he had hidden in a wardrobe and seen, through the crack in the door, my father and his cohorts insult and beat his parents and sisters as they took them away. A young woman couldn't stop shivering while she recounted the slaying of her own family and many others who had been taken to a field up the valley in the middle of the night.

How come she had been spared? As the abducted group was prodded off the truck, she had become separated from her family. She was standing by herself at the back of the crowd, shaking and snivelling, when a soldier had tapped her on the shoulder. At first, she'd recoiled, but then she'd taken the open hand he'd offered and allowed him to lead her to a nearby bush. A couple of other children were already hiding behind it. From there, she'd seen and heard my father order the soldiers to open fire.

Was that possible? Wasn't it pitch dark? No, it wasn't pitch dark — the military trucks' headlights were shining on the scene, so she'd seen everything: the slaughter, the removal of the bodies and the trucks' departure.

More testimonies followed, each one describing not only the abductions and the killings, but also Ernesto Céspedes' arrogance and cruelty. By now, the audience was more subdued — only a few boos and hisses were heard. As the testimonies continued, there was silence in the room and my father looked fatigued. Then, she came in.

At first, I didn't recognize her. Her hair was cropped and she was wearing western clothing: an A-line blue skirt and a short-sleeved blouse with a busy, flowery pattern in reds and greens. Her appearance contrasted drastically with the fair-skinned, elegantly dressed Peruvian witnesses who had preceded her. Of course! "Indians" didn't have the right to vote in 1925, so the Chilean army and the Patriotic Leagues had targeted middle-class families of European descent. So, why would an "Indian" be testifying against my father?

Next thing I knew, I was standing, my hands on my mouth. She looked in my direction and offered me a slight nod and a smile. My heart was beating so loudly I couldn't hear anything else. I willed myself to sit down and stay calm, not to black-out, to just breathe, breathe deeply. But in spite of all my efforts, tears began streaming down my face and I couldn't stop them. I decided that it was okay to cry, as long as I remained quiet; I could manage that.

Name: Mercedes Mamani. Occupation: domestic worker. Place of residence: Tacna, Peru.

So, she had returned to Tacna. Who did she work for now? Had she brought up and loved another little girl? A pang of jealousy ran through my body.

"How do you know the accused?"

"I worked at his house for fourteen years."

She looked at my father with contempt. I couldn't suppress a smile.

"How do you know he was involved in the massacre of Peruvians in Tacna in 1925?"

"He held meetings at the house, late at night. I heard him give the orders, plan the abductions. I heard him say that they had to kill as many Peruvians as possible. He boasted about how he and the others had already killed hundreds. Laughed about it. They all laughed about it."

"How could you hear the accused and his cohorts? Wasn't your room separate from the house, at the back of the yard?"

"Yes, but I wasn't in my room. I was going back and forth between the kitchen and the dining-room, where the men were sitting around the table. Whenever there was a meeting, the Captain ordered me to stay up and serve food and drinks."

"Tell us what happened on March 10, 1925."

"There was a flood. The Caplina River swelled and rushed down into town carrying bodies — the bodies of the Peruvians the captain and the other men had killed."

"How do you know they were the bodies of Peruvians killed by General Céspedes and his cohorts?"

"Lovely saw them."

"Who?"

"Lucía. Lucía, the captain's daughter. She was playing at the river with her friends when the water came down carrying the bodies. She saw them."

"But again, how did you know that these were the bodies of Peruvians killed by General Céspedes and his cohorts?"

"Everybody knew. Everybody in town knew. For weeks, months, people had been disappearing — it was said that maybe they'd left town, but after the flood, everybody put two and two together and realized that the Chilean military had been killing them. And I put two and two together and knew that these were the people the captain and the other men talked about when they met at the house."

"When did your employment at the Céspedes' household end?"

"March 11, 1925. The day after the flood."

"What was the reason?"

"The family moved away. On the afternoon of March 10, shortly after Lov... Lucía came back from the river, the captain went out. He didn't come back that night. But the next morning he stormed into the house and ordered me to pack all their belongings because they were leaving."

"And they left."

"Yes, just like that, they left. A military jeep came and took them away."

"Do you know where they went?"

"No. I just guessed that they were going to Chile."

"Did you ever hear from them again?"

"No. Never again."

"What made you decide to offer your testimony today?"

"I had never told anybody about what I'd heard at the house or about Lucía seeing the bodies in the river. But then, just a few months ago, there were calls on the radio to come forward if you knew anything about the massacre. At first, I didn't want to do it. I told myself to forget about it all. After all, I had kept it a secret for so many years. But then, then... I realized how important it was to come forward. Also, I just couldn't... couldn't keep it a secret anymore. So, I went to the government building and told them what I just told you."

The defence did its best to break Mercedes.

"Mmmm... You put two and two together. You did not see the bodies yourself, you believed the account of an impressionable child, took the gossip going around town as fact and concluded that these corpses in the river belonged to Peruvians killed by General Céspedes and his men," the defence lawyer said, a big smirk on his face.

"He talked about it! He boasted about it! I heard him myself and everybody in Tacna knew," Mercedes countered.

"Hearsay, your honour, hearsay," the defence argued.

But they didn't only question her testimony. They also called her a liar, an opportunist and an ignoramus. They made fun of her looks. They made fun of her accent. They asked her if she could read and write, if she had gone to school. The public was even worse; they booed, hissed and yelled out insults to her: ignorant beast, *chola asquerosa* — disgusting Indian, dimwit, whore... But she held her ground.

When the judge ordered her to step down, she walked out of the room with her head held high. I scrambled to my feet and followed her out the door.

MANUEL
· · · · · · · · · · · · · ·

December 1938 – January 1939

Artesa de Segre, Barcelona
and the Spanish–French Border

WE BURIED ROSA IN the Artesa de Segre cemetery.

It was early in the morning, during a lull in the fire. The rain was pelting down, and a greyish light was doing a poor job of getting through the thick clouds. Jean-Louis had already left the area and the Catalonians were nowhere to be seen; so, Helmut, George and I took turns digging the grave with a rickety, rusted shovel we'd found in a nearby barn.

Among so many crosses, her tomb was perhaps the only one marked with a crude slat of wood we'd yanked off the barn and on which I'd carved: "Rosa Fromm, Photojournalist, Anarchist Revolutionary, 1911–1938."

Once more, my mind took me back to La Coruña, where I had written my sister Eva's name on a slat of wood; to the soccer field, where we had buried her, together with so many others.

Next thing I knew, my friends were dragging me through the mud. The battle had resumed. The deafening noise had returned, and the air was thick with smoke. Up above, the muzzle flash broke through the gloom with bursts of light.

"What happened?" I managed to ask. My head was in a whirl.

"You fainted," Helmut said.

"At the graveyard," George added.

"Let go of me! I can walk," I said, while I scrambled to plant my feet on the ground.

But my legs had turned to wool and my friends had to keep on dragging me all the way to the barn. I felt like a sissy. As a twelve-year-old boy, first in La Coruña and then in Iquique, I had acted like a man. Now, as a twenty-five-year-old man, I was acting like a girl. A wimpy girl. Rosa would've been ashamed of me.

"I'm sorry... I don't, I don't... know what came over me," I stuttered, sitting up against a post.

"You haven't eaten for days, have you?" Helmut asked.

"I don't know. I don't remember," I answered. I truly didn't remember when I had last munched on a piece of stale bread. Now my friends were inviting me to sink my teeth into a piece of roasted rabbit.

"It's fresh. We caught it last night, at dusk," Helmut said.

At first my stomach turned, but once I got going, I couldn't put the meat down. Finally, the world stopped turning. I took a swig from my canteen and got up. "For a moment I thought I was burying my sister Eva all over again," I said.

George gave me a hug. Helmut patted me on the head. A louse ran down my neck and under my shirt. I let it do its thing — perhaps it'd engage in active combat with the flees that had taken residency on my body; perhaps they would kill each other and leave me in peace at long last.

The Republican forces resisted the Catalonian Nationalist offensive for more than a month. During that time, hundreds of thousands of civilians started their exodus towards the Pyrenees and across the border into France. We could see them, farther east, a mass of people walking towards the mountains in anticipation of the Nationalists breaking the Artesa lines. Helmut decided to go with them, but George and I made our way back to Barcelona.

The city was in chaos. Martial law had been declared, but nobody seemed to pay any heed to it. The streets were crowded with refugees on their way to the border. Food rations were small, it was cold as hell, and an overall feeling of anxiety and despair permeated everything.

The Hotel Palace was deserted except for half a dozen foreign correspondents who had bunked in the lobby, where they kept warm by feeding the fancy furniture to the fireplace. "Serves the fucking bourgeoisie right," I thought, as I chuckled.

We brought bedding down from one of the empty rooms and joined them. They told us that the Republican government had ordered the mobilization of men up to forty-five and militarized all industry. They also said that Stalin had sent more tanks and weapons, but that they'd been sitting at the Marseille port since mid-December, confiscated by the "neutral" French government.

The front was shrinking fast and by mid-January, Nationalist troops had occupied almost half of Catalonia. Their armies outnumbered ours six to one, were well fed and supplied, and continued to have full Nazi and fascist support. For weeks we had known that their offensive could not be stopped but didn't want to believe it. On January 22, reality hit us in the face like a Joe Louis sucker punch.

Early that morning, bombs began to fall on the city. All over the city. Not only on military targets but also on the working-class neighbourhoods, the factories, downtown, everywhere. Yes, German and Italian planes were dropping their murderous cargo on the people of Barcelona and wouldn't stop for four consecutive days.

Shortly after the bombing began, we figured that the pilots were turning their engines off some distance out of Barcelona, gliding in, dropping their bombs and then turning their engines on again to take their escape. That meant that the detectors that triggered the alarms weren't able to warn the city in advance. Why else would the alarms be going off practically at the same time as the bombs hit the ground? Of course, this gave our anti-aircraft units no time to intercept the planes and the civilian population no chance to get into shelters.

The goal of the fascists and their Nazi friends was clear: destroy Barcelona and annihilate its population. Building after building went down in pieces; hundreds of corpses carpeted the streets. Rats the size of cats scurried around in plain daylight.

We welcomed dozens of refugees into the Palace. Some stayed for one night or two; others, until the evening before the city fell. We'd discovered that the hotel had a sizeable basement, where old furniture and other junk were stored, plus a very well-stocked wine cellar and a larder with a good supply of salted cod and tinned sardines. So, we brought down all the mattresses and bedding we could fit in and opened our doors to women, children, the wounded and the elderly.

A matronly *catalana* with a substantial moustache took charge of doling out the food and wine. She ordered a self-declared teetotaller to guard the cellar and plunked herself by the door to the larder. She would've made a great quartermaster general. In a flash, she took stock of her troops and the available supplies and devised a distribution strategy that kept everyone happy while ensuring that the supplies lasted for as long as possible.

There were no bathrooms down there, so the hotel's small backyard became an open latrine. Whenever somebody opened the back door, waves of stink wafted into the place. I had visions of the Nationalists coming into the yard, skidding and slipping on the mounds of shit, falling flat on their faces and dying of asphyxiation.

By the end of the second day of bombings, of all the journalists at the Palace, only George and I were left. The evening of January 25, the bombings stopped. Then we knew that we had to get the hell out of Barcelona. Clearly, the Nationalists would be entering the city in the next few hours. I went out the front door to look up at the sky in case any more planes were visible. Hundreds of people were running down Las Ramblas.

"What's going on?" I asked a *miliciano*.

"The fascists crossed the Llobregat River," he shouted and kept running.

The Llobregat was a scarce fifteen kilometres from Barcelona. We prompted the people downstairs to get out of the city as quickly as they could. Then, George and I ran to the censor's office and sent off our last dispatches.

A few other journalists were doing the same, including an American by the name of Jackson, who offered us a ride in his rickety Wyllis. Eight of us squeezed in his vehicle and began our slow trek north on the coastal route.

A column of people on foot filled the width of the road for kilometres on end. Women carried huge bundles on their heads, knapsacks on their backs and baskets in their hands; they were also helping the wounded, while children and the elderly carted rucksacks, suitcases, even chairs — most likely for the disabled or an old grandma or grandpa to take a rest along the way. A young woman had slung her guitar over her shoulder, as if it were a rifle. Some refugees looked excessively corpulent in relation to their thin necks and legs; they were carrying their complete wardrobe on their bodies. Still, most were not dressed for the biting cold.

I felt ashamed. Here I was, sitting inside an enclosed moving contraption, while these fellow human beings were walking and would be walking for days, completely exposed to the elements. I whispered to George how I felt.

"I know. I'm feeling the same way," he said. After a while, he added: "But we have to get to France as fast as we can. The world needs to hear about this."

Obviously, like me, he had considered offering his place in the vehicle to one of the refugees. But he was right. The world did need to hear about this, and it was our responsibility to make sure they did. As soon as possible. Still, I felt like shit.

We drove all night. I'm sure I nodded off once or twice, but for the most part, I stayed awake. By dawn we had made it to Figueras, a few kilometres from the border. Then, the bombings began. The German Condor Legion was dropping bombs on the refugees! We came to a screeching halt, jumped off and got under the car. A couple of minutes later, Jackson lost it. He crawled out, stood up, lifted his arms and started shouting at the skies:

"Fucking cowards! These are innocent people, you assholes! Come down here, come down so that I can kill you with my own two hands, you pieces of shit!"

He kept going and going, so George crawled out and pulled him by the ankle. He fell on his side but got up again like a spring and kept on shouting. Finally, both George and I crawled out, pulled on his ankles and dragged him back under the Wyllis. This time, he didn't resist. He stayed put, was silent for a few seconds and then started to howl as if he'd been stabbed in the heart.

On the morning of January 26, we crossed the border into France. The crowd of refugees seeking asylum spread out like a restless, murmuring sea.

"Barcelona has fallen," they were saying. "Barcelona has fallen."

LUCÍA

· · · · · · · · · · ·

February 1939

Santiago

SHE WAS PERCHED ON the edge of a bench in the hallway, knees glued together. I sat beside her. She turned her head towards me and took my hands in hers. "Remember Amarú?" she asked.

I nodded. "'Amarú woke up,' you said to me that day and made me promise that I wouldn't forget what I saw. I never forgot. I remember it as if i'd seen it yesterday."

She squeezed my hands. "You will testify, won't you?" she said then, her eyes probing mine.

"Yes. Of course, I will," I responded.

"I knew you would. You were never like him... or like your mom, for that matter. You always had your own, strong mind," she said. "How is your mom?"

"Passed away," I answered.

"Oh, Lovely!" she said, squeezing my hands. "When I first went to work at your house, I was in awe of her — so beautiful and glamorous. Then I started to feel sorry for her — trapped in that life... with that man. But then, when I realized that she actually loved her life, I wasn't sure how I felt about her."

"I know what you mean," I said.

"What about you? How are you?" she wanted to know. "You don't live with your father, do you?"

"Oh, no, no! When we left Tacna, we went to Iquique. But in

October of that year my parents sent me to Valparaíso to live with my aunt, my mom's sister. Now I share a place with my friend Pilar and her daughter Alexandra. My aunt is around the corner from us; she's like my real mom, you know... after you, after we left you," I responded.

She looked at me, pity in her eyes. I wanted her to wrap her arms around me and hold me tight. But she didn't, and her rigid posture and gaudy blouse stopped my urge to reach out for her.

"Come live with me in Valparaíso, Loly," I heard myself say. "Come live with me and Pilar and Alexandra. They're my family now. They and my aunt. Come live with us, not as the maid or the nanny, no, no. Just like you, like Loly."

She let go of my hands and smiled with sad eyes. "Lovely. Lovely. I have a family of my own now. After what happened, after I lost you, I promised myself to never get attached to somebody else's child again. A few years after you left, I came back to Tacna, met a man and got married. I have two children; my mom's looking after them while I'm here. But my husband turned out to be a drunk and a womanizer. He left us a few years ago. But I have my kids; they and my mom are my family."

How pretentious of me to assume that Mercedes would be chomping at the bit to live in my home again, as if that was the only thing she'd ever wanted! Of course she would've built her own life after so many years of living at the periphery of somebody else's! I guess a good part of me was still a selfish petit-bourgeoise. Or maybe that was not it. Maybe it'd just been my desperate twelve-year-old self begging her to be my mother again.

"Oh Loly, I'm so happy for you!" I managed, flushing hotly. "We'll keep in touch then. Maybe one day the four of you will visit?" I offered.

"Maybe," she answered.

But we didn't keep in touch. In Tacna I'd loved her with the abandonment and innocence of a child. Now, in an instant, I'd come to realize that she'd moved on, but somehow, in spite of all the good things in my current life, I was still holding on to that love. She'd let go of her former life — her braids, her indigenous garments, her years of servitude and, of course, her motherly love for me. For her, the past was where it belonged, in the past.

She'd had the tools to do that. After all, when we'd been forced apart, she was an adult. I, on the other hand, hadn't known how to deal with the hole her absence had bored inside me. Her unexpected reappearance had opened it up again and exposed my long-standing yearning for her. Unknowingly, I had been holding on to that yearning for all these years. It was time to let it go.

My testimony lasted for two and a half days. When I walked into the courtroom and took the witness stand, the crowd shuffled and stirred. When I stated my name, Lucía Céspedes, some people shouted "What?!" others "Who?!" and many booed and heckled.

I looked straight ahead and proceeded to answer the prosecution's every question as clearly and with as much detail as I could.

As expected, the defence's cross-examination was brutal. They brought up the episode of high fever I'd had on the train, on our way to Iquique. Wasn't the alleged conversation between Ernesto Céspedes and his colleagues something I had concocted inside my feverish, twelve-year-old head? They also brought up my membership in the Communist Party. Had the party ordered me to come to court and tell these lies about my own father? A Chilean hero? A true patriot? What kind of daughter was I?

"Isn't it true that your distorted, Bolshevik ideology, coupled with your feeble mental health have driven you to accuse your father of abominable acts that he never committed?"

"No. I know that he committed those acts. I saw the corpses in the river and the next day, on the train, I heard him brag about the killings," I answered, looking at my father for the first time.

Unlike his usual self, he was slumped in his chair, his gaze lowered. For a second, I felt sorry for him. But then, he sat up straight, looked up and held my gaze. There was contempt in that gaze. Defiance and contempt.

A couple of days later Judge Morris ruled that there was not sufficient evidence to extradite Ernesto Céspedes to Peru.

MANUEL

. . . .

January – February 1939

Argelès-sur-Mer

JACKSON, GEORGE AND THE rest of my travel mates were driving on to Paris, but I stayed in the area. My boss had asked me to join the refugees, bear witness to their ordeal, hear their stories and report on them.

Saying goodbye to George was not easy. I'm sure we exchanged a few lice and flees while I buried my face in his chest, but it was hard to let him go. His heart was beating hard and fast, and he smelled of unwashed clothes, stale sweat, shit, piss, cigarette smoke and fear. He smelled of war.

"Ay, Manolito, ay Manolito," he repeated, squeezing me tight.

After a few hours of waiting, a nasal voice started yelling into a megaphone and the gendarmes prodded the crowd into forming columns. From what we understood, the refugees would be taken to nearby camps. There was a lot of pushing and shoving, swearing and screaming, as panic spread and families tried to stick together. Right beside me, a little boy was crying his eyes out and having a hard time breathing. I picked him up and sat him on my shoulders.

"What's your mother's name?" I asked him.

"'Mama,' but she can't hear me because she's far away," he responded in between sobs.

"Who are you with?" I asked then.

"My grandma." Louder sobs.

"What's her name?"

"Grandma." Increasingly louder sobs.

"That's what you call her, right? But what do other people call her? The neighbours — what do they call her?" I asked, looking up at him.

"Federica," he answered this time, wiping his nose with the back of his hand.

So, I started shouting "Federica" with all my might, and sure enough, a desperate face, a few metres ahead, looked in our direction and cried out: "Aleix!"

Aleix sobbed and laughed like a little madman, extending his arms towards Federica as if he were being reunited with his grandma after a twenty-year separation. Obviously, for him, it had felt like twenty years.

Federica was walking with her elderly mother, one of her daughters and a few children. Her husband, son, son-in-law and another daughter had joined the *maquis*, a contingent of fighters preparing to wage guerrilla warfare against the Nationalists.

"We may be losing the war, but the fight is not over, *chilenito*. There's a resistance movement underway," Federica's mother whispered to me, as she pointed in the direction of the Pyrenees.

Little did we know then that the *maquis* would play a key role in World War II, fighting the Nazis in southern France, and that their armed struggle against Franco would go on until the 1960s.

Federica must've been in her mid-forties but looked ancient — her body had been reduced to a bundle of skin and bones, her face was a mesh of tiny roads on barren land, her mouth was practically toothless, and even her eyes seemed old — cloudy and dull. Had she looked like this before the war? I doubted it.

The nasal voice on the megaphone started to announce the names of the refugee camps we were going to, and the gendarmes, to split the crowd and steer the groups in different directions. Our group was sent to Argelès, up the coast.

As we marched on, Federica told me her story. She had worked at the Puig textile factory for most of her life. There, she'd met a young man called Pep and they had got together when she was nineteen.

"I wanted to get married — not in a church, just a civil marriage, you know, but Pep wouldn't hear of it. He's a hard-core anarchist and hates everything that has to do with the state. 'The state has no business in our private lives' he said. So, after more than twenty-five years we're still not officially married, but in fact we are... if you know what I mean," she said.

For a few years she'd stopped working as she raised her three children, but then she'd returned to the factory. "Pep's salary was not enough. We couldn't make ends meet, so my mom took charge of the kids and I went back to work" she explained.

"Pep didn't want me to get involved in politics. He'd say that I had enough with work, the house and the kids, but my friends kept pushing me to go to the union meetings with them, so I finally did. Behind Pep's back. It didn't take long for him to find out, though. He yelled and screamed, threw tantrums and made scenes, like a two-year-old, you know, but I didn't really care. I just kept going to the meetings. My mother and I figured that as long as there was a plate of food on the table when he came home and the kids were kept out of his hair, he wouldn't have reason to complain. And that's exactly how it was.

"Back then I didn't know how to read and write, but the CNT, the Workers' National Confederation, set up literacy lessons. I started going to those and little by little I learned how to read; writing, not so much, but I got to be pretty good at reading," she said, a tinge of pride in her voice.

Eventually, Pep had come around and let go of his resistance to Federica's political involvement, particularly when she helped to organize the rent strike of 1931. "He never said it out right, but I know that he was proud of me," she said, a smile in her eyes.

"The landlords kept hiking the rent, but our salaries stayed the same. Things got so bad that nobody could afford to pay their rent anymore. So, we just stopped paying. Period. More than a hundred thousand families stopped paying rent. This went on for months. The government clamped down on us. Put our leaders in prison, you know, the usual. But we kept on going. In the end, some laws were passed to put a cap on the rent hikes, nothing major, but at least something," she explained.

Federica and her family had lived in the Sants neighbourhood, home to most textile factories and their workers. I had gone there one day, when I'd first got to Barcelona, looking for the places that Aunt Asunta had told us about — her own little apartment in an old, ornate building on Santa Caterina Street, the Escola Barrufet, where she'd taught, the headquarters of the Association of Freethinking Women on Rosés Street. Most likely, now they were all in ruins.

"Sants was the first neighbourhood the fascists bombed. They hate us, you know. They hate us because we're enemies of the bourgeoisie. Because of the revolution. They want to get rid of us. Kill us all. That's what they want," Federica said, anger in her voice.

After a heavy pause, she went on: "You should've seen the chaos — the dust, the smoke, bodies strewn all over the streets, stuck in between the rubble... Little children, our neighbours... Our apartment building came crumbling down as if it'd been made of domino pieces. It's a miracle we survived."

"We survived because our place was at the back, on the bottom floor, and the bomb hit the front. Tons of debris rained on us, but we weren't hit straight on," Federica's mother explained, parting her hair and showing me a gash on her head, crusted over with blood and grime. "We got cuts and bruises all over but nothing serious."

They had grabbed what they could from the wreckage and started walking. Now they were on their way to what they hoped would be a place of refuge, but the Argelès camp turned out to be just another version of hell.

It had been set up in open areas among sand dunes along the

coast, with no protection from the elements whatsoever. There were no bathrooms, no buildings, nothing. Just a bunch of flimsy tents flap-flapping in the wind, the roar of the sea in the background. The area had been enclosed with barbed wire, as if the Spanish refugees had been hard-core criminals that the French needed protection from. Clearly, this was not a refugee camp. It was a concentration camp.

We were given a couple of water canteens, a pail of anemic soup, bread, blankets, candles and matches, and told to find an empty tent. We looked and looked, but there were none; they were all taken. I went back to the entrance and explained. The gendarme just shrugged his shoulders, while he kept checking people in.

I walked up and down the camp; definitely there were no empty tents left. Then I figured that we could dig a small cave in the dunes. We found a good spot and went to work. The sand had been hardened by the rain, but after a while we had a large enough shelter to accommodate everybody. I went to look for driftwood and after many attempts, got a feeble fire going.

Compared to the interminable walk in the rain and the cold, our cave, the fire and the meagre food we'd been given felt like heaven. The children found refuge in the women's crooks and crannies, and it didn't take long for the family to start snoring.

Sitting in front of the fire, I thought of Rosa. If she'd been with us, she would've captured everything with her Leica — our march to the camp, Federica with her bundle of bedding on her head, the children in their flimsy sweaters and tattered shoes, their faces covered in snot, their little bodies shivering like wet chicks, the old woman, a blanket wrapped around her shoulders and a pair of bedside slippers on her feet.

Yes. Rosa would've been going snap-snap at the Argelès concentration camp, while she cursed the fascists, the French government and its fucking gendarmerie. She would've assured the women that in the end everything would be all right, that she, the *chilenito* and all the other foreign correspondents would let the world know what was going on, that in no time the French would be forced to start treating them like human beings, that other countries would open their doors to them.

"You'll see. The French will have to eat shit for what they're doing to you people," she would've said.

I kept the fire going for as long as I could.

"Tomorrow I'll forage for food," I told myself, a flash of my childhood at La Coruña and my afternoons at Bellavista Beach zigzagging through my head.

When I woke up, it was morning and the sun was in my eyes.

LUCÍA

. . . .

February – March 1939

Valparaíso and Santiago

MY TESTIMONY AND MY father's acquittal made the front page of every newspaper and was featured as the lead story in all newscasts in the country. Ernesto Céspedes was put on a pedestal as a Chilean patriot, while I was presented as his heartless, lying daughter, and a Bolshevik *marimacha* to boot. Somehow, they had managed to find out about Pilar and me. So, in their eyes, Céspedes was an exemplary hero and I, an abominable freak.

Photographers followed me everywhere, while reporters thrust microphones in my face. Hideous anonymous letters and death threats were mailed to our home and the academy. *All* my students withdrew and asked for their money back. Our neighbours stopped talking to us; some gave us dirty looks when we stepped out of the house and a few hurled insults: *tortilleras, marimachas, degeneradas.* Fortunately, Alexandra was still on summer holidays, so she didn't have to put up with abuse from her teachers and classmates.

Pictures of me and Aunt Encarnación and of Pilar and Alexandra made it into the rags, so the Castillos and my aunt suffered indignities as well. The bakery lost many customers and my aunt's neighbours turned their back on her. Needless to say, the Castillos were devastated — the bakery was their livelihood. Also, their contempt for Pilar's and my relationship was reignited and they blamed us for everything: "If you two were *normal* people, none of this would've happened." Clearly, their communist ideals of equality for all did not include homosexuals.

What kept us afloat was my aunt's love and the support of many friends and comrades. Madame Moreau was one of them. On a balmy Sunday night, she showed up at our door: "I doubt very much that those filthy rags will pay photographers to work at this late hour on a Sunday," she said in her smoky voice and thick French accent. She was right. They had left about an hour earlier.

She wanted to let me know that she believed every word I'd said at the trial. "Now I understand why you lived with your aunt and not your parents. It must've been awful to reside in a mass murderer's home, especially when the murderer is your father," she said, arching her eyebrows.

I nodded.

"What about your mother?!" she asked.

I felt a wave of sadness wash over me. "It's a long story, but basically she didn't believe me. She didn't *want* to believe me. If she had, her glamorous, comfortable life would've gone up in smoke," I answered.

Madame Moreau was silent for a while. "I understand," she said finally. "I was married once. Even though the man alleged he had fallen in love with the dancer in me, after the wedding he forbade me to dance or teach. When I protested, *me sacó la cresta* — he beat the shit out of me, so I shut up. But it didn't do any good — he'd knock me around whenever he felt like it anyway. I'm not proud to say that I stayed with him for years because I couldn't bring myself to give up the luxuries he provided. But one day I woke up and realized that I had turned into a boneless prostitute. A battered, boneless prostitute. So, I ran away, recreated myself and started a brand-new life here, in Valparaíso," she explained.

I reached for her hand and squeezed it. "That's why you liked *Amapola, the Prodigious Seamstress* so much. It resonated with your own story."

She nodded.

"I'm very glad you found the courage to leave your husband," I said.

"Me too, Lucía. Every single day I thank the heavens for my peaceful, simple life, and for allowing me to do what I love the most: teach others how to dance," she said. "I heard that you don't have any students left. Is that right?" she asked then.

This time I was the one to nod.

"Some of my students have withdrawn too; after all, people know that we've been working together for years. But I still have plenty, so you would be welcome to work with me, but of course this would not solve the problem, only spread the mess around. Besides, I think you deserve better. Perhaps this is the opportunity for you to move to Santiago and try something different? Your latest choreographies have been excellent, Lucía. I'm in touch with colleagues who I know would like to see what you have to offer," she said.

I felt elated. Yes, it would be wonderful to move on, to go to Santiago and play in the big leagues. But it didn't take long for my elation to turn into apprehension. What about Pilar and Alexandra?

Pilar had no second thoughts: "Go. Your professional life here has been shattered. Valparaíso tries hard to be a big city, but in fact it's just a small provincial town populated by simple-minded people — including my parents — who can't see beyond their noses. Never mind your father, the murderer. Never mind the massacred Peruvians. For them, we're perverts and that's all there is to know. Leave this swamp. Go and try your luck in Santiago. It's a big city. In a few weeks the rigmarole of the trial will have blown over and nobody will remember your face. Once you're settled, Alexandra and I will join you. And your aunt. And maybe even my parents. Who knows? They might come around and realize that they're in the wrong. Go!" she said.

Madame Moreau gave me letters of introduction to several companies, and sure enough, a week later I had already landed a couple of contracts. She had also recommended a pension on Ejército Street

— a large, old house with high ceilings, cracked marble floors, arched windows and a turret, where the landlady let me put my gramophone and do my work. I had to share a bedroom with three other women, but the rent was cheap and the place was clean and within walking distance of the theatre district.

Following Madame Moreau's advice, I reinvented myself. I changed my last name to González — my aunt and mother's name, got the glasses the eye doctor had prescribed and I hadn't bought out of plain and simple vanity and cut my hair short. My transformation not only changed my looks but also managed to lift a huge burden off my back. It felt like a good chunk of my past had been cut off together with my long hair, as if the two had been braided together. Most importantly though, I was not a 'Céspedes' anymore. Now I was ready to face the future.

Pilar was right. In Santiago people in the arts didn't give a hoot about my father, his trial or me. If they had, they'd already moved on. Life for my family in Valparaíso, however, became unbearable. Many parents of Aunt Encarnación's students demanded that their children be put in a different class or just registered them elsewhere. Alexandra was facing daily abuse from classmates — shunning, shaming and even physical attacks. So much so that Pilar decided to pull her out of school. Sales at the bakery were still way below normal and the Castillos couldn't make ends meet. All in all, it was a disaster. The family would have to join me in Santiago as soon as possible.

Pilar and Aunt Encarnación agreed. The Castillos didn't. They wanted to stick with the bakery. "If Pilar isn't behind the counter, our customers will return," her mother said. As hurtful as her words were, they proved to be true. It only took a few weeks of Pilar's absence for the bakery to turn into a booming business once again.

I found a lovely one-storey adobe house with a central courtyard on Carmen Street. As soon as the family got to Santiago, we registered Alexandra in Liceo Javiera Carrera and it didn't take long for her to start making new friends. My aunt got a job at Escuela Paula Jaraquemada and Pilar at Panadería Milhojas, a bakery just around the corner from our home.

It was good to have my aunt under the same roof again. When I told her that I'd found the perfect house for the family, she'd assumed that she'd be living in a separate place. "Could you look for a little house or an apartment for me, Lucía?" she'd asked. "You know what I need — something close to your house and affordable, of course."

"Auntie, we'd like you to come and live with us," I said. Pilar and I had discussed it and agreed that this would be the best arrangement all around.

"Oh, no, Lucía! Your little family needs its own space, just like you explained to me when you and Pilar decided to live together. You don't want an old hag like me meddling in your lives," she said.

"That was then. Now it'd be best if we lived together, Auntie. In that unfamiliar, big monster of a city we'll all need all the support we can get. Pilar, Alexandra and I will need to have you close to us, Aunt Encarnación. But we'll understand if you want to live on your own," I said.

I was back in Valparaíso for a couple of days and was at my aunt's place having a cup of tea. She burst into tears. "Ay, Lucía! No, no, no. I mean yes. I mean I don't want to live on my own. Yes, I'd love to live with you three," she said, holding me tight.

"By the way, Auntie, I love old hags," I said, wiping my own tears and breaking into a smile.

MANUEL
. . . .

March – July 1939

Argelès-sur-Mer and Paris

ON MARCH 27 THE Nationalists captured Madrid, and on April 1 Franco declared victory and announced that the war was over.

Josep, a longshoreman from Tarragona, had a ham radio. So, while the rest of the camp slept, a few of us would join him to listen to whatever information about Spain we could get. There was a ten o'clock curfew on penalty of being shot if you broke it, which certainly turned the expedition to Josep's tent into a real challenge. It also brought out the serpent in me. I would literally slither and snake my way there, while I dodged the floodlights and avoided encounters with the guards. Many a time I had to freeze in my tracks and lower my head, which inevitably made me gulp a good helping of sand. It doesn't taste good.

That's why, on one of those nights, when a gendarme poked his head into Josep's tent, we thought we were dead meat. But, in his ungrammatical, although well-pronounced Spanish, he asked if he could listen to the radio with us. It took us a while to start breathing again.

"How do we know you're not a mole?" Josep finally asked.

The gendarme's eyes opened wide. "Ay, no! Ay, no! I could get in real trouble if they find out," he responded, pointing with his chin towards the gendarmes' headquarters. "My father is from Spain. He came here as a little boy. We've followed the war. We're on the

Republican side," he went on.

We let him in. He seemed to be a good young man turned gendarme out of necessity.

"Can't survive as a farmer anymore," he explained when we asked him why he had become a cop.

It turned out that the best shortwave signal was Radio Moscow's, so we swallowed our anarchist pride and tuned in to their nightly Spanish-language newsreel. That's how we learned that Republican Colonel Segismundo Casado and Socialist politician Julián Besteiro had staged a coup against Prime Minister Juan Negrín and replaced his government with a National Defence Council. Ostensibly, Casado, Besteiro and their allies believed that, unlike Negrín, they could negotiate a "good" peace deal with Franco.

Anyone could've told Casado and Besteiro that negotiating a peace deal, never mind a "good" peace deal, with Francisco Franco was as absurd as expecting a crow to sing the lead in *Madame Butterfly*. Sure enough, Franco sent them to hell and demanded an "unconditional surrender." Then, his troops stormed into Madrid, killed everybody in their path, incarcerated those who had survived and executed all Republican combatants.

At the beginning of the war, Franco and the Nationalists had declared that they were embarking on a "crusade" against Bolshevism and in defence of Christian civilization. Now they took pride in having defeated "anarchy," shut the door on a "Judeo-Masonic conspiracy" and eliminated hundreds of thousands of "agitators" and "Godless scum." Spain *needed* Franco's "authoritarianism" to bring order to the country, they said. "Authoritarianism," my ass. Their government sported the purest brand of *fascist totalitarianism*.

Every few days I had been making my way to Perpignan to send off my articles and pick up money transfers and correspondence from my boss. Towards the end of March, I got a cable ordering me to leave immediately for Paris. The Chilean government had appointed Pablo Neruda as special consul in that city with the specific task of offering asylum to Spanish refugees. My boss wanted me to cover that story. I went back to Argelès feeling buoyed. I could not only "cover the story" but also help my friends leave the concentration camp and resettle in Chile.

The dire situation at the camp had not improved. On the contrary, it had got worse. Many children and elderly folks had died, as well as a few adults and youth. The exposure to the elements, the scarcity of clean water, the crummy food and the unsanitary conditions had all conspired against the refugees. Montse, one of the kids in Federica's family, had been one of the victims. She'd been coughing for days and when we finally convinced the gendarmes that she needed a doctor, it was too late.

As I dug Montse's grave in the camp's expanding cemetery, La Coruña memories and Rosa's death came rushing back. But this time I didn't faint, like when we had buried Rosa. I just bawled. Bawled openly. Loudly. I didn't care if anybody was watching, and I didn't feel ashamed. Plainly and simply, I wailed like a hungry baby.

I was hungry, all right. Not only for food but also for justice. The Spanish refugees were being treated worse than criminals — at least convicts had a roof over their heads — and little was being done to remediate their situation. Now I had an opportunity to help. I gathered as much information as I could from as many people as possible and left for Paris.

I arrived at the Gare D'Orsay in the middle of the afternoon. While the architecture was similar to Mapocho Station in Santiago, this place was gigantic. Dozens of high arches rested on top of thick metal pillars, and a glass roof and wide windows let in natural light. The platforms went on forever and the lobby was the size of a soccer field. As I made my way through the crowd towards the exit, an enormous, ornate, golden clock was chiming three o'clock.

The streets of Paris were full of people enjoying the spring sun. Compared to Argelès, this was paradise. Greenery and flowers joyfully filled the spaces between the buildings and along the boulevards, while dozens of cafes and restaurants spilled onto the sidewalks with their bistro tables and chairs. I couldn't resist. On my way to the hotel I had an aphrodisiac café au lait, accompanied by a croissant that felt like silk inside my mouth.

Hôtel Georgette, on Rue Voltaire, was housed in a modest three-storey building with a bakery on the bottom floor and flower boxes hanging from every window. My room was on the third floor and looked onto the lively street. After months of freezing bird baths at the Argelès camp, I luxuriated in a tub full of hot water in the bathroom at the end of the hallway, changed into a clean outfit and walked to the Embassy.

An older woman cloaked in a navy-blue smock and wielding a broom in her left hand answered the door. When I asked for Special Consul Pablo Neruda, she wrinkled her nose, stared me up and down and then lifted her broom to point to a lone, florid armchair set at an angle by the majestic, spiral staircase that occupied the centre of the lobby. The chair swallowed me as if I'd been made of quicksand. I was still trying to extricate myself from its depths when a soporific voice behind me asked: "What can I do for you?"

I scrambled to my feet, turned around and there he was, the man himself, renowned poet Pablo Neruda, now the Chilean government's envoy in charge of sending Spanish refugees to Chile.

I started to explain to him who I was but didn't get very far. After a few words, Neruda lifted his right index finger to his pursed lips and with his left one, pointed to the dark corner behind him from which he had emerged. A narrow, windy staircase took us all the way to the fourth floor, which housed the servants' quarters *and* Neruda's office — a tiny cubicle with no windows, a small desk and a couple of unsteady chairs.

We squeezed in, Neruda closed the door, sat down and pointed to the other chair. After he'd caught his breath, he began to speak in a hushed voice: "The government of Chile has changed, but the functionaries at the Chilean Embassy in Paris have not. These 'career' diplomats despise President Pedro Aguirre Cerda, don't give a damn about me and hate the Spanish refugees. So, they are doing everything in their power to make my work as difficult as possible *and* my life miserable. They claim that there aren't any other offices available, as if this cubbyhole could be called an office," he chuckled.

"Even the servants are right wing at this Embassy. I guess they have to be — they need their jobs. But that's not the only reason. They come from the patient rain and the sad, sullied shacks of the countryside in the Chilean south. Now they're living in Paris. Paris, the City of Light! And they have dry, warm quarters and three straight meals a day! What else could you ever ask for? If I were them, I'd be right wing too!" He chuckled some more.

By then, Neruda had already published *Spain in my Heart*, a poetry collection in which he denounced the atrocities of the Spanish Civil War and declared his support for the Republicans. Until then, he had been the universally "adored" bard — he had written love poetry that made the whole world sigh and existential poetry that nobody understood but that everybody claimed was unique and profound. Now, he had dared write political poetry, and the fascists and their allies hated him for it. No wonder then that "the functionaries" had forbidden him and the refugees to use the elevator or the main stairs.

"We cannot let your... uhmmm... 'mission'.... ehem... interfere with our Embassy business," they'd said.

Obviously, what they meant was that they didn't want a communist poet and hordes of Spanish refugees "contaminating" their garish space.

Neruda was a tall, round man with a bald head, a long nose, thin lips and a pair of small, piercing eyes that changed from liquid-smiley to hardened-cold in a flash. His voice didn't quite match the size of the man nor the eyes. It was soft and high-pitched, quivery and, most strikingly, monotone. If you weren't looking at his eyes while he talked, you wouldn't know what kind of emotion his words carried.

Even though the man was a communist and I was an anarchist, we hit it off. I admired his writing and he liked mine.

"So, *you* are Tamarugo," he said after I'd had a chance to explain myself. He held my gaze as if he was seeing me for the first time and hadn't already shaken my hand. "I must confess that I didn't start reading your columns until recently — after I went back to Chile from Madrid. At first, I was weary — I'm not very fond of anarchists, I must say. But your stories are good. Your writing is good — nonpartisan, energetic, full of imagery, entertaining," he said, while he nodded and narrowed his eyes.

That first night, when we left the Embassy (through the back door), we went straight to Rafael Alberti and María Teresa León's apartment, where Pablo and his wife, Delia del Carril, were staying.

"Once in a while Rafael takes hold of the kitchen and cooks up a storm. Tonight is one of those nights," Pablo said.

It turned out that Alberti was an expert in Italian cuisine and had put together nothing less than a banquet: chicken cacciatore, spaghetti puttanesca, capresse salad and, to top it all off, tiramisu! I had never tasted any of these dishes before; our Chilean working-class repertoire of Italian cooking was small and humble.

As we ate and drank velvety French wine, stories came and went, theirs and mine. Pablo told about the house he and Delia had just got in a wild section of the Chilean central coast, which could only be reached on horseback. This made Delia beam; she loved horses and they were the main subject of her striking paintings. Rafael and María Teresa had led the operation that had saved the Prado Museum collection from the Nationalist bombs.

They wanted to know how I'd become a journalist. I wanted to know about Neruda's life in Asia and Delia's upbringing as the daughter of wealthy landowners in Argentina. They wanted to know about life at the Argelès camp. I wanted to know about *El mono azul* — *The Blue Overall,* the literary magazine that María Teresa had founded and directed until recently, and why Rafael had abandoned his practice as a visual artist and become a poet instead. They wanted to know about the La Coruña massacre. And on and on.

By the end of the evening, Neruda had appointed me his "assistant." "Report to me tomorrow at nine o'clock sharp at the service door of the Chilean Embassy," he ordered, with a chuckle.

"Yes, sir!" I replied, coming to attention.

For weeks, we worked shoulder to shoulder. We interviewed and assessed each and every one of those who made it up the windy staircase at the back of the Embassy. There were Republican generals and soldiers, carpenters and plumbers, construction workers, cooks, maids, textile workers and medical doctors. Engineers, nurses, lawyers, farmers and fishermen.

Then, the telegram arrived:

Got news of your plans to bring Spanish refugees to Chile Stop Disavow this surprising information at once Stop Signed Pedro Aguirre Cerda President of the Republic of Chile Stop.

No wonder the highest-ranking Embassy functionary delivered the telegram in person, a big grin on his face.

Pablo couldn't believe his eyes. A few months earlier, Pedro Aguirre Cerda had summoned him to La Moneda and entrusted him with this mission: "Bring me thousands of Spaniards. We have work for them all. Bring me fishermen; bring me Basques, Castellans, Extremadurans," he had said.

Was this telegram for real then? Had the president forgotten that he had sent Neruda to Paris to implement *his* decision to repatriate Spanish Republicans in Chile? What to do now? Say "sorry" to the hundreds that had already been approved and turn our backs on them and all those who were still waiting to be interviewed?

That evening we went to the Allard, one of the exiled Republicans' favourite meeting places. As usual, around thirty men were there, cursing the Nationalists, commiserating, blaming each other for the defeat, proposing strategies for the resistance movement and, of course, drinking inordinate amounts of wine. Juan Negrín, the former Republican president in Spain and now head of the Republican government in exile was sitting with a couple of his ministers at a corner table. We joined them and Pablo explained the situation.

Then he said, his voice even more high pitched and quivery than usual: "In my view, there are three possible solutions. The first one is indeed abominable: simply to announce the cancellation of the repatriation program to Chile. The second, dramatic: to publicly voice my disagreement with the president's astonishing new position and to put a bullet through my head. And, the third one, definitely defiant: to forge ahead, fill a boat with Spanish refugees and take them to Chile."

I had never seen Neruda so excited. Even his voice was going up and down. A bit. But enough so that the whole room was now in silence and all ears and eyes were on him.

Negrín listened unperturbed and after a pause asked in a straightforward, calm voice: "Have you thought of a fourth option, *poeta*: phoning the president?"

A tense silence filled the room. Then Pablo burst out laughing and soon enough, everyone, including Negrín, was guffawing.

First thing the next morning, Pablo asked the functionary in charge to dial up the president's office in Chile.

"We're not allowed to call the president directly," the functionary responded.

"Who are you allowed to call, then? The telegram that I need to discuss came directly from the president!" Pablo responded, waving the piece of paper in front of the functionary's face.

"I'll connect you with the minister of foreign affairs," the man stated, dialing the operator and asking her to place the call.

What ensued was an exchange of dozens of "What did you say," "Can't hear you" and re-dials, interspersed with Pablo's cursing and fists on the table, while the functionary smiled away and shuffled the piles of papers on his desk.

By the end of a good fifteen minutes, Pablo was exhausted. We made our way up the stairs and as soon as we walked into the "office," he collapsed in his chair, his head in his hands. I feared the worst. The minister had probably said that the refugee program had been cancelled. Period. But after a couple of minutes, Pablo recovered his voice and told me that even though he couldn't be sure of what the minister had actually said, he had understood that new instructions would be arriving soon.

Sure enough, the next day, a grim-faced functionary handed Pablo a new telegram, this time from the minister of foreign affairs. It explained that in the last few weeks the president had been subjected to undue pressures which had caused a lot of "confusion." However, now he had taken his decision-making powers back and had given the go-ahead to the repatriation of Spanish refugees.

On August 4, 1939, the *SS Winnipeg*, a cargo steamer that had been refurbished and converted into a passenger ship, left the port of Trompeloup-Pauillac with 2336 Spanish refugees on board, including many of my friends from the Argelès concentration camp. Its final destination was Valparaíso, Chile.

Nobody from the Embassy showed up — only Neruda, who kept busy making sure that everything was in order, shaking hands, offering hugs and dabbing his eyes with a white handkerchief as the refugees boarded the boat. As the *SS Winnipeg* sailed away, Neruda remarked: "Never mind my poetry or anything else I've ever done. This is the most honorable mission I've brought to bear in my entire life."

LUCÍA
· · · · · · · · · · ·

March 1940

Santiago

A YEAR AND A half after parting ways in Lima, Manuel and I met again. He seemed to have shrunk — his clothes hung loose on his small frame — and his face looked leathery and creased. Even his eyes had changed; while they still sparkled with life, now they were also shrouded in a mist of sadness.

Internationally renowned *Editorial Ercilla* had collected his chronicles about the Spanish Civil War and published them as a book with a preface by Pablo Neruda. Today, the two men were sitting at a table on the stage of Teatro Caupolicán, launching the book and discussing its contents. It was heartening to see that Neruda had endorsed Manuel's work and was honouring him with his presence. Clearly, Spain and the war had left an indelible impression on them both. In Neruda's case, his experiences had found their way into his poetry.

You will ask what happened to the lilacs?
and the metaphysics wrapped in poppies?
and the rain that would often hammer his words
opening holes and filling them with birds?

These were the first lines of "I Explain a Few Things," a poem in which Neruda recounts how the bloodbath he witnessed in Madrid at the beginning of the war had led him to use his poetry as a tool of denunciation and resistance. I had heard him recite it on the radio not long before, and his words, particularly the poem's last few lines, had taken root in my mind.

You will ask why his poetry
doesn't speak of dreams, of leaves
of the great volcanoes in his native land?

Come and see the blood in the streets, come and see
the blood in the streets
come and see the blood
in the streets!

The sight of the two men on the stage made me smile. Neruda looked humongous next to Manuel, and his high-pitched, monotonous voice couldn't have been any more different than Manuel's upbeat, animated storytelling. Manuel may have looked withered and pensive, but he was still full of spunk.

I stood at the end of the line and waited for a good twenty minutes to have my book signed. When I got to the front, Manuel didn't recognize me.

"What's your name?" he asked, distractedly.

"Lucía," I answered.

He signed the book and then looked up. He tilted his head. "Lucía?!" he exclaimed, springing off his chair and walking around the table to give me a hug.

"What happened to your hair?" he asked, holding me at arms' length. He introduced me to Neruda as "a childhood friend from Iquique." I had brought a copy of *Spain in my Heart* with me and asked the poet to dedicate it to my aunt, Pilar, Alexandra and me.

"That's what I would call a communal book," he said, his eyes smiling, as he scribbled our names and his signature in green ink.

Manuel invited Neruda to join us for lunch, but he declined. "*La hormiguita* promised me a succulent *charquicán*, and I wouldn't want to disappoint her. Besides, I'm sure you two have a lot of catching up to do," he said.

We parted ways at the door.

"*La hormiguita*" — "the little ant," is Delia del Carril, his wife," Manuel whispered, as we walked away.

We headed to Restaurante Las Tejas, just a couple of blocks from the theatre. While we waited for our *cazuelas*, we began to talk over a bottle of Don Melchor. Manuel wanted to hear everything about the trial. He knew the generalities — he had read the press coverage and his colleagues at *Rebelión* had filled him in, but he was hungry for my experience and impressions. So, even though thinking, never mind talking, about the trial filled me with anxiety, I described the scene and recounted the witnesses' stories to him; I also told him about Mercedes' testimony and our reunion.

"Mercedes?! The woman who brought you up in Tacna?!" he cried out. "The defence found her and brought her down to Santiago?! Wow! That must've been hard on her... and you!"

"Her testimony was flawless, Manuel, but the defence and the public treated her like dirt. It was horrible," I said.

"And you were able to talk to her?"

"Yes, afterwards, in the hallway."

"How was that?" he wanted to know.

"Painful. Brought back all kinds of feelings I thought weren't there anymore. And I acted like an ass, Manuel," I confessed.

"What do you mean?"

"I asked her to come live with us."

"Mmm... What did she say?"

"The obvious: that she has her own family now and her life is in Tacna. It was as if I was a little girl all over again, Manuel."

Manuel patted my hand. "Lucía, you were literally snatched from your mother at age twelve. Mercedes *was* your mother. No wonder seeing her again brought those old feelings to the surface."

"Pilar and my aunt said the same thing. I've recovered, I'm fine, but it was tough seeing her after all these years," I admitted. I also told Manuel about the trial's aftermath: the insults and the slander and our eventual move to Santiago.

"Yes. I read a few of those... revolting articles. Sorry I wasn't here to offer support," he said.

"Oh, yeah! You were gallivanting in Spain, weren't you?" I joked. He chuckled.

"In the end, those assholes did us a huge favour," I continued. "Moving to Santiago was the best thing that could've happened to us."

"How so?" he asked.

"Things have worked out very well for us, Manuel. I'm a full-time choreographer now, Pilar opened her own bakery with her parents' help, Alexandra's happy, my aunt is still teaching. And of course, we haven't stopped being staunch communists," I said, a big grin in my face.

"Good, good," he said, smiling his crooked smile.

"Tell me about Spain, Manuel," I said.

He took his time. "It was La Coruña all over again, Lucía," he said. "But a thousand-fold. Yes, a thousand-fold," he repeated.

"It's all in here," he said then, resting his hand on his book, which I had set on the table.

"I read all your chronicles, Manuel. It must've been a living hell. But you were so good at telling the real stories, the stories of all those poor people," I commented.

"Well, not *all* the stories," he said after a moment. Then he told me about Rosa. "Remember how on the sailing to Lima we talked about falling in love and all that?"

I nodded.

"I don't know if I fell in love with Rosa or not. But what I do know is that I don't want to be in love. Ever. And I don't want to have children either. Life is too cruel," he went on.

"I hope someday you change your mind, Manuel. It's good to have somebody to love and who loves you," I said.

"Who knows... maybe... but I doubt it," he responded.

"What are your plans now that you've released *Nights and Days of War and Hope*?" I asked.

"Well, for one, to keep on working at *Rebelión*. But I've also been thinking that given the outcome of your father's extradition trial, I should write a book about him. Use the trial's transcripts, the Peruvians' testimonies, your testimony and the stories you've told me, recount what happened at La Coruña. Expose the bastard, let the world know that he is nothing more than a mass murderer at the service of the state and the bourgeoisie!" Manuel answered. His voice had gone up an octave.

I waited a few seconds before responding. "That's a great idea, Manuel, but it's dangerous. He's a powerful man."

"Yes, you're right. It's a risk. But this is an opportune time, given that your Popular Front is in office. If not now, when?!" he countered.

"*My* Popular Front?" I asked.

He chuckled. "In all seriousness. What do you say?" he asked.

A surge of excitement mixed with fear rushed through my body. The Popular Front government, as progressive as it was, could not protect Manuel from Ernesto Céspedes's rage. At the same time, my father would not be able to act with complete impunity as he had in Tacna and La Coruña. Back then, the fascistic governments of Alessandri and Ibáñez had given him carte blanche to use whatever means he saw fit to ensure that Peruvians wouldn't vote in the plebiscite and that the workers' movement was quashed. Neither of the two massacres had made the news because of gag legislation. These were different times. Freedom of expression was protected by law now, and if anything were to happen to Manuel, the story would be covered by every media outlet and my father would be exposed.

I shared my thoughts with Manuel.

"I agree with you," he said. "That's why I believe this is the time to write and publish that book."

We made plans to meet again and talk some more. I offered to help with the research. I also invited him to the opening of *Amapola, the Prodigious Seamstress*, which was finally being produced by the National Ballet at the Municipal Theatre. I told him that I was dreaming up a choreography based on his chronicles, the story of the *SS Winnipeg* and Neruda's "I Explain a Few Things." I invited him to our home so that he could meet Pilar and Alexandra and see my aunt again. I gave him the address and we agreed on a day and a time. But he didn't come either to our home or the theatre. Then I noticed that nothing of his had been published in *Rebelión* for quite a few weeks.

I made my way to the magazine's office on San Isidro Street. The receptionist, a perky young woman clad in pants and a striped blouse informed me that Manuel was on a leave of absence.

"Comrade Garay stopped working three weeks ago," she said, looking up at a calendar on the wall.

"When is he coming back?" I asked.

"Unfortunately, I don't know the answer to that question because his leave is indefinite," she answered, offering me an apologetic smile.

"Did he leave an address, a way he can be reached?"

"Not that I know of. But let me check with Comrade López. He may have an address for him.

She came back a few moments later. "No. Comrade Garay didn't leave any contact information with us. So sorry," she said.

Where was he? Was he okay? I went back to *Rebelión* a couple more times, but the answer remained the same: no news of Manuel's whereabouts.

Six months later, he showed up at our door. He had put on weight and looked a lot healthier than at the book launch. Over tea, he explained that shortly after the launch, he had fallen into a void.

"It happened very quickly. I woke up one day and didn't feel like getting out of bed, just wanted to stay there, under the covers. Didn't even feel like writing..."

"The tragedies in your life caught up with you," I commented.

"I guess so. The Spanish Civil War was behind me, *Nights and Days of War and Hope* was out in the world, and I felt completely empty. I had told you and promised myself that I'd start working on the Ernesto Céspedes book right away, but I couldn't do it. I had neither the energy nor the desire. Spain, La Coruña, all my dead kept haunting me. I'd try to put them to rest by thinking of the future, but all I saw in front of me was a black cloud. In a way, I still do, Lucía. Europe is at war and fascism keeps gaining ground, but at least now I can function and am looking forward to start writing again."

"I know what you mean. It's difficult to stay optimistic, but we can't lose hope, Manuel. I know that you're very critical of Stalin, but we communists are confident that the Soviet Union will play a key role in stopping the spread of fascism and Nazism," I said.

"You may be right," he conceded.

"How did you come out of your depression?" I asked.

"I went to Iquique, stayed with my grandma and my sister, spent time with Moncho, went foraging for food at the beach, found Mr. Bacic and had endless conversations with him. Being with my people lifted my spirits."

"Love, eh? Loving and feeling loved. That's the best remedy for our woes. That's what Pilar says, and she's right. She helped me come out of the depression I fell into after my mother died. And you're better now?"

"Yes. I feel good and I'm ready to set to work on the book about your father. Will you help me?" he asked.

"Of course!" I responded.

Over the next year he came over often. Alexandra took to calling him "Uncle Manuel." Aunt Encarnación welcomed him with open arms, treated him to her scrumptious casseroles and sent him home with good-sized care packages. Pilar also grew fond of him and made sure to supplement my aunt's foodstuffs with goodies from the bakery.

He'd show up with his signature collection of school notebooks, each one dedicated to a different aspect of the book, and proceed to report on his latest findings: "Did you know that Ernesto Céspedes was also implicated in the murder of more than seventy communist leaders in Vallenar in 1931 *and* the massacre of more than a hundred countryside workers in Alto Bío Bío in 1934? The man is a killing machine!"

His big dilemma was in which style to write the book. "Céspedes emerged from the trial as a national hero and I'm about to expose him as a mass murderer," he said. "So, I don't think it'll be a popular book. It may provide the left with good ammunition; a few academics and intellectuals may read it, but other than that… So, I'm leaning towards making a straightforward and impersonal presentation based on facts."

"No, Manuel! No, no, no!" I countered. "You're a storyteller! That's your forte and people need to hear *your* voice! The book will become as popular as you want to make it, and that will hinge on how personal it is, not on the facts. Of course, the facts are key, and they will find their way into the story, but you must write it in your distinctive, personal style!"

Pilar and Aunt Encarnacion agreed.

"Look at how popular *Nights and Days of War and Hope* turned out to be, Manuel. Of course, the content had a lot to do with it — the Spanish Civil War had such an impact around the world — but people love your book because of the way you wrote it, because of how you infused those stories with your own voice," Pilar claimed.

"I have to agree with Lucía and Pilar," my aunt added. "You have to write this book as if you were telling a story. Remember when you came to our place in Valparaíso and recounted how you'd got the job at *The Northener*? About the composition you'd written for school and that the gentleman that ran the magazine liked so much? Think of it that way, Manuel. As an expanded and enriched version of that composition."

He paced around the room in silence. Then he grabbed his things and walked to the front door. "Thanks ladies," he called out as he put his coat on. "Don't expect to see me for a while. The time to turn into a loner has arrived. I need to mull things over. Also, I'd better stop procrastinating and get down to the writing, don't you think?" he said with a smirk, as he walked out the door.

We didn't see Manuel for months, but he popped into my head often. I had decided that if Manuel had the guts to write a book about Ernesto Céspedes, I would muster the courage to create *Amarú*, a ballet about the Tacna massacre. So, as I paced, sketched, took notes, listened to music, danced, relived the past, sat down to sketch some more and got up to dance again, I imagined Manuel going through his own version of the creative process.

On a balmy summer evening, Manuel showed up at our door once again, this time with a bundle of typed-up pages. He wanted feedback on the first couple of chapters of the book.

"What approach did you decide on?" I asked.

"You'll find out by yourself when you read these two chapters," he answered, tapping the stack of papers with his hand.

He had gone for the personal approach and the story read as a mix of memoir, reportage, historical account, political essay and thriller. It was believable and it was touching. Manuel succeeded in presenting my father as who he was: the embodiment of the most extreme views within the bourgeoisie, a man who saw himself as an almighty god, a zealot at the ready to eliminate anyone and everyone who did not belong in his patriotic, inhumane world.

My ballet *Amarú* came to life long before Manuel's *General Ernesto Céspedes, the Mass Murderer: Survivors Speak Out*. It took him years to finish it and a few more to get it out in the world. Nobody wanted to touch it, not even Ercilla, the publisher that had released his book about Spain. Finally, *Rebelión* decided to take the risk and published it in March of 1948. A few months later, President Gabriel González Videla, who had been elected under the banner of the Popular Front in 1946, outlawed the Communist Party and began to write a new chapter in the annals of the persecution of the Chilean left.

PART III

1949

LUCÍA AND MANUEL

Pisagua

RUMOUR HAD IT THAT a second boat had arrived at dawn and that its human cargo included several women. He had come a few days before, together with a thousand other men — communists, anarchists and homosexuals — "the scourge of the earth," according to the Chilean state.

While lining up to get his morning mug of tea and breakfast roll, he saw them — four women were shielding a fifth one from the men's eyes so that she could wash herself at the lone, anemic tap in the middle of the square. He could only see their backs, but recognized Lucía at once: tall and slim, not to mention her signature blonde waves. Then it had been her turn to use the tap and he had found himself yearning to shield her slender body with his, to protect her from the hardships of the concentration camp.

He also wanted to bury his head in the curve of her shoulder, lose himself in her wide eyes and stay there until it was safe to come out. He was desperate for refuge. This surprised him and scared him — he had pressed through much more severe hardships before without feeling this vulnerable.

Pisagua — nothing more than a barren, narrow strip of land — was in the Atacama Desert, wedged between the Pacific Ocean and a tall, thick hump of rock and sand which closed it off from the rest of the world. The government could not have picked a better place for a concentration camp. No need for barbed wire here. Getting to or leaving Pisagua was virtually impossible unless you had a good-size boat and knew the ocean's idiosyncrasies.

At the beginning of the century, during the golden age of salt-petre mining, the capitalists had "discovered" Pisagua and turned it into a port. They had built a railway that zig-zagged its way down the mountain, a luxurious theatre and a few other Victorian structures to house and entertain the magnates and their families during their brief stays there. But all that was in advanced stages of decay, and now Pisagua was nothing more than an abandoned, derelict village.

In 1938, before leaving for Spain, he had written about the formation of the Popular Front coalition, which included the Communist Party. At that time, he had denounced the Party as a puppet of the Soviet Union and called it "naïve" and "opportunistic." What had happened to the feisty proletarian organization of the first part of the century, the one that had fought so fiercely for the Chilean working class? Why was it compromising its principles and building alliances with wishy-washy social democrats and right-wing politicians, he had asked.

In 1939, when he returned from Paris, he had conceded that many of the government's policies were beneficial to the working class. At the same time though, he had warned the left of the dangers of playing the role of "little brother" in a coalition that was leaning more and more to the right.

Now, Gabriel González Videla, the third Popular Front president in a row, had outlawed the Communist Party and unleashed a wave of repression against its members and others who posed a danger to "Western, Christian civilization." As if communists, anarchists and homosexuals belonged in the same corner. Which now they did: at the Pisagua concentration camp.

He waited for the women to finish their ablutions, and as they began to walk away, he made his approach. "Lucía!" he called softly.

She turned her head and looked in his direction, shielding her eyes with her hand. "Manuel? Is that you?" she asked, as she stepped towards him.

They wrapped their arms around each other.

"Manuel, I'm so sorry I encouraged you to write the book," she whispered in his ear.

"Lucía, it was my decision and I stand by it. I'm the one who should be sorry for having dragged you into it," he answered.

"No, Manuel, I don't see it that way. I'm glad you wrote it and even more glad that I was able to help, even though it meant that... we ended up here," she said, drawing an arc in the air with her hand. "My father is a vengeful man," she added.

"No question about that," he said.

"Are we allowed to walk on the beach?" she asked.

"Yes, during daylight hours," he responded.

"Let's go to the beach, then," she proposed.

Dozens of prisoners were sitting on the rocks, while others walked barefoot in the surf. Guards were posted at the back, their guns at the ready. Lucía and Manuel took their shoes off and let the ocean caress their feet. The freshness of the water sent a bolt of energy up their bodies. Lucía felt like dancing.

"Are we allowed to swim?" she asked. Maybe she could "dance" in the water?

"Nope. They claim that we could escape, even though not even a dinghy would make it out of here, never mind a person," he chuckled.

"Why?" she wanted to know.

"Apparently the undercurrents are deadly," he responded.

"Obviously, your father sent me here because of the book. Do you figure that's why you're here too?" he asked after a short pause.

"I think so... and because of *Amarú* and because of the trial..."

"But the trial happened a decade ago! If he'd wanted to do something about it, he would've done it back then, don't you think?"

"Who knows why, but he didn't. For a while I was quite paranoid. I was sure that he would have me arrested, or beaten up, or at least have my company closed down. But nothing ever happened…"

The ocean stretched out like a diamond-studded skin in the morning light. They listened to the pulse of the waves and breathed in the salty air.

"We meet again by the oceanside," she said quietly.

"Twenty-four years later," he added.

"And a few lives and deaths along the way," she concluded.

FOR THE LONGEST TIME, Ernesto Céspedes could not understand his daughter's behaviour. He had been a doting father, forever making sure that she had everything she needed and more, even after she had turned on him and he'd sent her to live in Valparaíso with that communist whore. He still got worked up when he thought about it.

By the time he had found out who Encarnación González really was, it was too late. Lucía was no longer a girl and had refused to come back home. Of course, his demands could have been followed by more forceful measures, but did he really want his Bolshevik daughter in Iquique? She would've not only gone on with her subversive activities but also spread lies about him all over town. Antonia had sworn up and down that she'd never known about Encarnación's true circumstances — that her sister had been cunning and dishonest. He hadn't believed her and told her so. She had burst into tears, flung her arms around his neck and begged him to take her at her word. In the end, he'd let the matter go.

Still, he wondered why his daughter refused to understand that he was a Chilean patriot and that his actions were guided by his unconditional love for the fatherland. Chile had won the War of the Pacific. The display of valour and the supremacy of its heroic Armed Forces had resulted in the annexation of a sizeable piece of territory that had formerly belonged to Peru and Bolivia, including the city of Tacna. But thirty years later, the damn plebiscite had threatened to reverse what had been gained with such ingenuity and bravery. In his mind, the plebiscite was nothing more than the continuation of the war and he had felt compelled to act. Didn't she understand that he could not just sit there and watch Peru usurp his and *her* beloved Tacna? In the end, the fucking rains and the flood had spoiled the Army's and the Patriotic Leagues' hard work and Tacna had been lost. But at least he could say with a clear conscience and pride that he had fought for it to the bitter end.

What baffled him the most was how Lucía had gone from loving him as the adoring father he'd been to hating him with a vengeance. The first time he'd seen Lucía in her mother's arms, he couldn't help but be smitten with her. She looked like a delicate porcelain doll. Along the years he had witnessed with delight how she had grown into an angelic beauty — fair skin, blonde hair, a pair of huge blue eyes and a slender, graceful body to boot. She was also charming and well-behaved. How could things have gone so wrong? It was beyond him. But perhaps there was a viable explanation, which he began to consider at the time of the trial.

When he saw her take the witness stand, he couldn't believe his eyes. He'd been distracted — after so many days of listening to the sappy stories of a parade of Peruvian scum, including the Indian whore who'd been his servant in Tacna, he was more than ready for a drink and a nap. So, when he'd heard yet another witness being called to testify, he'd thought: "Here comes another fucking *cholo*." But it was Lucía.

How dared she humiliate him like this? As if turning into a Bolshevik *and* a *marimacha* hadn't been more than enough?! He looked at the beautiful woman sitting across from him and felt the urge to kill her with his own two hands. Yes, he wanted her dead. He paused and reconsidered. Was it possible for a father to feel compelled to kill his own flesh and blood? That's when he began to contemplate the possibility that perhaps Lucía was not his daughter.

He had met Antonia, his wife-to-be, at the *Apollo* on Estado Street in Santiago, where she worked as a cigarette girl. She had a pair of good, bouncy breasts with a deep, inviting cleavage that she made sure to flaunt when bending down to hand you a pack of smokes; her ass was meaty and jiggly, begging to be grabbed and massaged; and she had a pair of solid, shapely legs. Her face though had a pale, milky innocence to it; her eyes were child-like — curious and bright, and she had a fleshy, pouty mouth that would open into a wide smile at the drop of a hat. The combination of her womanly body and cherubic face endowed her with a sensuousness and allure that Ernesto Céspedes, just like every other man in the theatre, found difficult to resist.

He had never had any special feelings for a woman. Perhaps the only exception was his mother, for whom he felt a tepid affection. But overall, he found women to be irrational and temperamental. They were also ignorant and shallow — incapable of entering a conversation about anything other than the weather, movies and fashion; and if they happened to be married, you also had to put up with their endless babbling about servants and children.

Antonia was no exception, but her charm and sex appeal had managed to play havoc with his mind. He was assailed by an insatiable thirst to fuck her every minute of the day, coupled with the desire to kill every man who looked at her, never mind talked to her or invited her out. He would get sick with rage just imagining Antonia being fucked by other men. So, he asked her to marry him. She would be his and nobody else's.

When Ernesto Céspedes proposed, Antonia reacted with a mix of bewilderment and hesitation. She didn't utter a word, shook her head and burst into tears. Why? Was it because she couldn't believe her ears or because she was not ready to give up her whorish ways? Didn't she see that he was offering her comfort and security for the rest of her life? Any other woman would've jumped at the opportunity! Perhaps she had sentimental feelings for another man. If so, who? One of the Apollo's patrons? Somebody at one of the cafés where she worked during the week? But then, Céspedes showed her the one-of-a-kind diamond and ruby ring he had got her at Dulcamara's Fine Jewelry, and Antonia's face lit up; she gasped, opened her eyes wide and cried out "Huh! Oh, no! Yes! Yes, Ernesto! Wow! Yes, yes, yes!" She extended her right hand, and as Céspedes slid the ring onto her finger, she went on: "Thank you! Thank you! Oh, Ernesto, it's beautiful!" Then she threw her arms around his neck and promised to be a faithful wife and to do everything in her power to make him happy. "I swear to God that I'll be the best wife ever, my love," she added.

That's exactly what he had wanted to hear — a pledge of devotion and compliance. In a few months he was being transferred to Tacna, and having a beautiful, obliging wife on his arm would be an asset. First of all, it would show the other officers that his taste in women was unparalleled. Secondly, he had had enough of the bachelor's life and was ready for a home of his own. Antonia would take care of that.

He registered her in the Academia de las artes personales y domésticas — Academy of Personal and Domestic Arts, and in a few weeks, she had swapped her provocative outfits for ritzy, stylish ones and her heavy make-up for a subtle, sophisticated look. Also, she had learned everything to be known about setting up a well-appointed home and managing an efficient household.

During those weeks he had not seen her every day. Sometimes her classes had run into the evening; on other evenings, he'd been busy at the regiment. Had she kept on "entertaining" other Apollo men? Had she slept around in Tacna? Unlikely, because shortly after they'd got there, she'd announced that she was pregnant. But now that he thought about it, Lucía had been born "early" by a couple of weeks. Was Antonia already pregnant when he'd married her?

Ernesto Céspedes was certain that they would have a son — his spitting image and a boy eager to follow in his father's footsteps. But then they'd had a girl, and while he was disappointed, he told himself that the next child would be a boy and that it would be good for him to have Lucía as an adoring, big sister.

However, as much as Antonia and he had tried — fucking at all hours of the day for weeks, months and even years on end, she didn't get pregnant again, and he had no choice but give up on his dream of raising another Ernesto Céspedes. The doctors couldn't figure out what the problem was, but he concluded that Antonia's sleeping around had caught up with her and she had become barren on account of excessive fucking at a young age.

Now he had no choice but to wonder. Was *he* the infertile one? Was that why Antonia hadn't been able to get pregnant after giving birth to Lucía? If that was the case, he was not Lucía's father. She was not his flesh and blood. She was a sham and a lie. An impostor. No wonder she had turned out the way she had! She had taken after her mother — a first-class whore, a cheat and a conniver. A traitor. Too bad Antonia was already dead. Otherwise, he would've made sure that she died a slow, painful death. But Lucía was alive and he would find a way to have his revenge.

A decade later, the opportunity had presented itself on a platter. Manuel Garay, the son of the La Coruña Bolshevik he'd neutralized in 1925, the worm who had befriended Lucía in Iquique and now called himself a journalist and author, had dared to publish a slanderous book about him — a piece of trash that Garay had obviously written with her help. The book related details no one but Lucía could have known. Obviously, they had not counted on the third Popular Front president outlawing the Bolsheviks and perverts. They had believed that they would get away with their opprobrious campaign against him, but they had been wrong. Dead wrong. The time for Céspedes to take revenge had finally come.

ERNESTO CÉSPEDES, GENERAL IN Chief of the Chilean Armed Forces, arrived in Pisagua on a Focke-Achgelis helicopter that caused havoc at the camp. The main square and the beach were evacuated in a flash and the prisoners sent to their respective dormitories. From their bunks they heard the deafening roar of the chopper's engine and the military march playing at full blast over the loudspeakers, which until then had been used solely to deliver homophobic and anti-leftist propaganda and to impart house-keeping directives.

Captain Augusto Pinochet, the camp's director, offered Céspedes a snappy report on the camp's situation. When he finished, Céspedes asked: "What about the women? How many are there?"

"There are five female prisoners, my General, all young — most likely not real Bolsheviks, but followers, you know how women are... not much up here," he chuckled, pointing at his head.

"For the most part you're right, Captain, but don't forget that there are always exceptions to the rule and if those women are here it's because they did something to deserve it," Céspedes replied.

"Yes, General!" Pinochet cried out, coming to attention.

He was relieved to see that Pinochet had not figured out that Lucía was his daughter. One less complication to deal with. But the young captain seemed to have a soft spot for the female sex and may react adversely if he neutralized a woman. Pinochet showed promise and he wanted him on his side. There was plenty of time for the captain to learn that the enemy is the enemy, whether in pants or skirts. But for now, he would acquiesce. Lucía's punishment would be to witness Manuel Garay's ordeal. That would be enough. If she chose to continue slandering him, he would reconsider. The future was long, and life had taught him to be patient.

He wondered if this decision also had to do with those years when he was Lucía's devoted father, when he made her laugh with his riddles and took her to her dance and music lessons, when he showered her with presents, when he was her hero. Absolutely not, he concluded.

IN THE LAST COUPLE of weeks, Manuel and Lucía have become close. During their daily walks on the beach they have delved deeply into their own and the other's psyche, talked about the things that make them happy and the things that make them sad. What angers them and what gives them hope. She's told him about her choreographies, how they go from her mind to her journal and then, after much work, to the stage. He's told her about his writing, the diary he's kept since age twelve, the year they met at the beach in Iquique.

"It's my confidant," he said.

"What do you write about?" she asked.

"What's inside me. My articles and the two books have been about what happens outside. My diary is about what happens inside," he answered, placing his open hand on his chest.

She turned to face him. "And what happens inside, Manuel?" she asked, placing *her* hand on his chest.

He hesitated, looking at the ground for a few moments. Then he replied, his eyes moist: "The La Coruña massacre and my sister's and Papa's murders bore a hole in my chest, Lucía. Then came Aunt Asunta's disappearance and the hole got even bigger. It's a deep, black hole, always threatening to grow and take over my whole body. The only way to keep it in check is to write. So, I fill it with memories. My memories of the *pampa*, of Spain. Not of what happened there, but of how I felt during those times. Those things that I haven't said out loud to anyone."

"Like that you actually fell in love with Rosa?" she asked.

"Yes, like that. And about my fear of falling in love again. But also about this dream I have of bringing up a child of my own. I write about this child, who perhaps will look like my sister Eva... that kind of stuff. And also, about the profound hatred I feel for your father and all the fascists and murderers in the world."

Now, the 2117 prisoners, their 91 military guards, Captain Augusto Pinochet and General Ernesto Céspedes are asleep. Manuel and Lucía have snuck out of their respective quarters and are lying shoulder to shoulder on the beach, sheltered by a cluster of rocks. It's a starry night, like all nights in the Atacama Desert, the driest in the world. The brilliant cloud of the Milky Way has made its way to the centre of the sky and turned the surface of the water into a resplendent skin. A crescent moon hangs in the horizon like a hammock.

The Pacific Ocean comes and goes, comes and goes, kissing their feet with its foamy crests, its pulse in concert with their hearts. The sound of the ocean fills their ears as they lie, silent and still on the beach.

"He's here now," Lucía says finally. "He sent us here and now he's come."

She reaches out for his hand. "I'm scared, Manuel. Are you scared?"

"Yes. I'm scared," he says, squeezing her hand.

The ocean water is ebbing, and a cool breeze has turned its surface into an army of white caps. Lucía shivers. The drumming in her chest has shut out the roar of the waves. She frees her hand and places it on Manuel's chest. His heart is galloping as crazily as hers. She slides her hand up and feels his face. It's wet, just like hers.

They lie there, shoulder to shoulder, silent and still. Silent and still, in the starry night, on the beach, in Pisagua, perhaps realizing now that their lives have been intertwined in more ways than they had ever considered —woven together by thick threads of pain rooted in a common source.

He takes her hand and puts the tip of her fingers in his mouth. He sucks. What ensues is perhaps love, perhaps sex. Perhaps something else. There are tears, there are kisses. There is a coming together, a coupling. An exchange of bodily fluids, the pleasurable sensation of skin against skin, bellies touching, legs entangling, fingers running through hair, lips brushing the roundness of a shoulder. But above all, there is a sharing of grief, life-long grief.

The following morning, they are both summoned to the camp's headquarters, at the crumbling King Edward Theatre. They're handcuffed, blindfolded and prodded into a space at the back of the stage. A door slams shut behind them. Their blindfolds are taken off and they're made to sit on the floor. A bright light goes on with a loud click, which makes Manuel think of Aunt Asunta's "revolutionary tool" — the battery-operated flashlight that he was so smitten with. But this is a flood light — powerful and blinding.

"Lucía González and Manuel Garay!" Ernesto Céspedes says bombastically. Lucía and Manuel cannot see him, but they don't need to. They know his voice well.

"Lucía González, Antonia González's daughter. A Bolshevik and a degenerate *marimacha*, a pervert, an impostor and a traitor," he says, bitterly.

"Manuel Garay, son of the Bolshevik agitator I had the pleasure of neutralizing in La Coruña and putative nephew of Asunta Vila, the Spanish whore who came to this country with the sole purpose of causing trouble, but who I also had the pleasure of neutralizing in Iquique," he adds after a pause.

Manuel roars, springs to his feet and charges towards Céspedes. Two soldiers are quick to restrain him and slam him against the wall. Lucía screams. Manuel moans.

"Lucía, I have a riddle for you," Céspedes announces cheerfully. "Remember how you used to love my riddles when you were little?"

"Why did the woman change her last name from Céspedes to González?" he intones and then pauses. "Because she was never a Céspedes in the first place! And why was she never a Céspedes? Because her mother was a liar and a whore!"

He approaches Lucía, pulls her off the floor and holds her up by the collar of her blouse. His face is hardly an inch from hers. His breath is rancid. "You are *not* my daughter, Lucía González and your mother *was* a whore. As for who your real father is, your guess is as good as mine. All I know is that I am not!" he shouts and lets her fall.

Lucía is not sure if she's heard him right. What did Céspedes actually say? That her mother got pregnant by another man? Is it true or is he making it up? If it's true, how did Céspedes find out and how long has he known about it?

Manuel has felt short of breath and dizzy since the soldiers slammed him against the wall. Now he's lying on the floor, trying hard to stay vigilant, all his senses on high alert. He doesn't care about what Céspedes does to him, but he will protect Lucía every way he can, to the death.

The ceiling lights are switched on.

Céspedes is standing in a corner, his hands behind his back, two soldiers on either side of him. They're wearing brass knuckles and have chains and truncheons in their hands. Their eyes are trained on Céspedes. The General nods slightly and the four of them charge against Manuel. To Lucía it feels like the thrashing goes on for hours, but it only takes the four henchmen a few minutes to beat Miguel to a pulp. He's beyond moaning and yelping now. His jaw and ribs are broken, one of his shoulders has come out of its socket and his whole body pulsates like a gigantic, gangrenous wound.

The soldiers have not laid a finger on Lucía. Her body is shaking uncontrollably, but she's unharmed.

A few minutes later Manuel and Lucía are brought out of the King Edward Theatre and taken to the beach. Lucía is walking on her own. Manuel is being dragged by the shoulders. His face is beyond recognition and his tattered clothes expose a wreck of bruised and lacerated flesh.

All the prisoners and guards are there, waiting for the "learning opportunity" they've been promised. Manuel is propped up against a pole that has been planted in front of the thick hump of rock that conceals Pisagua from the world. Lucía is ordered to stand across from him.

Haughty, squared-shouldered General Ernesto Céspedes joins the scene. He's dressed in his formal uniform, two rows of medals pinned to his chest. Five soldiers stand facing Manuel, rifles in hand.

Ernesto Céspedes raises his arm and shouts "Fire!" but neither Manuel nor Lucía hears him. They're already elsewhere, far away from Pisagua.

After Aunt Asunta disappeared, sitting on a rock at Bellavista beach, Manuel had wondered why he had been spared. Why he had lived on while so many others had been killed. Then he'd realized that his purpose in life was to write. To tell stories. To bear witness, protest, denounce, provoke and propose. Along the way he had promised himself that his writing would be a tool, a weapon in the struggle for justice and an instrument of hope. His writing would turn horror into beauty, shame into dignity and deceit into truth. And that's exactly what he has done since age twelve.

Now he's sitting on his favourite *tamarugo* tree, contemplating the never-ending, rugged skin of the Atacama Desert. His ears welcome the cheerful whistling of the wind, while his eyes revel in the enormity of a clean, blue sky...

Lucía is with Pilar, Alexandra and her aunt at the opening night of *Amarú*, her most ambitious choreography to date. They're all smiling, filled with excitement. Years before she had decided to honour Mercedes and the dead in the river by creating a ballet that would intertwine the legend and the massacre. It had been a challenge, but her skillful colleagues had rallied behind her, and finally *Amarú* had become a reality. She smiles as she thinks of her childhood ruminations on how to portray *Amarú* on stage —- the ruminations that kept her awake after Mercedes had finished recounting the story. More than twenty years later she had turned those tender imaginings into a real choreography — the principal ballerina in a scarlet tutu representing the *qantu* flower–turned hummingbird, the gigantic llama head carried by four hidden dancers, Amarú's iridescent scales and creamy wings. Advances in technology and the genius of the set designers had resolved the "making Amarú fly" issue. The young girl in her is thrilled...

Manuel and Lucía are on the ground. Manuel is lying on his side, his limbs bent and contorted, his head thrown back. A torrent of blood spouts out of a hole in his neck. The rest of his body is also riddled with bullets. His blood is quickly sucked up by the arid, fine sand.

Lucía is in a fetal position, her hands covering her ears.

Soon after, the Focke-Achgelis helicopter that brought Ernesto Céspedes, General in Chief of the Chilean Armed Forces to Pisagua, carries him away.

A few weeks later, Lucía is released. By then, she knows she is with child.

PART IV

2021

Lucía González Centre for the Performing Arts
Vancouver

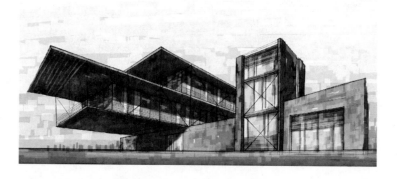

Established on June 19, 2021,
in Honour and Memory of Lucía González

Chilean-Canadian Choreographer,
Artistic Director and Human Rights Activist
Tacna, January 15, 1913 — Vancouver, March 4, 2002

EL MUNDO — ARTS AND CULTURE

· ·

Santiago, July 17, 2021

President's Award in the Performing Arts Posthumously
Granted to Choreographer & Artistic Director Lucía González

M. Correal

IN A SPLIT DECISION, a three-member jury granted the President's
Award for the Performing Arts to late choreographer and artistic
director Lucía González.

"Lucía González revolutionized the world of dance," National
Ballet's principal dancer Camila Prado, the jury's president, stated
in a press conference yesterday. "This award was long overdue. Lucía
should've got it twenty years ago, when she began to be recognized
around the world. Back then she received the Governor General's
Award in the Performing Arts in Canada and the Berlin Golden
Swan. In the ensuing years she got awards in Japan, Brazil, Spain,
England, France, Mexico. Now, a few months ago, a state-of-the-
art, brand-new centre for the performing arts was named after her
in Vancouver. But as usual, following our infamous tradition — let's
not forget that Gabriela Mistral received the President's Award for
Literature six years after, and I repeat, six years *after* getting the Nobel
Prize — Chile has been the last one to honour this extraordinary artist. Shameful, really," she added.

Theatre director Carlos Cruz, also a member of the jury, voiced his dissent: "Lucía González chose to live and work abroad for more than half her life. I don't think Chile should be honouring people who have not made a contribution to *this* country's arts' scene for the last forty-odd years. Besides, she was a Canadian citizen, not a true Chilean," he stated.

Choreographer Gabriela Echeverría, the third jury member, disagreed with Cruz: "Lucía González *was* Chilean. She didn't *choose* to leave Chile. Augusto Pinochet chose for her. Actually, it's a miracle that she survived the torture she endured as a political prisoner in Villa Grimaldi in 1973. What was she supposed to do? Stay in Chile and get murdered? She deserves this award because she is a world-renowned *Chilean* artist whose contributions pushed the boundaries of modern choreography and opened the world's eyes to the predicaments, the music and the art of non-Europeans. Not only that. She took concepts such as non-linear storytelling and abstract spatial dynamics to new levels, not to mention her use of multimedia and visual art. Finally, I would like to say that she had the guts to inject social and political awareness into the field of dance. Princesses and love stories were not her thing. Justice, human rights, the rights of working people, of aboriginal peoples — that's what she tackled. With depth and compassion, she brought those issues to the stage. She told relevant stories; important stories. They may not have been pretty, but she made them beautiful. She had the rare gift of turning darkness into light," she concluded.

EVA GARAY-GONZÁLEZ, LUCÍA GONZÁLEZ'S daughter, traveled from Vancouver, Canada, to receive the award on her mother's behalf. She offered the following exclusive interview to *El Mundo*:

EM: Did your mother resent not receiving this award while still alive?

EG-G: Oh, no! She wasn't that kind of person at all. She didn't really care about the awards — she just cared about her work as an artist and an activist.

EM: You grew up in Santiago. If I'm not mistaken, you were in your early twenties when you and your mother left.

EG-G: Yes. I was twenty-three when our family left.

EM: And your mother was already a well-established artist here in Chile. What are your memories of growing up with Lucía González?

EG-G: She was always very driven. We used to live in an old house not far from here, on Carmen Street, and I remember hearing Rachmaninoff's Piano Concerto Number 2 over and over again, as my mother paced around the courtyard singing along and scribbling things in her notebook. As a kid I grew to hate that music [chuckles]. Now I love it, but back then... [chuckles again]. Later on, in the sixties and seventies, she collaborated with Víctor [Jara] and his wife Joan [Turner], who was a dancer and a choreographer herself; with Violeta Parra, Inti Illimani, Isabel Parra, Cuncumén, Patricio Manns, the National Ballet. As you may know, together they created beautiful and affecting pieces that they took all over the country. All these artists used to come to our house and work with my mom in the courtyard.

EM: What about her work in Canada? We understand that her more innovative initiatives began after she left Chile. What propelled her to push the boundaries of dance the way she did?

EG-G: Pain, maybe? Mourning? Grief? My sister Alexandra disappeared after being abducted from our house. Many friends were murdered — Víctor Jara was one of them, of course. We lost our country. I don't know... What I do know is that it took us a few years to find our niche in Vancouver — I had to go back to university, my mother and her life-companion

Pilar had to work as janitors for quite a while.

EM: So, when did she actually start working as a choreographer and director again?

EG-G: Oh, she started right away — she joined exiled artists from Chile, from other countries in Latin America, Palestine, Iran, and also Canadian artists. They started producing shows at the Russian Hall, a modest venue in Vancouver. These collaborations also opened her eyes to different artistic sensibilities, which propelled her to try new, different things. But these were alternative initiatives. She and her colleagues never got paid a penny for that work. It took years for mainstream institutions to start paying attention. The breakthrough came when she got a contract with City Ballet and collaborated with Aboriginal artists to create a show that integrated Canadian West Coast aboriginal myths and visual art, Latin American and European music, projected slides portraying people from around the world fighting for their rights — yes, in those days it was slides in a carrousel [chuckles] — and an assortment of dance traditions. At that point we were living in a housing co-op in East Vancouver, and my mom's colleagues would come over to discuss their ideas with her. Back then I didn't know who they were, really, but it turned out that they were world-renowned, like visual artist Bill Reid, composer Ann Southam. Well, the show was a huge hit. And the rest is history.

EM: Did Lucía González see herself as Chilean or Canadian?

EG-G: Both — she identified herself as Chilean-Canadian.

EM: We understand that you never knew your father.

EG-G: No. He died before I was born. He was executed by firing squad in 1949 in Pisagua, the infamous concentration camp that President Gabriel González Videla opened back then. You probably know that at that time Captain Augusto Pinochet was the camp's director. Ironic, eh? Twenty-four years later

General Augusto Pinochet–turned dictator ordered the execution and disappearance of thousands, including my sister Alexandra. He also reopened the Pisagua concentration camp. So, no, I never met my dad, but my mom told me all about him and I've read his books and all the columns and articles he wrote along the years, so I feel like I do know him.

EM: You're a published author yourself and he was a journalist. Do you think you inherited your talents from him?

EG-G: Maybe, eh? I did inherit his looks, that's for sure [smiles and tilts her head]. Also, he was a fantastic storyteller and I love to tell stories, so it's likely that I got that from him too [smiles and shrugs].

EM: You have written a few novels and short story collections about the 1973 military coup, the dictatorship, life in Canada. What's your next book about, if I may ask?

EG-G: Sure. About my parents... their life stories... fictionalized, of course. It'll be a novel, an homage to them, two extraordinary human beings, really...

EM: Do you have a title for it?

EG-G: I haven't quite decided yet, but I may call it *Atacama*.

AFTERWORD

· ·

WHILE *ATACAMA* IS BASED on historical events, the original impetus for the novel came from my parents' stories.

My *mamá* loved to recite poetry, but she hardly ever told anecdotes about her childhood. However, when she was on her death bed, she revealed to my brothers and me the one, all-important story that she had kept to herself for seventy years — the episode that Lucía narrates early in the novel about the corpses in the Caplina River. My mother spoke until she had no breath left and concluded by saying: "That's why I always hated my father." Her confession, nearly thirty years ago, prompted me to start researching the Chilean occupation of Tacna and the massacre of 1925, which my grandfather, a military officer, had masterminded and led. That was the genesis of *Atacama*.

As I learned about the events surrounding the Tacna massacre, I stumbled upon another historical event: the La Coruña massacre, also in 1925. It didn't take long for my mind to start making connections between the two tragedies and to begin devising ways to incorporate my father's childhood stories into the novel as well.

Unlike my mother, my *papá* was an engaging and skillful storyteller. The son of a miner and a laundry woman, and a child labourer himself, he grew up in abject poverty and learned about hardship and adversity at an early age. But it took me years to comprehend the unjust nature of my father's life, because he always made sure to infuse his stories with adventure and humour, not to mention animated and colourful depictions of his native landscape in northern Chile. A few of Manuel's experiences in the novel were, in fact, my father's, e.g., scavenging for food, nearly drowning while trying to retrieve a washing trough for his mother and working as a crusher cleaner at a saltpetre mine. However, Lucía González and Manuel Garay are fictional characters and their overriding stories are also fictional, including Part IV, which takes the narration to present-time Canada and Chile. The stock illustrations represent my mental picture of Lucía in her eighties and an imagined centre for the performing arts named after her.

While Parts I, II and III of *Atacama* focus on the first half of the twentieth century, Part IV makes reference to a later chapter in Chilean history: the military coup of September 11, 1973, led by General Augusto Pinochet. On that day, the Chilean Armed Forces overthrew democratically elected President Salvador Allende and put an end to his "Peaceful Road to Socialism." They also unleashed a brutal wave of terror throughout the country, beginning with the bombing of the presidential palace and Allende's assassination. That event marked the beginning of a seventeen-year dictatorship.

Under military rule, Chile became a testbed for unfettered neoliberal policies, which were then entrenched in a new constitution created by the dictator and his cohorts in 1980. Everything was privatized, from education, to healthcare and pension systems; every bit of the country was sold to the Chilean bourgeoisie and multinational corporations, including all sources of potable water and the ocean; and agrarian reforms implemented by previous governments were obliterated. Since the end of the Pinochet regime in 1990, successive administrations have continued to follow the neoliberal model and govern by the 1980 constitution. This has resulted in the accumulation of extreme wealth by the elites and the impoverishment of the majority of the population.

On October 18, 2019, protests by high school students triggered a massive wave of unrest. Artists, pensioners, students, teachers and workers from every socio-economic group took to the streets by the millions to demand change. After several months of continuous demonstrations, the government was forced to commit to a democratic process aimed at writing a new constitution for the country. The Chilean people paid a staggering price for this momentous victory, as the militarized police responded to the uprising by killing, injuring, torturing and jailing thousands.

On October 25, 2020, Chileans went to the polls and voted overwhelmingly in favour of drafting a new constitution by means of an assembly composed of one hundred and fifty-five delegates elected directly by popular vote. On May 15 and 16, 2021, they went to the polls once again, this time to elect such delegates. The results were resounding: the traditional and independent left coalitions obtained a decisive victory, while the right failed to elect the number of delegates necessary to block anti-neoliberal language in the new constitution. Additionally, gender parity in the allocation of seats was achieved — thus making Chile the first country in the world with a constitution drafted by an equal number of women and men, and seventeen seats were reserved for and filled by representatives of Indigenous Nations.

At the beginning of the twentieth century, the Chilean working class and their allies believed that sooner rather than later they would defeat capitalism via an armed revolution. Later on, they attempted to do it through the polls. Today, Chileans from all walks of life have united to fight against the latest incarnation of capitalism: neoliberalism. Will they succeed and show the way to the rest of the world?

ACKNOWLEDGEMENTS

SEVERAL PEOPLE READ DIFFERENT versions of the manuscript and provided invaluable feedback: Dafne Blanco, Denise Bukowski, Alan Creighton-Kelly, Valentina Vega Eck, Rose Gaete, Cynthia Flood, Bonnie Klein and Jane Warren.

The riddles that Ernesto Céspedes asks Lucía in the first part of *Atacama* were taken from *The Lunch Bag Chronicles*, a delightful book by my friend, fellow writer and educator Don Sawyer. I thank him for allowing me to use them and apologize for making such cheerful and amusing words come out of the villain's mouth.

My friend and colleague John Kirk introduced me to Stephen Kimber who introduced me to Beverley Rach, managing editor of Fernwood Publishing. The result? The book you have in your hands. I thank John and Stephen for helping me find the best possible home for *Atacama*. Roseway, the literary imprint of Fernwood Publishing, "aims to publish literary work that is rooted in and relevant to struggles for social justice," an aspiration that also informs my writing and work as an educator and activist.

I am grateful to Beverley and the Fernwood/Roseway Publishing team for their hard work and commitment to offer *Atacama* to the world in its most favourable form and to ensure that the book is read as widely as possible.

I am indebted to editor Linda Little. Following nine years of hard work, I was certain that I had finished *Atacama* and that she would be guiding me through minor changes to the text. However, with gentle firmness, she prodded me to engage in a whole re-write of the novel, which was followed by three more rounds of revisions. I cannot thank her enough for her insight, skill and support through this process, which also taught me invaluable lessons on editing.

Copy editor Brenda Conroy went through the manuscript with a fine-tooth comb, revised punctuation and grammar, and checked for inconsistencies. I thank her for her meticulous work.

The Canada Council of the Arts and the British Columbia Arts Council provided invaluable financial support. Their timely grants allowed me to do field research in Peru, Chile and Spain, and also made it possible for me to dedicate uninterrupted periods of time to writing and doing archival research.

A residency at Historic Joy Kogawa House (HJKH) in 2017 resulted in the first draft of the novel. I thank Joy Kogawa, an accomplished writer and a Canadian treasure, Ann-Marie Metten, HJKH's executive director and its board of directors for this gift.

I was fortunate to grow up in a family that valued the arts. In addition to being a skillful storyteller, my father was an avid reader and encouraged my brothers and me to follow in his footsteps. My mother's love of poetry was complemented by her talent for painting and ceramic art. She was also an accomplished seamstress, knitter and embroiderer. My brothers enjoyed singing and playing the guitar, and from an early age I attended the music conservatory and took dance lessons. These experiences proved to be crucial to the development of *Atacama*.

My deepest gratitude goes to my family. My writing life would be unbearably lonely without their love and our frequent gatherings. A special "thank you" to Alan Creighton-Kelly, my partner in life, for his unwavering support and encouragement throughout.

SELECTED BIBLIOGRAPHY

The Anarchist Library <theanarchistlibrary.org>.

Aranda, Vicente. Las libertarias (film). Spain, 1996.

Biblioteca Nacional de Chile <bibliotecanacionaldigital.gob.cl>.

Biblioteca Nacional del Perú <bnp.gob.pe>

Canal UNED <canal.ued.es>

Historia Alternativa <althistory.fandom.com/es/wiki>.

Kolontai, Alexandra. Selected Writings. New York, W. W. Norton & Company, 1977.

Lenin, Vladimir Ilyich. El estado y la revolución. Madrid, Editorial Ayuso, 1976.

Marx, Karl and Frederick Engels. The Communist Manifesto: A Modern Edition. London and New York, Verso, 1998.

Marxists Internet Archive <marxists.org>.

Memoria Chilena <memoriachilena.gob.cl>.

Neruda, Pablo. Confieso que he vivido. Barcelona, Plaza & Janés, 1994.

Neruda, Pablo. España en el corazón - – Himno a las Glorias del Pueblo en la Guerra. Sevilla, Editorial Renacimiento, 2004.

Orwell, George. Homage to Catalonia. London, Penguin Books, 1975.

Preston, Paul. La guerra civil española (Ed. actualizada). Barcelona, Editorial Debate, 2016.

Rooum, Donald. What Is Anarchism?: An Introduction. Oakland, PM Press, 2016.

Rossif, Frédérik. Mourir à Madrid (film). France, 1962.

Saña, Heleno. La revolución libertaria: los anarquistas en la Guerra Civil española. Pamplona/Iruña, Editorial Laetoli, 2010.

Social History Portal <socialhistoryportal.org>.

Vitale, Luis. Interpretación marxista de la Historia de Chile, Vol. 3. Santiago, LOM Ediciones, 2011.